D1365042

SWAP

SWAP

JENESI ASH

HEAT

HEAT
Published by New American Library, a division of
Penguin Group (USA) Inc., 375 Hudson Street,
New York, New York 10014, USA
Penguin Group (Canada), 90 Eglinton Avenue East, Suite 700, Toronto,
Ontario M4P 2Y3, Canada (a division of Pearson Penguin Canada Inc.)
Penguin Books Ltd., 80 Strand, London WC2R 0RL, England
Penguin Ireland, 25 St. Stephen's Green, Dublin 2,
Ireland (a division of Penguin Books Ltd.)
Penguin Group (Australia), 250 Camberwell Road, Camberwell, Victoria 3124,
Australia (a division of Pearson Australia Group Pty. Ltd.)
Penguin Books India Pvt. Ltd., 11 Community Centre, Panchsheel Park,
New Delhi - 110 017, India
Penguin Group (NZ), 67 Apollo Drive, Rosedale, North Shore 0632,
New Zealand (a division of Pearson New Zealand Ltd.)
Penguin Books (South Africa) (Pty.) Ltd., 24 Sturdee Avenue,
Rosebank, Johannesburg 2196, South Africa

Penguin Books Ltd., Registered Offices:
80 Strand, London WC2R 0RL, England

First published by Heat, an imprint of New American Library,
a division of Penguin Group (USA) Inc.

First Printing, September 2008
10 9 8 7 6 5 4 3 2 1

HEAT is a trademark of Penguin Group (USA) Inc.

LIBRARY OF CONGRESS CATALOGING-IN-PUBLICATION DATA:
Ash, Jenesi.
    Swap/Jenesi Ash.
        p. cm.
    ISBN 978-0-451-22494-1
    I. Title.
    PS3601.S5226S93   2008
    813'.6—dc22   2008002652

Set in Centaur MT
Designed by Ginger Legato

Printed in the United States of America

To Anne Bohner.
Thanks for guiding me through this book
from concept to completion.

ONE
ONE

Jamie dropped the old sweater onto her bed and held up her hands. "So let me see if I get this straight. You have sex every night, and you often experience multiple orgasms." She stared at her friend in disbelief. "And this is a problem how?"

"I'm not complaining!" Mia insisted, her words echoing in Jamie's attic apartment of her bungalow house. She immediately lowered her voice. "It's just that . . . well, having sex with Aidan is . . . I don't know how to describe it." Overwhelming? Unnerving? If she told that to someone like Jamie, that would be considered a plus.

Jamie shrugged and tossed the sweater into the bag for charity donations. "So change it."

"I've tried." She did exactly what the magazine articles and tips suggested to take charge and try something new. But no matter what she did, she never felt like an equal in her boyfriend's bed. "Aidan is very dominant."

"So? Wasn't that a requirement for you?"

It had been, but she had a very definite idea of what it would be like. She thought she could handle someone like Aidan and control the relationship. She was wrong on both counts. "Never mind." She picked up a pair of jeans from Jamie's pile of discarded clothes and started folding them.

"No way. You brought it up." Jamie yanked the jeans from Mia's hands. "You specifically went after Aidan because he was a take-charge kind of guy. You wanted a man who knew what he wanted in bed and knew how to please a woman."

"I know."

"And now you don't want it?"

Mia was about to argue but stopped. "I don't know. I like it. I'm not sure that's what I want every night." And she didn't think she wanted it for a lifetime.

"You know what your problem is?" Jamie tossed the jeans in the bag and pointed her finger at Mia. "You've only had sex with one man."

Mia pressed her lips together. The idea had crossed her mind on occasion, but she had always pushed away the disloyal thought. There were nights when she felt as if she had passed the beginner's stage and gone straight to the advanced level.

But she wouldn't change that, even if she could. She wasn't like Jamie, who had seen her virginity as a condition that needed to be dealt with right away. Mia hadn't seen it as a precious gift that had to be saved for the honeymoon, either. She had waited for the one man who was worth the effort.

"The moment I saw Aidan, I was attracted to him more than any other guy I met," Mia confessed.

"You were so focused when you went after him." Jamie shook her head at the memory as she balled up a shirt and tossed it in the bag. "I never thought you had that in you. I was so impressed."

"And I got him," Mia said with a triumphant smile.

"And now you're bored with him."

"I'm not bored!" Aidan was never boring. He was intense, passionate, and probably the only unpredictable element in her comfortable life. Boredom was never the problem, but she was wondering if she had gotten in way over her head.

Jamie placed her hands on her hips, her threadbare tank top riding high, exposing her golden brown skin. "Or maybe this has nothing to do with sex."

"How could it not?"

"He's pushing to move in here once I leave, isn't he?"

"Yeah." It had been discussed since Jamie announced she was moving on. It would make a lot of sense for Mia and Aidan to live together in the bungalow she had inherited from her grandmother.

"Are you going to let him?"

Mia looked away. "I haven't decided."

"Aha!"

"Drop it, Jamie. I'm telling you, that is a different issue." And yet maybe it wasn't. If she was serious about Aidan, shouldn't she have immediately suggested he move in? And why did she feel guilty because she was holding back?

"Okay, fine." Jamie returned her attention to the heap of clothes. "I won't say another word about it."

"Thank you," Mia said tightly. "But what am I going to do about my problem?"

"I would tell you, but you're not going to like it." Jamie didn't look up as she dug through the pile.

Mia had a feeling that might be true. Jamie was known for her outlandish ideas, but she also came up with creative solutions. "Come on, Jamie. Lay it on me. What am I going to do about the sex?"

"There's only one thing you can do," she said as she scooped up all the clothes and dumped them into the bag. "Change the guy."

Mia blinked. "Excuse me?"

"You need to do a little research," Jamie said matter-of-factly as she stomped the clothes into the bag with her bare foot. "Maybe Aidan was a good starter lover, and it's time for you to move on."

Starter lover? Move on? Mia's stomach gave a sharp twist. "I'm not going to dump him so I can have sex with someone else," she said in a scandalized whisper.

Jamie looked up and held Mia's gaze. "Then don't dump him."

"If I don't dump him, then"—Mia's eyes went wide as her mouth dropped open—"*cheat* on him? You want me to be unfaithful to Aidan?"

"Oh, please, it's not that big of deal. Do you have an exclusive contract with him?"

"We've been monogamous for a year, so I'm going to say it's implied."

"Okay, then maybe you'll need to get his permission."

Mia laughed at the outrageous suggestion. "Oh, right. I can see it now. 'Hey, Aidan, I'm going to pick up a guy at the corner bar and sleep with him. Don't wait up for me.' Yeah, that will go over well."

Jamie brushed off the concern with a wave of her hand. "It's all in how you present it." Jamie stood still, and a smile slowly grew on her full lips.

"Uh-oh. I know that look. What are you planning?" Mia wrapped her arms around her stomach as the familiar mix of dread and curiosity bubbled inside her. "I'm telling you, I'm not cheating on Aidan."

Jamie tilted her head. "How do you feel about swapping?"

"Swapping?" She dragged the word out of her mouth.

"I'll give you Caleb, and you give me Aidan."

Mia took a step back, her heart beating wildly. "Are you crazy?"

"It's the best way to explore without dumping Aidan. And, even better, you know Caleb. He's hot, don't you think?"

"He's not my type." She didn't know what to think of Jamie's standby lover. Caleb was a wanderer, yet Mia sensed he was searching for something or someone to hold on to. Jamie might be drawn to his mysterious nature, but that was the one thing that put Mia on edge. She sensed the man had secrets and was not as easygoing as he appeared.

Mia didn't care if the guy was sexy and knew how to keep Jamie coming back for more. The very idea of sleeping with him made her jumpy, and it felt like her heart was going to burst through her rib cage. Mia shook her head. "I am not screwing with my best friend's lover."

"Why not? I'm giving you permission."

And that changed everything, didn't it? If her best friend gave permission—went so far as to encourage it—was it cheating?

Mia and Jamie had been friends since kindergarten and shared everything from clothes to chicken pox. Jamie was always generous with her, but this was taking it a step too far. Mia had to stop her before she approached the guys with the idea.

Mia tried to come up with a valid reason why this idea wouldn't work. "Caleb isn't interested in me."

"Caleb likes women, and he likes sex," she countered with her usual bluntness. "He's the perfect guy to experiment with. I can vouch for him."

"Thanks for the recommendation," Mia responded drily, "but Aidan isn't going to agree. And, no offense, if Aidan wanted to sleep with you, he would have done so already."

Jamie's smile tilted slyly. "Leave it to me."

Oh, God, what would she do? "No, Jamie. I've participated in a lot of your insane plans, and I backed you up every time we got caught and you improvised your way out of trouble, but I'm not going to do this one."

"Why not?" Jamie threw an arm around Mia's shoulders and gave it a good squeeze. "Come on, you know you want to."

"Not really. Being in a relationship means saying no to other possibilities." Mia frowned. That hadn't come out right.

"Doesn't have to be."

Mia stepped away from Jamie and held up her hands. "This conversation is over."

"It only has to be one time," Jamie promised.

"Only?" Mia's voice rose. "One time is all it takes to ruin everything."

"I don't understand. Are you worried that you're going to ruin things with Aidan, or are you afraid that you might want something more than what Aidan can provide?"

"Both!" Mia winced when she realized what she said.

Jamie pursed her lips as her eyebrows lifted up. "I think we have made a breakthrough."

Mia wished she could take that answer back. She wasn't afraid of anything. If her relationship with her boyfriend wasn't working, she would end it. She wasn't hanging on to Aidan because he was her first.

"Listen," Mia said quietly as she picked her words with care. "Things are good with Aidan and me. So what if I want something more or different in the bedroom? I'm not going to rock the boat."

"Then I'll do it for you. What are friends for?"

"No, Jamie." Mia grabbed her friend's arm before the woman went downstairs and confronted Aidan. "Forget I said anything. It's not worth the risk. I'm not going to act on it even if you hand me the opportunity on a silver platter."

Jamie gave her a long, searching look. "Okay, fine," she finally said. "If that's what you want."

"Fine?" That was all she had to say? Jamie was giving up her idea too easily. "What are you up to?"

"Nothing." Jamie shook off Mia's hold. "You don't want to do it, so we won't."

Mia watched her friend with narrowed eyes as she gathered the bag of clothes. Jamie looked up. "Don't you trust me?"

"No."

Jamie smiled, not the least bit offended. "I won't bring it up again. Pinky swear."

Mia watched as Jamie held her little finger up. Jamie never broke a pinky swear, but Mia felt like she was missing a loophole. Then again, Jamie was moving out of town in a week. How much trouble could she cause in such a short time?

"Mia?"

Mia stiffened when she heard Aidan's low, rough voice at the foot of the stairs. How long had he been there? "Do you think he heard us?" she whispered.

"I wish he did," Jamie muttered. "It would make everything so much easier."

"Shush!" Mia took a deep breath and called out to Aidan. "Yeah, honey?"

"Are you going to be up there all night?"

"I'm coming down right now"—she looked at the mess in Jamie's attic bedroom—"unless you need me here."

"Go on to bed. I'm fine," Jamie assured her. "Anyway, Caleb is coming over soon. Perfect time to empty out my sex toy drawer, don't you think?"

Mia's stomach clenched at the mention of Caleb. She couldn't believe Jamie had offered to lend him. She didn't think she could look him in the eye ever again. "All in one night? I don't think even you can handle that kind of marathon."

"Not all of the toys are for me." She wagged her eyebrows suggestively.

Mia playfully covered her ears. "I don't want to know."

Jamie's smile grew wide. "Yeah, you do."

"Good night, Jamie," she said with a hint of warning. "I'll help you out some more tomorrow before I go to work."

"Sweet dreams."

Yeah, right, Mia thought sourly. Jamie knew exactly what Mia was going to dream about because she had put the idea in to Mia's head!

Mia headed for the stairs and saw Aidan waiting for her at the bottom step. Her heart gave a funny flip, and she felt a burst of energy warming her. It didn't matter if she'd just seen him an hour ago. Her senses always responded to him like that.

She walked down the stairs and took in his appearance. Aidan wasn't tall or muscle-bound, but she could have sworn that he filled the doorway. She noted, not for the first time, that he was a study in contrasts. Aidan's black hair was cut ruthlessly short, but he always sported an unshaven look. He wore only casual clothes like T-shirts and jeans, yet his stance was anything but relaxed.

As a personal trainer for the local gym, Aidan followed a rigorous exercise regimen that would exhaust a lesser man. His body was hard and powerful, but he could be very tender and gentle with Mia.

"Sorry, Aidan." She grabbed his hand and linked her fingers with his. His touch still made her pulse skip a beat as heat coiled deep in her belly. "I was helping Jamie pack, but she has so much stuff she needs to get rid of."

"I'm not complaining. I know you want to spend as much time as possible with her before she leaves." He drew her close until she was hip to hip with him, and Mia was tempted to curl into his side. She always felt petite and delicate against Aidan.

She didn't want to think about her best friend leaving. She knew once Jamie crossed the state line, nothing would ever be the same. Jamie might come back for a visit, but she would never return to stay. Clover Bud was too small a town to hold someone like Jamie for long.

Mia, on the other hand, reveled in the cozy atmosphere the sleepy town had to offer. It was comfortable knowing everything about her neighbors. She knew every inch of Clover Bud and enjoyed the gentle rhythm of the seasons and traditions.

The only time her routine was disrupted was when she was in the bedroom with Aidan. When she was with him, she was a different person. She took risks. She was wild and bold.

But it wasn't the real her. Or, at least, she didn't want it to be. Sometimes it scared her because she felt out of control. She would often beg Aidan to tie her up or pin her down. It made her feel safer.

She wanted to be strong, powerful, and fearless, but when she was with Aidan, she clung to him and needed his guidance, knowing that otherwise she would get caught up in swirling dark emotions. She didn't like her submissive tendencies or her need for bondage. She was almost embarrassed by her transformation in bed.

She needed to change that, Mia decided as she silently guided Aidan to her bedroom. Tonight she was going to accept her wild abandon. She would not ask to be tied up. In fact, she would take charge.

Mia stopped at the threshold of her bedroom and turned to Aidan. She stood on her tiptoes and linked her hands behind his head, claiming his mouth with hers.

She kissed Aidan aggressively, a potent mix of excitement and trepidation sparkling in her blood. But his mouth didn't soften against hers. Was he surprised? Or turned off?

Mia retreated slightly, nibbling his mouth and swiping the tip of her tongue along his bottom lip. Aidan gave a sexy murmur and parted his lips, allowing her entrance. Triumphant, she drove her tongue into his mouth.

She ground her lips against his, the white heat zipping through her veins. Her nipples tingled; her breasts were full and heavy. Mia wiggled her hips, fighting against the swelling, wet sensations flooding her body.

Gliding her hands over his chest, she murmured her approval of his chiseled muscles and the steady beat of his heart. Aidan loved having his chest rubbed. He groaned, the sound vibrating deeply. Mia needed to get closer and dipped her hand under his T-shirt. His skin was warm, and her fingertips caught in the whorls of his springy dark hair.

She shoved Aidan's shirt up, exposing his washboard abs. As she pulled the shirt over his head, she trailed her fingers along the defined muscles of his arms, shivering as she remembered how they flexed and tightened. How could she overpower such a man? And did she really want to?

Mia shivered as Aidan's large hands roamed over her back, his fingertips gently teasing her spine. Her resolve was disintegrating, and she wanted to cling to him, but the tension in his movements alerted her that he was holding back. Why hadn't he taken over?

Was he biding his time, or could he tell that she needed to be in charge, just this once?

Mia reluctantly pulled away until he couldn't touch her. Aidan frowned as his hands dropped to his sides. She darted her tongue against her lips, not sure what her next move should be.

She decided to strip off her clothes. It would have to be quick, and she had to keep out of his reach, because Aidan could never keep his hands off her naked body. Mia took off her pink camisole top with more force than necessary. She felt her small breasts bob freely as she pulled off the shirt and tossed it on the floor.

Mia kept her gaze on Aidan, watching his eyes flare with lust as she shimmied out of her gray hipster shorts. She hooked her thumbs over her thong, already damp from her arousal, as she dragged it down her legs.

She stood proudly in front of him with her hands on her hips. Her nipples puckered, and her skin was hot to the touch. Mia reached up and pulled the rubber band from her hair, giving her long blond tresses a good shake. She was aware of the rapid rise and fall of her chest. Mia stood on the balls of her feet, ready to move fast if Aidan lunged for her.

Aidan stayed where he was, his hands clenched to his sides. She saw a tremor sweep his strong body and knew he was definitely holding back. A renegade thought occurred to her: Had he heard her discussion with Jamie? A heavy knot formed in her stomach. She studied his face and dismissed the idea once she saw the desire gleaming from his dark brown eyes.

"Touch yourself," Aidan said hoarsely.

Mia knew she should refuse and tell him to touch *himself.* She would enjoy that, but not as much as she would have fun putting on a show for him. Even better, if she masturbated in front of him, she would control the pace.

She covered her breasts with her hands, fondling them the same way Aidan would. She squeezed tightly, pushing them together. Mia pinched her nipples hard, gasping when they stung.

Aidan took a step toward her and then stepped back. He folded his arms across his chest, as if he knew that was the only way to keep from touching her. "Lean against the bed," he suggested.

It was a good idea. Her legs felt a little wobbly, but she didn't want to lie down. That was when she was vulnerable. Leaning against the bedpost would keep her on an equal level with Aidan.

Mia rested against one of the posts, the hard wooden corner biting into her shoulder. She jutted her hips out and cupped her sex. Sliding her finger along her wet slit, she bit her bottom lip to prevent a guttural moan escaping from her throat.

"Show me how you like it," Aidan said.

Oh, she'd show him. Mia widened her legs and showed him her glistening pussy. She caressed her clit with one finger, her movements quick. She rocked her hips against her hand, but it wasn't enough. She needed something more. She needed Aidan's touch.

"Kiss me," she moaned as she felt the urgent need winding tight in her pelvis.

Aidan slowly walked over and stood before her. He unfolded his arms but didn't touch her. His body heat enveloped her as her lips tingled in anticipation of a kiss.

"Keep touching yourself," he said.

Mia frowned and wondered why he wouldn't touch or kiss her. She stroked her clit, her breath snagging in her throat as pleasure rippled gently through her body. She wanted to feel powerful and strong, but she didn't want to do everything by herself.

"Lick my nipples," she told him, but her raspy voice ruined the commanding tone she was going for.

A wicked gleam shone from his eyes. "Feed them to me."

Mia cupped the underside of one breast and arched her spine, offering him a taste. Aidan lowered his head, never taking his gaze off her face. The tip of his tongue darted from his mouth, and he swirled it along her nipple.

She gasped, his touch sending a fiery jolt through her bloodstream. Mia reached up and cupped the back of his head, her fingers spearing through his short black hair. She tried to draw him closer, but Aidan resisted.

"Keep touching yourself," Aidan said as his tongue flicked against her tight nipple. "Otherwise I'll need to tie you up."

Mia closed her eyes as his words triggered a quaking through her. She lowered her hand and stopped in midair. She couldn't deny the piercing longing. It didn't matter what she had planned; she really needed to be tied up tonight.

She defiantly placed both hands on the back of his head and guided him closer to her aching breasts. From Aidan's smile, she knew he approved of this decision. He stepped away and walked to the chest of drawers.

Pulling out the bottom drawer, Aidan retrieved two leather cuffs. Mia's core clenched when the metal chains caught the light. Her pulse skipped a beat as the thin skin prickled around her wrists.

She licked her lips as she watched Aidan approach her with the bindings in his strong hands. Why did she make this decision? How was she supposed to feel strong and powerful when Aidan chained her to the bed?

Mia was surprised when Aidan took one of her wrists and expertly bound her to the bedpost. She thought he would ask her to lie down on the mattress like he usually did. He took her other wrist and bound it on the opposite post. Her arms were stretched as she stood naked at the foot of the bed, facing him.

Aidan stepped back and gave a devilish smile as he studied his handiwork. "Now I will lick your nipples."

He went down on her hungrily, the edge of his teeth scraping her nipples as his fingers crushed her breasts. She writhed under him, the metal chain rattling as she pulled at her bindings. Her inability to move made every lick, every bite more intense.

As her moans echoed in her ears, Aidan knelt down, licking a trail down her stomach. Mia watched his descent and felt an incredible rush of power. This was what she liked: Aidan on his knees, pleasuring her.

He knew exactly how to touch her. The muscles in her stomach bunched as he stabbed his tongue into her navel. She shied away when he brushed the gentlest kiss on her hip bone.

Aidan pushed her legs apart and kissed along her inner thigh. Each breath she took was painful as she found the anticipation tormenting. When he finally covered her pussy with his mouth, Mia cried out. She bucked against his face, her cuffs jingling.

She instinctively tried to reach for him, and the cuffs yanked her back. The burn racing down her arms heightened the pleasure throbbing in her core. "More," she whispered.

"More?" His breath was hot and steamy against her skin. "Like this?"

Aidan teased her with her mouth. His tongue circled her clit without pressing down on the swollen nub. Mia swiveled her hips, desperate to feel the pressure of his mouth against the insistent throbbing, but Aidan clenched his hands on her hips and held her still.

"Harder," she told him. She knew her tone was sharp and abrupt, but she didn't care. So what if she was bound to the bed? He was on his knees pleasuring her. She could have just as much power as Aidan.

"Like this?" he asked innocently as he laved his tongue along her slit. Sparks popped under her skin as she felt the rush of heat down her shoulders and back.

Mia closed her eyes as the desperation clawed at her. Aidan wasn't going to give what she wanted until she surrendered to him. The quest to gain power was clouded by the urgent need for satisfaction.

She sagged forward, her head dipping down in defeat. "Please," she whispered.

Her body trembled as she waited for his next move. Aidan captured her clit with his thumb and forefinger. She reared back as he pinched the nub, as the wild lust uncoiled deep within her, whipping through her body.

Mia cried out as if the desire lashed her. She felt like she was splintering into a million pieces. She froze when Aidan delved his tongue deep in her core. She came violently as he licked her drenched pussy.

Shivers continued to rack her body as he greedily lapped her wetness. When he was done, she could barely stand up; the bindings were the only things holding her up. Aidan got to his feet, and she noticed his movements were shaky as he ripped off his jeans.

He stood before her naked, and Mia's stomach fluttered at the sight. Aidan's hard cock eagerly pointed up and slapped against his tight stomach. He grabbed one of her legs and hooked it over his hip. He wrapped his hand around his cock, wincing at the touch, and guided the wet tip against her sex.

Mia took a deep breath right before he thrust into her. His cock filled and stretched her. His hot, sweat-slicked chest rubbed against her breasts as his fingers dug into her hips and legs. She barely noticed any of this, her world centered on meeting each savage thrust.

Aidan bent his head and placed his mouth behind her ear, suckling a sensitive spot there until she was struggling against her bindings. She wasn't trying to get away—she was trying to get closer.

Mia knew then she would never be as strong and powerful in bed as her lover. She shouldn't bother trying. Whenever she was near him, she felt naked. She was defenseless to Aidan's sexual allure and too weak to fight her addiction for his touch.

Yet she couldn't help but wish that one day she would conquer Aidan with her own sexual power.

TWO

Jamie collapsed on the bed next to Caleb. She gulped for air as her heart pounded in her ears. She was sweaty and bone-tired, but that didn't prevent her from curling her leg around his. His skin was hot to the touch, but Caleb didn't move away. Jamie wasn't much into cuddling, but she was tempted to nestle into his arms.

She reached up and plucked the blindfold from his face. Caleb blinked and Jamie was mesmerized by his soulful brown eyes. His forehead creased as he looked around to gather his bearings. He glanced at the window and saw the first streaks of dawn. "It's morning already?" he asked.

"Time flies when you're having fun." And when she was cleaning out her goody drawer. Fortunately, Caleb had the stamina to try some of her toys out one last time.

She was going to miss him. Jamie was surprised by that realization, probably because it had more to do than with Caleb being the perfect playmate. When she was with him, she didn't have to worry about him seeing her at her worst.

Jamie knew she was difficult and didn't get along with others.

As far as she was concerned, there was no need to change. She didn't do relationships and refused to be pinned down. She ran from any expectations and made it clear not to rely on her for anything.

Mia was the exception. Their friendship was the only constant thing in Jamie's life. While boyfriends came and went, Mia had accepted Jamie wholeheartedly, taking the good and the bad and never trying to change her.

It had been that way from the beginning. There had never been any discussion or promises to be friends forever. Jamie would do anything for Mia. Her friend never had to ask for help, because Jamie was already there at her side.

Much to her surprise, Caleb was beginning to show the same unswerving acceptance. It made Jamie nervous, because she didn't do anything to earn it, and it was simply a matter of time before she made a mistake and ruined everything, just like she always did. She wasn't purposely destructive in relationships—she just never got the hang of them.

Jamie glanced at Caleb, taking in his longish brown hair and his narrow face. He wasn't handsome or even cute. But there was something about his face from his aristocratic nose and high cheekbones to his dark eyes that had grabbed her attention.

It had taken her a while to figure out what made him fascinating. It turned out to be something very simple: He was everything she wasn't. His body was as lean and lanky as she was all voluptuous curves. Her skin looked golden against his paleness. She was loud and brash, while he laughed quietly.

They appeared to have nothing in common, but it turned out they had the same greedy approach to life. They wanted to live in the moment, experience everything new and different. Caleb was just as willing as Jamie to step out of their comfort zone in search of something exciting.

Jamie brushed her damp hair from her forehead and watched Caleb's smooth chest rise and fall and found her breath matching his. She realized she'd been with Caleb longer than with any other guy. Okay, so there had been other guys on the side, but he knew that. Jamie didn't do exclusive.

A random thought entered her mind. She could take Caleb with her when she left Clover Bud. Jamie could easily see him in the passenger seat of her old car, encouraging her to ignore the map and go where the road led her.

She knew Caleb wanted to go with her. He had offered several times, but she had instinctively shot him down. For a moment she wavered, ready to invite him. Caleb was someone she could count on. She trusted him, which said a lot. But was she ready for this type of commitment?

No, she wasn't going to play it safe. Now wasn't the time to hold on to something familiar. Jamie rolled away before she said something she'd regret.

She needed to make a clean break from the people she knew and the only town she had lived in. That meant walking away with nothing to pull her down or hold her back. She was determined to travel as light as possible, taking only what she could fit in her car.

She should have moved out months ago, Jamie thought as she sat up in the bed. If she didn't leave now, the one relationship she relied on would be in danger. She should have known that she would eventually mess up her one true friendship, all because she lusted after the one person she couldn't—shouldn't—seduce.

Jamie didn't know if it was becoming obvious. She needed to leave before Mia figured it out. Mia already could see that Jamie was hiding something. Jamie already felt guilty, and she didn't need to see the hurt in Mia's eyes every day for retreating.

Sighing deeply, Jamie pushed the thought aside and bunched the blindfold in her hand. She tossed it in the box next to her bed. Looking at the jumble of sex toys she was throwing away, Jamie wryly decided it was a sort of timeline of her sex life. Some of the toys had been used once and then forgotten. They were too tame or not powerful enough for her. They were a lot like the men she met in Clover Bud.

The other toys she hadn't played with very often because of lack of opportunity. The few men who could keep up with her didn't like toys. They had hang-ups when it came to vibrators and dildos. The only man who showed any enthusiasm was Caleb.

She looked in the drawer and smiled. "Only one toy left," she told Caleb.

She hooked the strap-on harness onto her finger and lifted it from the drawer. Her pussy tingled as she studied the contraption. The black vinyl and thick purple dildo looked fierce and threatening. Dangerous. Jamie couldn't wait to wear it. Every time she buckled it on, she felt a rush of power that she couldn't find anywhere else.

Caleb was the only guy who bent over for her. The only man who didn't fight for control. The primitive need to take the dominant role coursed hotly through her blood.

She wanted to invade Caleb's body. It had to be rough and fast. Jamie inhaled slowly as the need pulsed heavily in her. She would do this just once more, and then she'd toss the dildo away. There was no telling when she'd get the chance to do it again.

Caleb groaned and closed his eyes, knowing he was in for a wild ride. "Let me catch my breath."

"Wimp."

She jerked when she heard the rattle of the old pipes in the house. Just like clockwork, Mia was up and taking a shower. Jamie gave an impatient sigh. Unlike her friend, she couldn't stand routine. When each new day brought the feeling of déjà vu, it was time to shake things up.

Only she might have shaken things so much that she couldn't put them back in place. Jamie winced, wondering why she had to push her luck with Mia right before she left. She always had bad timing. Hadn't she learned from her past mistakes?

"What's wrong?" Caleb asked.

She stiffened, unaware that Caleb had been watching her. Worse, he was beginning to read her easily. "I think I went too far with Mia," she confessed.

Caleb turned toward Jamie and tucked his arm under his head. "What did you do?"

Where did she begin? "Mia was a virgin when she met Aidan," she said with an incredulous chuckle and shook her head. "Can you believe that?"

Caleb's eyebrows rose. "And she's a friend of yours?"

"Ha. Ha." Jamie playfully swatted at him. "Believe me, I didn't understand her decision to wait for Mr. Right"—she rolled her eyes at the term—"but that was what she wanted."

His eyes narrowed with suspicion. "So where do you come into this?"

Jamie wasn't sure how to explain her role. It was going to make her look bad. Normally she didn't care what people thought of her, but Caleb's opinion of her was beginning to matter more than it should.

She stood up and looked away, keeping her hands busy by sliding on the vinyl. If there was one way to distract a man, it was putting on a dildo harness. "Once I leave, Mia is going to get stuck in a rut," Jamie said. "She never tries anything new unless I'm dragging her into it."

"Never?"

"Never," Jamie repeated as she adjusted the straps and buckles. She knew she wasn't exaggerating about Mia. Her friend was practically allergic to change. "Which is why I made a"—she tried to think of a noninflammatory word—"suggestion. I told her to try out some other guys before she settles on the first man she slept with."

She gave a quick glance at Caleb. Her heart took a dive when she saw his mouth sagging open. Great, she'd managed to drop a bombshell on the one man who couldn't be shocked. It was official: She had gone too far with Mia.

"Jamie," he said in a growl of warning, "don't interfere with Mia and Aidan."

It was so cute when Caleb put his foot down. Jamie stroked her silicone cock, already warming up under her hand. "I'm only making sure that Mia will be happy," she said in her own defense. "I'm not going to be around to keep an eye on her."

"Aidan can do that," Caleb pointed out.

Jamie made a face. "Aidan is going to protect his own interests." She gripped the silicone cock in her fist, enjoying the sense of power flooding her.

Caleb's eyes drifted to her hands, and she saw the ruddy color seeping into his face. He shook his head and rubbed his eyes with his hands in an attempt to stay focused. "Okay, Jamie. Spill it. What exactly did you suggest?"

She gave a little shrug and crawled back onto the bed. "I suggested to Mia that we swap sex partners."

Caleb's eyebrows shot up. He opened and closed his mouth, but didn't say anything as if words had escaped him.

"With your agreement, of course," she hastily added.

Cynicism flashed in his eyes. "Of course."

"But it's not going to happen," she said with a pout as she straddled Caleb's chest, the purple dildo thrusting in his face. "Aidan would never agree."

"Don't be too sure about that," Caleb said as the dildo diverted his attention. "You are offering a man a sexual fantasy few get to enjoy."

She had a feeling Caleb had already experienced that kind of fantasy. Several times. One of the things she liked about Caleb was that he had no boundaries when it came to sex, just like her. He'd seen and done it all, and kept coming back for more.

His vast experience wasn't what made him the perfect lover. Jamie had been won over by his refusal to judge her. She could be wild and nasty or sweet and romantic. Her moods and secret desires never fazed him. For someone who scandalized the entire town on a daily basis, this could be somewhat unnerving.

Jamie guided the purple dildo and teasingly circled it around Caleb's lips. "Would you do it if I asked?"

"Do I need your permission?" he asked, his voice suddenly cold. "I thought we had no claim on each other. If I wanted to sleep with Mia, I would go ahead and do it. Wasn't that our agreement?"

Jamie winced, knowing she stepped into that one on her own. The first time she took Caleb to her bed she had told him he had no claim on her. She would have sex with whomever she wanted, and he had no say in the matter.

Now she was being a hypocrite when she specifically asked him to have sex with Mia. She clenched her teeth and continued to rub the silicone dildo against his lips. "I'm asking this as a favor."

Caleb grabbed the dildo and stopped it, his long fingers wrapped around hers. "If I did you a favor, won't you feel obligated to me?"

Jamie clenched her teeth harder. Caleb was really testing her on this. She refused to be obligated to anyone. "No," she answered tightly, "you would get something out of it, too." Namely sex with Mia.

"What would you get out of it?" he asked.

"I would make sure that Mia had a chance to explore her sexual boundaries." And, if she got Aidan in the swap, she would teach him how to take commands.

"Mia's sex life is none of your business."

"Oh, Caleb," she said with a smile. The guy was clearly misguided. "How long have you been around me? Everything Mia does is my business."

"And what about me?" he asked, his voice rough and low. "Is everything I do your business?"

"For the moment," she answered. "But that's all I can promise. Push me for an answer, and I'll push you out of this bed."

Caleb's eyes narrowed but he didn't say anything. He could easily push *her* out of the bed or pin her down, but he wasn't going to. He knew she wasn't going to lie and give false promises just to tell him what he wanted to hear. Her answer was as good as it was going to get.

"That's a good boy," she taunted, brushing the dildo against his mouth again.

Warning gleamed in his eyes, but Caleb didn't stop her. He knew what she wanted and needed, and he was willing to accommodate her. Caleb always knew how to get back into her good graces.

"Suck my cock," she ordered, inserting the dildo past his lips.

Caleb playfully darted his tongue along the purple silicone. Goose bumps washed her skin as she shivered with delight seeing Caleb sucking a cock.

"You're very good at this," she whispered as she cupped his jaw and thrust her hips. "Lots of experience?"

Caleb's eyes twinkled but he didn't answer. Just as she refused to talk about the future, Caleb didn't discuss his past.

She backed away, pulling the wet cock from Caleb's mouth. Jamie scooted down his waist and hips until her dildo brushed against his erection.

Caleb's cock was longer and thicker than her purple silicone one. It was warm and twitched in her hand as she rubbed her dildo against it. She glanced up at his face. The skin was pulled tight against his face, his nostrils flaring as he watched.

Jamie slipped her other hand underneath his buttocks, seeking his anus. She pressed her fingertip against his rosebud and Caleb's hips lurched.

She caressed the puckered ring as Caleb squirmed against her hand. Jamie slowly worked her finger past his sphincter as Caleb clenched and twisted his pillow in his fists. He tossed his head from side to side as he uttered a low moan.

Jamie withdrew her hands and reached for the bottle of lube on her nightstand. She poured the liquid onto the palm of her hand and rubbed it on the bright purple dildo. She liked slicking her hands up and down the silicone as it warmed up in her hands. It felt foreign and yet amazingly powerful as she stroked her "cock."

"Turn around and lie on your stomach," Jamie ordered Caleb. He silently obeyed as she squirted some lube onto his rosebud. She rubbed the liquid, dipping her finger into his puckered hole as he rocked his hips and moaned. Caleb made no secret that he enjoyed how she prepared him for anal sex.

"Wait," she told him. "I forgot the vibe."

"How could you forget that?" The pillow muffled his voice. "Isn't that your favorite part?"

"Hush." She smacked her palm against his ass. The sound echoed in the attic, and a bright pink bloomed on his buttocks. The vibrations allowed her to climax during sex, but it wasn't her favorite part. She was more interested in taking Caleb in the ass.

She reached for her bedside table and searched in the drawer until her fingers brushed against the mini vibrator. She grabbed it and slid it into the harness pocket next to her clit.

Grasping Caleb's hip with one hand, she guided the tip of her purple cock with the other. She slowly worked the dildo past his puckered hole, enjoying the way Caleb shuddered as he took her inch by inch.

"Oh, God, Jamie," he said in a broken whisper. "It feels so good."

She felt him slowly relax his muscles, and she pushed the dildo all the way in. She leaned over and surrounded him, her hips against his ass, her breasts crushing against his back. Jamie loved how he trembled beneath her.

Jamie reached down and turned on the mini vibe. She stilled as the sensations hit her in one big wave. She closed her eyes and pressed her lips together, fighting off the need to come. She wasn't ready yet.

She heard a knock on the door to the stairway. "Jamie?"

Jamie glanced over her shoulder toward the stairs and she felt Caleb stiffen in alert underneath her. *Oh, shit.* She had forgotten Mia's offer to help her with the packing.

Jamie withdrew just a little and stopped when she heard Caleb whimper. She grabbed both his hips and thrust deeply inside him.

He groaned and grabbed the edge of the mattress with tense fingers.

"What are you doing?" he whispered.

"Let's show Mia just how good it can be if a woman is on top," Jamie said in a low, confidential tone.

She felt the pleasure ripple through Caleb. "You want to have sex in front of your friend?"

Jamie gave a short buck of her hips and watched him twitch. "Is that a problem for you?"

"No, not at all," Caleb said, and Jamie could hear the wicked smile in his voice. "Just asking."

She heard the door creak open. "Jamie?" Mia asked softly. "Are you up?"

Heat blistered Jamie's skin as she heard Mia climbing the steps. Her friend was going to see her having sex, claiming her man in the most primitive way. Her blood was pumping furiously as she dug her fingers into Caleb's hips and withdrew only to plunge deeper into him.

Caleb groaned loudly, and Jamie almost missed hearing Mia's involuntary gasp. She heard a creak on the step and then . . . nothing. Jamie smiled. Mia wasn't running away. She wanted to spy on them. She needed to see Jamie mount Caleb.

"Do you like that, Caleb?" Jamie asked forcefully, hoping her voice carried over to her audience.

"Yes-s-s."

She picked up her speed, bucking her hips until her skin slapped against his. She watched her purple cock slide in and out of him, wishing Mia could see this. There was nothing like claiming a man this way. The power flooding through her was pure and addictive.

"Oh, God, Jamie," Caleb cried out.

His moan pulled at her as the vibe sent ripples under her skin. She wanted to give Caleb the most exquisite pleasure. She put all her weight and strength into each thrust, taking him harder, faster.

Caleb's moans lit a spark in her veins. Her core was swollen and wet. She loved watching him thrash underneath her. Sweat trailed down her back, and her muscles ached as the vibe pulsed straight onto her clit. Her knees shook as she took him with a ferocious pace.

She felt Caleb's body tense underneath her, his muscles shaking violently. Jamie knew he was about to find his release. She tensed her buttocks and gave one final plunge. Caleb's spine arched as he bellowed. The elemental, deeply masculine sound of surrender echoed around her before Caleb collapsed onto the mattress.

Jamie leaned forward and Caleb moaned at the deeper penetration of her dildo. She swiveled her hips, and his body shook from the overstimulation. Jamie knew it was time to stop. She placed a kiss on his neck as she heard the creak of the steps behind her.

"Thank you," she whispered in Caleb's ear.

He didn't lift his head. "You owe me."

Jamie smiled. She hadn't agreed to that, but this was one time she looked forward to returning the favor.

After taking a quick shower in her minuscule bathroom, Jamie threw on a bathrobe and didn't glance at Caleb, naked and spent, reclining on the bed. She hurried down the stairs, her bare feet slapping against the steps. The thin cotton clung to her wet body and was in danger of becoming transparent. Water streamed from her long hair, already twisting into sodden ropes.

She should have taken the time to towel off, but she needed to catch Mia before she went to work. Jamie found her friend in the cheery yellow kitchen, her focus on the colorful tea mug she held with both hands.

"Isn't this a great morning?" Jamie asked as she strode into the room, ignoring the twinges of her sore muscles. She headed toward the refrigerator and opened the door. "I'm starving."

"You are very chipper this morning." Mia said, not sounding pleased about it at all.

"Of course I am. I went through my whole goody drawer." She grabbed a small container of yogurt and ripped the foil lid off. "Now I have extra room in my car."

Mia didn't seem to be listening. She continued to stare at her tea, as if the brown liquid held answers to a deep, dark mystery.

"You are more than welcome to take anything in the box," Jamie said as she grabbed a spoon and swirled it into the pink tinged yogurt, "because it's just going into the trash. It's not like I can donate it to charity."

Mia absently nodded but didn't say anything. Jamie licked the yogurt off the spoon while studying her friend. Mia's behavior worried her. Had she gone too far? She had tried to pique Mia's curiosity, but had Jamie shocked her so much she was ready to run back to her safe little haven?

"After all," Jamie continued with her spoon in her mouth, "we share everything."

Those last three words jolted Mia, and she sat up straight in her chair. "Jamie," she said very carefully, "I was thinking. . . ."

"Yeah?" Jamie asked as casually as possible as she bit the inside of her mouth. It was too tempting to rush and complete Mia's question.

Mia slowly turned to face her. "Are you still up for swapping guys?"

"Yes," she said with a shrug of her shoulders as victory swelled inside her chest. "After all, I'm the one who offered."

Jamie didn't know what exactly tempted Mia. Was it the possibility of dominating a man? Or was the main draw the idea of having sex with Caleb?

She wasn't going to question it, but Jamie knew she had to warn her friend of the consequences. "If we do this, there is no going back."

"I know," Mia replied and looked down at her mug again. She gnawed on her bottom lip. "Will Caleb do it?"

"Of course," Jamie answered with confidence as the tension left her body. Right after breakfast, she'd let Caleb know that Mia had agreed. Jamie couldn't wait to see his expression.

Caleb would do anything she asked, never requiring conditions or guarantees. She didn't know why Caleb trusted her, other than he was probably more devious than she was. Jamie frowned and pushed the thought away. She could handle Caleb, and now wasn't the time to question that.

"Okay," Mia said in a shaky voice as she nervously fiddled with her long blond hair. "Now I just have to convince Aidan."

Jamie smiled. "Leave it to me." She knew that men were visual creatures. All they needed was the possibility laid out and ready for them. A little nakedness would also help her argument.

Mia watched Jamie carefully. "You've done this before? Swapping partners?"

Jamie quickly schooled her face. "Don't you think I would have told you something like that?" she asked, sidestepping the question.

"True. We share everything"—Mia's smile grew naughty—"including men."

THREE

Aidan stirred awake when he heard someone move around in the bedroom. He blinked his eyes open and saw the pink-and-green floral wallpaper. He was in Mia's bed.

When Mia had inherited the house, she didn't do a lot of re-decorating. Mia wasn't big on changes. The bedroom was very feminine and old-fashioned, from the floral wallpaper to the lace curtains. She had a pale green overstuffed chair, a chest of drawers, and a canopy bed.

Every time Aidan stepped into the room, he felt like he was in foreign territory. Once he moved in here, he would get rid of every frilly, girly thing. The only thing that would remain would be the bed, minus the canopy. The bed had proven to be sturdy on many occasions.

But those plans were academic. No matter how much he brought up the subject, Mia had not invited him to move in. He was beginning to wonder if it would ever happen.

Aidan heard the careful sliding of wood against wood. He

tilted his head and saw Mia closing the drawer before tiptoeing to the overstuffed chair.

She got ready to go to the hospital where she worked in the lab. The blue medical scrubs she wore were baggy on her petite frame. He never liked how her uniform concealed her small curves from him, and his hands itched to slide under the material and roam over her warm body.

She wore very little makeup except for a swipe of lip gloss, which was usually chewed off before she got to the hospital. Her long, wavy blond hair was pulled back into a bouncy ponytail. A few wisps were already escaping around her face.

The diamond studs he had given her for Christmas twinkled in her ears. Heat flared inside him when he saw them. Every time she wore those earrings, Aidan saw it as a sign of his possession. It was the only way he had branded her.

Or maybe not, he thought as he caught sight of a love bite behind her ear. He smiled as the heat roared in his veins. The colorful bruise was small but primal. Anyone who saw it would know that she had been taken.

He shouldn't be proud of the mark. He had gone too far last night. Aidan rubbed the sleep from his eyes and swallowed back a sigh of regret. He had tried to hold back, but all he managed to do was let it build up until he was out of control.

Aidan propped up on one arm. Mia whirled around and saw him before he could say good morning.

"Oh, you're awake," she said in a high, startled voice. "I'm running late. Would you lock up for me?"

"Sure." He noticed she wasn't making eye contact. Her gaze darted everywhere else in the room. That was never a good sign. "Are you okay?"

She gave a guilty start and dared a glance in his direction. "Me?

Yeah. Sure." Mia looked away and gave her full attention to tying her white shoes. "Why do you ask?"

Aidan wanted to tell her there was no reason and to let it go. But he couldn't. He had overheard Mia's conversation with Jamie last night.

He knew Jamie wanted to swap because Mia had only had one sex partner. He clearly remembered Jamie's words: *Are you worried that you're going to ruin things with Aidan, or are you afraid that you might want something more than what Aidan can provide?*

It was Mia's answer that had floored him: *Both.*

Up until last night, he thought Mia and he had shared good communication. It was an essential part when playing with bondage. Obviously, Mia could tell him anything in bed, but out of it was a different matter.

"You've been acting differently since you helped Jamie pack last night," Aidan said, treading carefully around the subject. "Did you guys get into a fight?"

"No." She dragged the word out. She paused, looking straight at him as she gnawed her pink bottom lip. Aidan knew she was debating about telling him. He waited, his heart pounding hard, before she looked away. "I'm just going to miss her," Mia replied. "That's all."

Aidan's shoulders sagged as disappointment weighed down in his chest. She wasn't going to tell him.

Mia leaned forward, and he inhaled her clean, vibrant scent. She gave him a brief kiss on the mouth, her soft lips clinging against his before she stood up. "I have to go. Lock up when you leave, okay?"

"Sure." He barely got the word out before she was gone. She couldn't leave fast enough.

So she wouldn't tell him about Jamie's plan. Aidan exhaled

sharply. If she didn't tell him, how could he convince her to go along with it?

Aidan fell back on the bed, tucked one arm under his head, and looked up at the ceiling. He had to come up with a plan, and quickly. He didn't know how long he would be able to hold out before making a mess out of things.

The moment he had heard Jamie say, "How do you feel about swapping?" his body had clenched. He had become instantly aroused, and his cock had grown heavy as images flickered before his eyes.

The idea of swapping appealed to him, but not for the obvious reasons. Jamie was sexy and, from what he heard, an imaginative lover. Having sex with Mia's best friend would be a unique event, but he wasn't panting for Jamie.

He had always wanted Mia, but he'd waited to make his first move until she was ready for him. He had loved the way she went after him, and he was thrilled that he got to be the one to introduce her to a sensual world. Watching Mia's sexual awakening had taken his breath away, and she'd only just begun the journey.

But if Mia swapped with Jamie, then Aidan had an opportunity he couldn't miss. He could finally fulfill his secret fantasy—the one thing he couldn't tell Mia.

After all, how would Mia react? What would she think of him if she knew? Could he tell her that he wanted to watch her have sex with another man?

Aidan instantly imagined Mia with another man. She would writhe underneath the stranger, begging for more. Her high gasps and keening cries would reverberate through him.

Aidan rubbed his hand against his stiffening cock and hissed through his clenched teeth. He stared up at the white lace canopy, but his mind was traveling back a couple years.

He still remembered the night that had changed him forever. He had been at a wild party celebrating his soccer team's win. Eventually he had realized he hadn't seen his girlfriend Lacey for a while.

After a search through the house, asking everyone if they had seen Lacey, he decided to look out in the yard. There was no one out in front, but by the time he walked along the side of the house, he heard primitive grunts and moans.

He slowed down and saw a couple sitting on the steps leading to the back porch. The harsh light from a single lightbulb glared on them. He immediately recognized the woman's deep red hair. It was Lacey. The man, wearing a red-and-black soccer uniform, was one of his teammates.

Lacey leaned back on the short steps, her legs splayed wide and her denim skirt bunched up to her waist. Her discarded panties were next to her feet. She arched her throat and moaned with unabashed pleasure.

Aidan stepped out of the shadows, needing to see more. The raw jealousy he had felt at first disintegrated as fast as it had bloomed. The look of ecstasy on Lacey's face sparked something hot and dangerous inside him.

He watched his teammate kneel between Lacey's legs and drive his face between her thighs. He was wild and messy, which Lacey obviously enjoyed. Her moans and hoarse encouragements mingled with the smacking of lips and slurps.

As Lacey tossed her head from side to side, she caught a glimpse of Aidan. At first she jerked, sensing trouble, but Aidan had raised his finger for her to be quiet. She lay still, her body tensing as her lover shoved her shirt up and kneaded her breasts.

Aidan mouthed the word "more" and stroked his cock. Lacey's eyes widened in shock, but Aidan watched as understanding dawned on her. It was a mix of relief and dread when she realized he liked watching her with another man.

Her sly smile sent a chill down his spine, but he was too far gone to worry about it. Aidan couldn't stop her or walk away. He needed to watch the pleasure chasing across her face.

As Lacey leaned back on the steps and urged her lover for more, Aidan knew his needs didn't make sense. He had claimed her as his own. He wasn't a guy who shared easily. Why did he need to see this?

He almost came on the spot when the first orgasm rippled through Lacey. She tilted her head back and cried out. Aidan could have sworn the moan echoed in his body. He gripped his cock as he watched his teammate pushing down his shorts.

Lacey wrapped her long legs around the man. Aidan couldn't see it, but he knew the moment his teammate plunged into her. He felt the hot sensations kick the small of his back before they exploded inside him.

He watched his friend pump into Lacey. Lacey met each thrust with a buck and roll of her hips. Every move she made was for Aidan's benefit, giving him the performance of a lifetime.

And suddenly his teammate's rhythm grew chaotic. He couldn't hold back anymore. Aidan heard his friend's hoarse grunt as he pulsed into his girlfriend.

Aidan quickly stepped back into the shadows as his friend immediately withdrew. Aidan continued to stroke his hard cock as he watched his teammate stagger back into the house to join the party. Lacey lay on the steps under the porch light, her bunched-up shirt and skirt exposing her body to him.

Aidan walked toward her. His arms and legs felt heavy, as if they were no longer under his control. He stood before Lacey, taking in everything from her juicy pink core to the red streaks on her breasts and the wicked smile on her face. He slowly pushed down his shorts and knelt down. Grabbing Lacey's knees, he thrust into her wet heat, determined to give her the same pleasure she found with another man.

Everything had changed from that night. Lacey thought his silent acceptance was a sign of weakness. She believed it changed the dynamics of their relationship, giving her all the power. She couldn't have been more wrong.

And maybe he was weak. Aidan considered the possibility as he looked away from the canopy and sighed. He rolled to his side and sat up on the bed, the icy-cold gust from the air conditioner buffeting his hot skin. Why did he find the ultimate pleasure by watching? Why did he want to see his lover taken by another?

What would Mia think if he agreed to the swapping? She had once confessed that she liked to be tied up because too much sexual freedom made her go out of control. Would she act like Lacey? Would she think his voyeurism meant she had carte blanche to take any man anytime? He didn't want that.

What he wanted was to watch Mia find pleasure any way she could find it, as long as she included him. He wanted to set the boundaries for her, knowing she would follow his rules. If she sought his permission, he would grant it.

It was as simple and as complicated as that, Aidan decided as he got up from the bed and stretched. He staggered into the kitchen and saw Caleb at the table drinking coffee.

"Hey," Caleb said by way of greeting. The guy looked as exhausted and out of sorts as Aidan felt. Caleb wore a wrinkled T-shirt and pale worn jeans. His hair was uncombed, and the whiskers on his long, narrow jaw gave him a scruffy look.

Aidan grunted in response and shuffled to the refrigerator. He opened the door and grabbed the milk jug, giving Caleb a sidelong look. Did Caleb know about the idea to swap? Aidan wondered what his reaction had been.

He had gotten to know Caleb during the past year, since he was often around the house. Mia was under the impression that Caleb was deep and dark. Aidan rolled his eyes at the idea, shut the door, and grabbed a bowl from the kitchen cabinet. Just because the guy chose not to talk about himself didn't mean he was deep or dark. Just private.

Jamie enjoyed the fact that her lover was a rule breaker and every exotic fantasy rolled into one man. Caleb wasn't exotic, Aidan decided as he found a spoon and walked to the kitchen table. He simply knew how to play Jamie.

Aidan knew what Caleb was like. He had learned about Jamie's on-and-off lover over the year, and one thing he knew was that the guy wasn't impetuous. Caleb was watchful, and he hung back before he entered a situation. The guy didn't talk much about himself, but when he had something to say, everyone knew his was the voice of experience.

He sat down at the table and shook some cereal into the bowl, giving Caleb another look. Caleb had probably swapped women before. Aidan bet it wasn't a novelty, and if that was the case, what would make him agree to do it again? He wouldn't decline the offer, but he would have an end game of his own.

Aidan needed to know what everyone was planning to get out of this scenario. He couldn't bring it up with Mia or Jamie. Caleb was the best person to approach.

Aidan decided now was as good a time as any to ask, "Is Jamie still planning to swap sex partners?"

Caleb choked on his coffee. "You know about that, huh?" he spluttered.

Aidan shrugged his shoulders and poured the milk. He tried to mask his annoyance. Why had they informed Caleb and not him? "Mia's not going to go for it."

One corner of Caleb's mouth tilted in a smile. "Wanna bet?"

"Yeah." He spooned some cereal in his mouth and chomped down hard. He didn't taste a thing, too busy wondering why Mia was hiding this information from him.

Caleb paused for a moment and then shook his head. "Aw, this is too easy."

Aidan glanced up. "What are you talking about?"

Caleb slowly set his coffee mug onto the table. "Mia agreed to it this morning."

Aidan's spoon slipped from his hand and fell into the bowl. Milk splashed over the rim and moistened him on his hand. "She did?" Aidan asked very quietly as he reached for the spoon and held it tight.

Why had she changed her mind? It was because of last night. Aidan was sure of it. He *had* been too dominant. Damn. Aidan gripped the spoon harder and felt the metal give.

"Jamie and Mia think the only obstacle is convincing you."

The tone in Caleb's voice alerted him. Damn, the guy really did see too much. Aidan kept his eyes on the bowl of cereal so Caleb couldn't see his expression. "Is that right?"

"I told them they might be overestimating the problem." Caleb paused to take another sip of coffee. "What man wouldn't want the free pass to have sex with his lover's best friend?"

Was that what Caleb thought? Aidan would let Caleb continue to operate under that mistaken belief. "You already agreed to it?"

Caleb nodded. "Jamie thinks I'll be doing her a favor."

That just showed how smart Caleb was. Aidan wanted this guy as his ally. "Why do you want to do it?"

Caleb appeared surprised by the question. "Despite what you think, it's not to get into Mia's bed."

Aidan knew he should feel a spurt of jealousy, but all he could think of was Caleb and Mia in bed together. Her slender body would arch underneath Caleb's. She would grab his ass, her fingers digging into his tight muscles. Caleb would thrust into her, the sound of wet flesh and low growls echoing in the room. Aidan clenched his hand, bending the forgotten spoon.

"Settle down." Caleb stared at the bent utensil in Aidan's fist. "I'm not interested in Mia. I want Jamie."

Aidan tossed the spoon onto the table. "You have her."

"For another couple of days," he said with a hint of bitterness. "Then she's heading off to who knows where, and I don't plan to be left behind."

"Oh, I get it. You think if you instantly agree to swap partners, you gain brownie points. She'll know that you aren't holding her back or judging her." Aidan cast Caleb a look of admiration. "That might work."

Caleb nodded. "So the sooner we do this, the better."

"Don't hold your breath." Aidan pushed away the cereal bowl. "Mia might say she's ready, but it's going to take her a while to get used to the idea."

"If Jamie wants to do it before she leaves, it'll happen."

Aidan couldn't argue with that. "What's Jamie's strategy?"

"She wants Mia to explore her sexual boundaries."

Aidan rubbed his hand over his chin. "So anything goes?"

"Yep."

Aidan caught Caleb's sly smile and he went into full alert. "You have something else in mind, don't you? It's not just to get on Jamie's good side."

Caleb held his hands up. "I'm all for swapping partners. The swap may not work out exactly as Jamie hopes. . . ."

Aidan's eyes narrowed. If he didn't get Mia or Jamie, then that left . . . "Whoa!" He pushed his chair back as the fight-or-flight instinct pounded through his veins. "You and me?"

Caleb laughed. "Don't flatter yourself."

"Good," Aidan said with relief. But Caleb's explanation niggled at his mind. Jamie had a plan, and Aidan wanted to be prepared. "Did Jamie say how she wanted it to play out?"

"She didn't tell me anything." Caleb took another sip of coffee. "So how about it? Are you going to swap?"

Aidan knew now was the time to feign reluctance. It was the only way to get what he wanted without too many questions. "It's not that I don't trust you. . . ."

Caleb gave a snort. "Yeah, right."

"But if Mia agrees to this, I'm not going to interfere."

Caleb couldn't hide his surprise. "Really?"

Aidan nodded. "As long as I get to set some ground rules."

"Ground rules?" Caleb's eyebrows shot up. "Jamie doesn't do ground rules."

Aidan was fully aware of that, but Jamie didn't need to know that rules were already in place. Aidan rested his elbows on the table. "Then this is between you and me."

Caleb was quiet, as if he were debating the pros and cons of the alliance. "Okay." He leaned back in his chair. "Let's start with Jamie."

"I'll take it easy on her," Aidan promised.

"Screw that." Caleb made a face. "I want you to tie Jamie up."

Aidan's eyes widened. "Seriously?"

"I'm not suggesting you use force, pain, or anything like that," Caleb assured him. "She needs a taste of deprivation. I want her to learn a little patience."

Aidan closed his eyes, trying to imagine Jamie bound to the bed. She would try it because it was something new and different. But the moment the cuffs enclosed her wrists, she would act like a hellcat, determined to break free.

"It won't be easy," Caleb admitted, "and I don't know how you're going to get her to agree to it. But if you can achieve that kind of miracle, then she'll find out how good she has it with me."

"And after a night with me, you think she'll be clinging to you?" Aidan knew he should feel offended, but he knew it was the truth. Jamie could never handle someone like him. "Okay, fine. Anything else?"

"That's all I can think of. What about Mia?"

Aidan hesitated. He had to make this sound convincing. "I want to be there when you take her."

Caleb's mouth sagged open. "Excuse me?"

Aidan didn't reply. He wasn't sure how to explain it. If he used the wrong word, Caleb would find out about his secret fantasy.

Caleb's eyes narrowed. "I thought you trusted me."

"I do." Aidan wouldn't let any man have sex with his woman. That was a nuance Lacey hadn't quite understood.

"Oh, so you want to watch to pick up pointers—is that it?"

"Funny."

The laughter disappeared in Caleb's eyes. "Seriously, though, Mia might not want you watching her having sex."

Aidan raised his eyebrow. "And Jamie probably doesn't want to be dominated."

"Good point." Caleb shrugged. "But do you think Mia wants to explore while you're there watching?"

"She might feel more comfortable, especially if she knows I'm okay with it." Aidan paused, and decided to go for it. "In fact, I think it would be best if I tell her exactly what she should do to you and how."

Caleb chuckled and waved his hands for Aidan to stop. "No. No way. Aidan, you need to give up some control."

Aidan leaned forward, prepared to get the point across that this was nonnegotiable. "If you guys want me to swap, this is how it's going to have to be. Don't tell me you're not going to try to get your own way."

"I told you"—Caleb placed his hand over his heart—"I'm doing this as a favor."

"Bullshit. You're in this for something more." Aidan didn't have proof, but it was a feeling he couldn't shake. "It's not all about favors or finding someone to dominate Jamie."

"That's all I want."

"You're lying. If I can't trust you on this, I'm not swapping." Aidan gathered his bowl and spoon and scooted back to his chair.

"Okay, fine. There's something I want to happen," Caleb confessed. "I didn't want to tell you because you might be against it."

Aidan remained still, his gut twisting as he prepared for any potential bombshells. "What is it?"

Caleb looked away. "I'm hoping for Mia and Jamie to hook up," he muttered.

Mia and Jamie. Aidan forgot to breathe as he imagined the two of them together, naked and sweaty. Jamie's face would be nestled between Mia's slender legs. Mia's blue eyes would be glazed over with arousal as she climaxed, screaming her best friend's name.

Aidan felt the sweat bead on his forehead. The idea alone made him hot. His fantasies were always about Mia with another man.

But Mia with a woman? With Jamie? His knees went weak as lust flooded through his body.

"Like that idea, too, huh?" Caleb asked.

Aidan wasn't going to answer that. "Mia has never shown any interest in having sex with a woman."

Caleb shrugged. "What's your point?"

"Even if she had lesbian fantasies, she's not going to act on them. She's a Clover Bud girl through and through."

"We can join forces and give it our best shot," Caleb said. "We'll create a mood. Opportunities."

"And if it doesn't happen, then no big deal," Aidan continued. "They'll never know what we were up to."

"It's better than that," Caleb insisted. "Think about it: We'll live out every fantasy, and Jamie and Mia think we're being good sports about it."

Every fantasy? Aidan wasn't sure about that. "Do you really think we can do all this in one night?"

Caleb smiled. "Who says we only get one night?"

Aidan shook his head. The guy was getting ahead of himself. "We can manipulate the situation all we want, but this is a one-time deal."

"Doesn't mean I can't hope."

Aidan thought Caleb was reaching for too much. The guy wanted to hold on to Jamie as well as have more than one night of swapping. Not only that, he wanted Mia and Jamie to hook up.

Mia and Jamie. Aidan imagined their arms and legs tangled. Jamie would be on top, grinding her large breasts against Mia's. "I gotta go to work," he said gruffly.

"So are you in?" Caleb asked. "You're going to swap?"

"Yeah, I'll swap." A flash of excitement ripped through him.

He found it difficult to take his next breath. "When should we tell them?"

"We don't need to." Caleb leaned back in his seat and took a leisurely sip of his coffee. "I want to see how they're going to convince us."

"You mean trick us."

Caleb nodded and smiled. "And we'll trick them right back."

Aidan grinned as the anticipation swelled in his chest. "This is going to be good.

FOUR

FOUR

Several days later, Caleb pulled his battered pickup truck alongside the curb next to Mia's house. He put it in park, leaned his forearms on the steering wheel, and let the engine idle as he studied the modest bungalow.

He didn't think he could wait any longer for the swapping. It had been three days, and he was slowly going crazy from waiting. If he wasn't having sex marathons with Jamie every night, he would have already gone crossed-eyed.

When Jamie had told him Monday morning that Mia was on for the swapping, he made the mistake of believing something would happen that night. The idea of swapping and making some fantasies come true had revved him up, and he had been close to bouncing off the walls. He was the kind of guy who, when he decided on something, took action immediately.

Apparently, no one else felt that way. Caleb gave a long sigh and turned off the engine. The tension had been thick in Mia's house, but no one said a thing. His muscles bunched, were ready to pounce, every time someone made a move.

But nothing had happened. He had been ready to get the party started, but Jamie had asked him to play it cool and go along with her strategy. He had been willing, but he hadn't realized the plan was to make him wait until he grew old and gray.

On Tuesday, it was like the fates were against him. As a handyman, he usually made his own hours, but on that day, he received an emergency call from his best client. He had rushed to Mia's house late in the night, worried that he had missed out.

It turned out he had nothing to worry about. Aidan didn't drop by the bungalow that night. Caleb didn't know whether to be relieved or frustrated. Strangely, Mia and Jamie didn't seem disappointed.

He was beginning to think that they were playing a prank on him. Why mention swapping and then do nothing? Unless Mia and Jamie were getting cold feet. He didn't think Jamie suffered from second-guessing, but Mia might.

Caleb wondered if they had decided against the swap and forgotten to tell him. That was the most likely scenario, he decided as he got out of the truck and slammed the door, the vehicle shuddering and creaking from the impact. All Mia and Jamie talked about in front of him was the Herculean effort of getting Jamie ready for the move.

Or did they not include him in their plans because they thought he would be ready at a moment's notice? Part of that was true, but he wanted a say in how the swapping would work.

He was not sure how he had gotten a playboy reputation. Sure, he'd had some amazing sexual experiences, but that didn't reflect who he was anymore. A lot of those memories were hazy. He couldn't remember the names and faces, and he was sure his previous sex partners felt the same about him. It was disheartening, especially since, at the time, he had been trying to find somewhere he belonged.

Instead he had taken a path to find sexual nirvana but never found it though what he had discovered with Jamie was something special and he didn't want to lose it. Unfortunately, Jamie was ready to walk away from it all. She didn't see him as a partner. Sometimes he got the feeling that Jamie saw him as a sex toy that could talk.

The possibility troubled him. Caleb tucked his head down as he walked up the path to Mia's house. He knew that Jamie didn't mean to treat him that way; she was trying to protect herself. How was he going to prove to Jamie that he was much more? He had less than a week to get the point across.

Tonight he was going to push the idea of swapping out of his mind. It was distracting him from his ultimate goal: to leave Clover Bud with Jamie. He didn't know if Jamie had mentioned the possibility of swapping partners so he would stop talking about their future. He wouldn't put it past her.

Caleb pressed the doorbell and heard the chimes inside the old house. He folded his arms across his chest and waited. The scent of the flowers on the porch drifted toward him as the hot summer breeze pulled at his shirt. He looked through the window panels in the front door and saw Mia step out of the media room and hurry to let him inside.

She wore a pair of bright red shorts that hugged her slender hips. Her blond ponytail swayed from side to side as her small breasts bounced underneath her white tank top. Mia was a beautiful woman, but she didn't have Jamie's sexual zing.

Mia opened the door, and he felt the chill of her air-conditioned home. "Hi, Caleb," she greeted him with a smile. "Come on in. We're hanging out in the media room."

Caleb smiled at the term as she closed the door behind him. "Media room" sounded very contemporary and high-tech for a small old house. He didn't know what the room had been before, but every time he stepped in there, he knew Aidan had either been the architect or the inspiration.

"What are you doing there?" he asked as he followed Mia across the living room floor.

"Oh, we're playing some karate game on the Xbox." She waved her hand in the air. "I have no idea what I'm doing."

Her movement drew his attention to the jiggle of her breasts. Caleb stopped walking as everything around him went into slow motion. Mia wasn't wearing a bra, and he could see the dusky areolas beneath the thin white fabric.

Caleb closed his eyes and swallowed. That was unlike Mia. What was going on? Was tonight the night?

No, he wasn't going to spend another night wondering and waiting. He needed to focus on his top priority: Jamie.

Caleb walked into the media room, his gaze sweeping the corners. The computer sat on a desk in the corner, but it wasn't turned on. Loud yells and crashes came through the surround-sound system. He turned toward the wide-screen television and saw two scantily clad animated women kicking each other, their breasts bouncing as freely as Mia's.

Don't think about that. He purposely turned away from the TV and saw Jamie sitting on the big leather couch. She wore a tight green T-shirt and the tiniest pair of cutoff shorts he'd ever seen.

"Hey, no fair," Mia said to Jamie as she grabbed the abandoned game controller and sat next to her friend. "You can't kung fu me when I'm not in the room."

"All is fair in love and war," Jamie pronounced, pumping her fist in the air when the music started, indicating that the game was over. "Hi, Caleb. Take a seat."

Not exactly the sexy or loving greeting he would have liked, but he'd take what he could get. He walked over to Jamie and gave her a brief, hard kiss. Jamie gave him a distracted smile and returned her attention on the game.

He stepped back and studied the two sitting on the couch. It was rare for them to play Xbox unless he or Aidan invited them to join. Something was up. He tried not to speculate and ignored the tingling in his skin.

"Are you guys done packing?" Caleb asked as he sat on the armrest next to Jamie.

"Yes. Three days before I leave," Jamie said with pride. "Can you believe I didn't wait until the last minute?"

"That is Mia's doing," Caleb said. "You probably tried to put it off, but she wouldn't let you."

Mia smiled and nodded as she pushed the buttons on her controller to start another game.

"You know me well." Jamie frowned as she realized what she'd said. "I might as well go now. No sense hanging around."

Fear congealed in Caleb's stomach. He remained very still and bit down hard on his tongue before he did something stupid—like demand that she stay. Fortunately Mia beat him to the punch.

"Don't you dare!" Mia warned Jamie, taking her eyes off the television. "I helped you pack so we could have fun on your last few days."

"Okay, okay." Jamie raised her hands in surrender. "I'll stay. Let the fun begin."

The tingling was getting stronger for Caleb. He saw the silent exchange between Mia and Jamie. Mia's secretive smile set off alarms in his head.

Tonight was the night. He knew it. He didn't know how he knew, but he couldn't shake the feeling.

Caleb tried to breathe evenly as the anticipation swelled in his chest. He sat down on the floor next to the couch, his arm brushing against Jamie's leg. He curled his hand around her ankle and caressed her warm golden skin.

"Where's Aidan?" he asked as Jamie and Mia played the game. He couldn't help but see how poorly they competed. Why were they playing this game?

"He went to the corner store to get some beer," Mia said as she pressed her thumbs against the control buttons.

Caleb heard the back door swing open and the clink of glass bottles. He recognized the footsteps as Aidan's.

"Did you start without me?" Aidan called out from the mudroom when he heard the warrior cry from the karate game.

"I'm just practicing," Mia yelled back.

"Room for one more?" Caleb asked.

"Absolutely," Jamie said, chuckling evilly when she vanquished Mia's character on-screen. "But we can only play two fighters at a time, so let's make this a competition."

Oh, yeah. Tonight was the night. Her explanation was prepared. Caleb couldn't figure out her plan, but he was willing to go along with it.

"Sure you want me to play?" Caleb asked. "I always win."

Jamie looked down at him and waggled her eyebrows. "Your luck might change tonight."

Aidan walked in with three bottles of Corona. "Hey, Caleb. Didn't know you were here. You want a beer?"

"No, I'm good." He needed to keep on top of his game. He grabbed the controller. "Are you guys ready?"

They took turns playing against one another, and Caleb found out how badly Mia played. Jamie wasn't even trying, and Mia still came in last. Aidan was his only real competition.

Caleb thought it was amazing he was winning by a large margin because all he could think about was swapping.

It was time for him to make the first move. Caleb waited until he slaughtered his competition again. He listened to the swell of the music as the scores appeared on the screen. "I win again," he announced.

Jamie made a face, which didn't surprise Caleb. She was never a good loser. "You must be bored winning all the time."

"I can think of something to make it interesting." He paused, knowing that once he started this in motion, he wouldn't be able to stop it even if he wanted to. "How about the winner gets a kiss from the loser?"

Jamie wrinkled her nose, not impressed with idea. "I get kisses from you all the time."

He loved how she talked big, as if it was a foregone conclusion that she would win. "But this time the winner will tell the loser exactly what to do." He knew how he would claim his prize from Jamie. Her wide mouth would wrap around his cock right before she deep-throated him.

Interest flared in Jamie's eyes. "I'd like to point out that I don't lose all the time."

Caleb raised his eyebrow. "I know."

Jamie's lips parted in surprise as the tension in the room suddenly arced. Jamie slid a look to Mia, but Mia was watching Aidan under her lashes. Everyone waited breathlessly for Aidan's response.

Aidan, sitting on the floor near Mia, drained the rest of his beer bottle in one gulp and wiped the moisture from his mouth. "You're on."

The tension didn't evaporate. Instead it went up a notch. Caleb gave a silent thanks that Aidan didn't back down from the challenge. "What about you guys?" Caleb asked Jamie.

"Sure," Mia agreed for them, her voice high from nervousness. "Let's do it."

Caleb did his best not to look triumphant. He started the game for Jamie and Mia, who would play the first round. He glanced at Aidan, whose face was suspiciously blank.

Should he win this time? Caleb wasn't sure how to play this. He didn't usually throw a game, but he could tell that Mia was nervous. He glanced in her direction. Mia stared intently at the screen. Her shoulders were hunched as she hit every button on her controller.

He knew she wasn't ready. Caleb could tell that she was doing everything in her power not to be last. When the game ended, Mia crowed in victory.

So Jamie was the loser this time. He wasn't sure if she should win or allow the swap to happen between Jamie and Aidan. Caleb debated as Mia fought against Aidan, but she was no match for him. It was now time for him to compete with Aidan.

As they played, he glanced over at Aidan's hands. The man was doing his best to win. Caleb decided then he would lose. He lifted his thumbs and pretended to work the controllers. It was a matter of minutes before Aidan was the victor of the game.

"Shit," Jamie said as she stared at the screen.

"Excuse me?" Aidan said.

"I don't believe this!" Caleb made a show of complaining. "We just make it interesting, and I don't win."

"Okay, Aidan, a deal is a deal," Jamie said as she tossed her controller on the couch. "How do you want me?"

"Come here and find out."

It was obvious that Jamie didn't like Aidan's tone, but she rose from the couch and walked over to where Aidan sat. Without an invitation, she straddled Aidan's hips, her tiny shorts revealed her curvy ass. Jamie placed her hands on Aidan's shoulder and raised her eyebrows in silent question.

Caleb's chest tightened as he watched Jamie in full aggression mode. He always enjoyed it when she was on the prowl, but he couldn't tell how Aidan felt. He had heard the guy liked to be in charge and preferred submissive women, but who could reject such a bold, sexy invitation? Aidan showed no expression as Jamie lowered her mouth onto his.

Aidan reached around the back of Jamie's head and gripped her messy ponytail. Her mouth hovered above Aidan's. She parted her lips and looked straight into Aidan's eyes.

"That's not how I want you," Aidan said coolly.

Aidan made Jamie wait, her mouth just a kiss away from his. Anger flashed in her eyes. Caleb could tell that Jamie was about ready to tell Aidan off. Aidan must have sensed it as he made a swift move, roughly claiming Jamie's mouth, catching her off-guard.

This time Aidan was the aggressor. Caleb saw Aidan's tongue slide past Jamie's lips. Jamie's eyelids fluttered shut as she roughly returned Aidan's kisses.

Caleb cast a quick glance in Mia's direction. She watched with rapt attention as her boyfriend kissed her best friend. When Aidan finally let go of Jamie, they were both gasping for breath. Caleb suspected Jamie would scramble off Aidan's lap. Instead she sat still, her mouth wide-open. She stared blinkingly at Aidan, not saying a word.

Caleb got up suddenly. "I'm going to get a beer. Anyone else want one?" After all three made requests, he scooped up the empty bottles and walked quickly to the kitchen. He dumped the bottles

in the recycle bin and opened the refrigerator door, not really seeing what was on the shelves.

Get a grip. Caleb closed his eyes but he still had the vision of
Jamie kissing Aidan. He wanted to be in Aidan's position, claiming
Jamie's mouth and taking the kiss, rather than taking whatever she
was willing to give. He wanted to match Jamie's dominance and
aggression.

Caleb could get the same response as Aidan did, but not without consequences. If he tried to claim Jamie, she would run in the
other direction. He knew the only way to be invited into her bed
again and again was to surrender the control.

He did it well, which was a surprise. He was used to being the
aggressor. One of his ex-lovers had accused him of being a chame-
leon, ready to change and be the kind of man his lover needed.
Caleb hadn't denied it. It was his greatest strength as a lover, as well
as his weakness.

It didn't make him a great lover—more like the perfect sex partner. In his opinion, there was a difference. A lover gave and took,
while a sex partner was more like a vessel for someone's fantasies.

With Jamie, he had eventually understood that she wanted an
undemanding lover. He had easily slipped into the role, putting
aside his own wants to please her. He always found satisfaction.
Jamie wasn't a stingy lover. She was bold, daring, and impetuous.

And there were nights when he wanted to tame her and harness
that energy for his own pleasure. So why did he ask Aidan to
dominate Jamie?

It was because Caleb couldn't dominate Jamie. Too much was at
risk. If he couldn't dominate her, he would do it by proxy. It didn't
matter if he lived his fantasy through Aidan or through Mia.

Caleb stood up and looked in the direction of the media room, indecision swamping him. Should he have told Aidan the full truth about why he wanted help setting up some girl-on-girl action? He knew Aidan was under the impression Caleb had the common lesbian fantasy most men had.

But would Aidan have agreed if he knew the main reason why Jamie was leaving town? Did he even suspect that Jamie was becoming sexually attracted to her best friend?

Caleb knew that Jamie was bisexual, but he didn't know if she shared that information freely, even with her best friend. It was something that didn't go over well in Clover Bud, and protecting that secret was second nature to Jamie.

Aidan probably didn't know, but he was okay with the idea of Jamie and Mia together. That was good enough for Caleb, and he wouldn't give Aidan any more information. If Mia was intrigued by the idea, then Caleb would do everything in his power to give Jamie her fantasy.

He knew she wouldn't make a move on Mia, worried that it would destroy their friendship. But he might be able to make her fantasy come true without any repercussions. It would be his last gift to Jamie.

Caleb grabbed four beer bottles and went back to the game room. Jamie had returned to her seat, her legs crossed tightly and her arms wrapped around her midriff. Caleb could see that Jamie's nipples were poking hard against her tight shirt.

"Ready for the next game?" Caleb asked as he handed out the last beer bottle. The others agreed, and he watched Jamie and Mia fight each other on-screen.

This time Mia lost, as Caleb had predicted. Next, it was Jamie competing with Aidan. This time Jamie put her all into the game and lost by the narrowest of margins.

As Jamie curled up in her corner of the couch and sulked,

Caleb was ready for his match with Aidan. Unfortunately, the game didn't go as he had planned. Caleb did his best to win, but Aidan was clearly the winner.

"What the hell?" Caleb wasn't feigning surprise this time. He stared at the score on the screen. He had been annihilated by Aidan. "Have you been holding out on me, Aidan?"

He shrugged. "Call it luck."

Mia got up from the couch and stood next to Aidan, who sat on the floor, his legs sprawled in front of him. "Name your prize, Aidan," Mia said with a sweet smile.

Aidan grabbed the hem of his shirt and pulled it off. "Start at my waist and kiss your way up to my lips."

Mia got down on her knees and straddled Aidan's hips. She thoroughly kissed Aidan's stomach and chest, leaving not one spot untouched. Mia was almost reverent in her duty to the point that Caleb couldn't sit still from watching.

By the time Mia reached Aidan's neck, Caleb was doing his best not to find relief by rubbing his cock. Aidan captured Mia's face with his hands and gave her a long, wet kiss. Their moans made Caleb flinch.

"Do you guys want to go back to your room?" Caleb asked drily as his cock began to throb.

They broke off the kiss, and Mia shyly ducked her head, gnawing on her bottom lip.

"Sorry," Aidan replied, unperturbed. "Are you ready for another game?"

"Yes," Caleb said. He was determined to win this time. He wanted in on the action!

Mia and Jamie grabbed the controllers, and Caleb watched them play. Mia's color was heightened, and her eyes sparkled. She was primed and ready for him now.

When she lost, Mia showed no concern. Once again, it was between Jamie and Aidan. Jamie's jaw was set with determination as she sat perched on the couch. She wanted to win.

Caleb looked over at Aidan. He did a double take and frowned. It might look like he was playing but he wasn't even touching the buttons. What was he doing?

Jamie gave a whoop of joy when she beat Aidan.

"Congratulations," Aidan said to Jamie. He turned and caught Caleb's attention.

Caleb frowned when he saw Aidan mouth, *Don't win.*

Don't win? Again? Was he kidding? The guy was getting all the women, and Caleb was sitting with a hard-on watching them. If he lost, then Mia would have to kiss Jamie.

He eyes widened. Ohhh . . . Caleb smiled. He liked the way Aidan thought.

"I'm going to win this time," Caleb announced, riling Jamie's competitive spirit.

"Don't bet on it," Jamie said.

Caleb made the fight with Jamie very close and lifted his thumbs off the buttons right at the end.

Jamie was the winner.

Mia was the loser.

Caleb and Aidan exchanged a look. It would be interesting to see how the girls would try to get out of this.

"Okay," Mia said as she grabbed her beer and took a delicate sip. "Do-over."

"I don't think so," Caleb said, tossing the controller onto the floor.

Mia gestured at the score on the screen. "But Jamie won."

"I can see that," Caleb replied. "The rule is that the loser gives the winner a kiss."

Mia's mouth dropped open in surprise. "But—but—"

"There weren't any exceptions to that." Caleb turned to Aidan. "Were there, Aidan?"

Aidan tilted his head as he tried to recall the agreement. "No, there weren't," he answered.

"Caleb." There was a hint of warning in Jamie's voice.

He looked at Jamie, who looked uncertain what to do. That was a surprise to Caleb. Jamie was brazen and assertive. Why was she hanging back?

Was she afraid to have a taste of her secret fantasy, worried that it would not live up to her expectations? Or was she concerned that she might like it too much? He couldn't do anything about that, but he just offered her a fantasy that had no strings attached.

"Go for it, Jamie," Caleb said.

Jamie looked at him and then at Mia. She tried to show no expression but Caleb saw the excitement flickering in her eyes.

"Fine," Jamie said breezily. "Mia, lie down on the floor."

FIVE

FIVE

"Are you kidding me?" Mia asked, her heartbeat starting to race. They had to be joking.

Jamie motioned impatiently at the floor. "Lie down."

Mia looked at the beige carpet and then back up at Jamie. What the hell was going on here? Jamie and she were supposed to swap sex partners, not spit!

Mia glanced at Aidan, hoping to get some guidance. She was surprised by the hot, smoky look in his eyes. She blinked and looked again, but she still saw it.

She couldn't believe it. The idea of watching her kiss Jamie was turning him on. Why? She didn't get it. Sure, it was scandalous and taboo, but she got the feeling this wasn't why he liked the scenario.

She looked at Caleb, noticing the rapid rise and fall of his chest. Oh, God. Him, too. Why did men want to see two women get together? And why her? She had never kissed a woman, had never considered even trying.

"Go for it," Aidan urged her.

Mia hesitated. The swapping wasn't exactly going as she had planned. There was nothing she could do about it now.

Anyway, the whole point of swapping was to explore her options. Test her sensual boundaries. Of course, she had thought that meant with a *man,* which just proved how limited her thinking was.

Mia rose from the couch and slowly lay on the floor, her heart jumping in her chest. Why hadn't she considered this exchange might happen? It was because she had been so fixated on having sex with Caleb. This was what she got for trying to trick the guys into swapping.

She stared at the ceiling, holding her arms tight against her sides. It was no big deal, just out of her comfort zone. She wasn't opposed to the idea, but she wasn't prepared for it either.

And if she was going to kiss a girl, Mia would want it to be Jamie. Jamie could make anything a wild ride. And if Mia ever swung that way, she would with Jamie, the sexiest woman she'd ever known, over any hot actress or model.

But that decision didn't stop her from tensing up when Jamie crawled above her. Mia watched her with wide eyes. Why was she hovering above her like a jungle cat ready to pounce? All Jamie had to do was lean over and brush lips with Mia.

Jamie braced her forearms on both sides of Mia's head. Mia stared up her mind whirling chaotically as Jamie rested her pelvis against hers. Mia automatically parted her legs, allowing for Jamie to settle between her thighs.

Oh, why had she done that? A blush sizzled across her skin. The movement was too telling, too inviting. Mia didn't know what she was doing anymore.

She wished she could put her legs together but it was too late. She wasn't going to bend her knees or buck her pelvis against Jamie.

But it didn't seem to matter. Her friend leaned down and their breasts pressed against one another.

"Let's give them a show," Jamie whispered in Mia's ear. Her warm breath tickled Mia's skin.

A show? Mia thought her eyes were going to bug out. She was trying to think of a way to get the kiss done quickly so they could move on to the next game. There was no way she could put on a show when she was frozen to the spot.

Jamie dipped her head and placed a gentle kiss on Mia's lips. Mia's heart stopped. Jamie tasted of beer and lipstick, and her mouth was warm.

Mia tentatively responded to the soft caress. She had never realized how silky Jamie's lips were. Mia slicked the tip of her tongue along Jamie's bottom lip.

Her inquisitive touch jolted through Jamie. She felt the tremor sweeping her friend. Jamie plunged her tongue past Mia's stunned lips. Jamie's aggressive move shifted some dark, unnamed emotion inside Mia.

Mia didn't want to figure out what was going on with her. A part of her wanted to pull back and return to her safe little world. Another part of her knew it was already too late. Did she have the courage to explore?

Jamie's tongue tangled with hers. Mia's nipples puckered, and she felt a twinge in her core. She was embarrassed that her best friend could easily arouse her. Mia inhaled sharply as she felt her pussy swell and Jamie deepened the kiss.

Kissing Jamie wasn't what she expected. Her body tingled, her nipples stung, and her pussy pulsed with urgency. Mia wanted to ride out the sweet ache. She arched her spine, her hard nipples pressing hard against Jamie's large breasts.

She heard Jamie's groan. It vibrated deep inside her. She tilted her hips, and Jamie rocked against her. Jamie placed her hands on either side of Mia's head, her long nails tangling into her blond hair, scraping her scalp.

Jamie lifted her head. She was breathing heavy, her warm breath billowing over Mia's face. "Kiss me harder, Mia."

Oh. My. God. She knew this was for show, but Jamie's harsh tone pulled deep in her belly. Her friend knew how sexual commands turned her on. She couldn't help it any more than she could help becoming aroused by her best friend!

Mia wiggled her hips and felt the damp heat between Jamie's legs. She stilled under her friend. Jamie was getting turned on as well? Mia couldn't believe she had the power to excite her sexy friend. The sense of power crashed over her like a wave.

Jamie kissed her roughly, their lips grinding as she thrust her tongue into Mia's mouth. Mia liked the pressure. The sting of her mouth added to her pleasure. She immediately dueled her tongue with Jamie's, not caring if she won or lost this battle.

She felt Aidan's eyes on her. Mia kept her eyes shut as a blush bloomed on her skin. She had forgotten that Aidan and Caleb were there watching. What did they think of her now?

Mia captured Jamie's tongue and sucked it ruthlessly into her mouth. The intense pull made her shiver. Mia mewed and tilted her chin up, surrendering to Jamie.

She wrapped her legs around Jamie's bare legs and clung to her friend's back. Mia glided her hands up and down Jamie's back, noticing every flex of muscle and the lack of a bra. She swept her hands up and down Jamie's spine before she reached down and grabbed Jamie's ass with both hands.

Jamie reared back in surprise. Mia licked her swollen lips with the tip of her tongue under Jamie's watchful gaze. Mia smiled. It wasn't often when she could shock her friend.

But the kiss had already gone too far. It was supposed to be for show, and she had managed to forget she had an audience. Mia untangled her legs from her friend's, carefully watching Jamie's expression.

"One more game?" Mia asked as she sat up, surprised by how firm her voice sounded. She busied herself by fixing her hair, barely hearing the others agree. Her heart was pounding in her ears, her body ached for satisfaction, and whoever got her next was going to be lucky, because she was one hard thrust away from a ripping orgasm.

She grabbed the controller and only then noticed her hands shaking badly. "Someone else can go first."

Aidan took the controller from her hand and played against Caleb. Mia tried to focus on the game, but the colors blurred before her eyes.

Well, Mia thought, she hadn't had sex yet, but she was learning all sorts of things about herself. She hadn't expected to enjoy kissing Jamie, and she certainly didn't think she had the ability to arouse her friend. Mia wasn't sure if she wanted to explore any further and find out more about her sexual allure and power.

"Caleb," Jamie exclaimed, "you lost again!"

"I don't understand what's going on here," he complained.

"Give me the controller," Jamie said, offering no sympathy. "It's my turn against Aidan."

Mia silently watched the competition between Jamie and Aidan, with the characters on the screen doing superhuman moves. Mia knew she wouldn't be the loser this time—Caleb was—but she probably would lose in the next game if she didn't put a stop to this challenge.

But she didn't want to. Mia was curious who would win her next. She kind of wanted it to be Caleb because she had never had him before. But if she got Aidan, he knew exactly how to touch her so she would go off like a rocket.

"Damn!" Jamie said as she angrily threw down the controller. "Okay, what's going on, Aidan? Have you been practicing secretly?"

"No," he said with a smile, "but I've never had incentives like these before."

"It's your turn, Mia," Caleb said as he handed her the controller.

Mia accepted the controller and began hitting all of the buttons when the game started. She wasn't going to win this game, and her mind was already on the next. She was still hitting the buttons as the scores came up on the screen. Jamie's voice pierced through her fog.

"Mia won?" Jamie said incredulously.

Mia's hands froze on the controller. "Say what?" That couldn't be right. She was randomly hitting buttons without any strategy. Mia squinted at the scoreboard on the screen.

"You won Caleb," Jamie said.

How could that be? Aidan was better at this game. Both of the men were, which was why she and Jamie had set up the game. The odds of losing to Caleb were in her favor.

But now she had *won* Caleb? That couldn't be right. She wanted a recount! Mia stared at Aidan and noticed the gleam in his eye.

She realized what had happened. The truth mushroomed inside her until it felt like it was going to burst through her skin. She might not have won him fair and square, but what was she going to do about it now? She would have preferred if Caleb had won her. Mia knew she wasn't ready to give orders in front of an audience. What if Caleb didn't listen, or worse, what if he knew exactly what she wanted?

She should play it safe and ask for a kiss on the lips. Then she'd grab Aidan and take him to bed. He would wrench multiple orgasms from her. Her body clenched with anticipation. Aidan was satisfaction guaranteed.

But she didn't want a guarantee. She needed to know what it was like being with a different man. She had thrown away the chance of getting what was familiar the moment she'd agreed to the swap.

She watched Caleb crawl toward her. "How do you want me to kiss you?" he asked.

Mia nervously licked her lips and tasted Jamie's fruity gloss. It was now or never. She suddenly felt very jittery. She knew it was time to take a risk. Take everything. She might never get another chance.

"Kiss my breasts," she said quietly. She felt the stunned silence hit her. For some reason, she hadn't expected that kind of reaction. Mia was tempted to take a quick, reassuring look at Aidan.

No, she wasn't going to get directions from him. If she needed guidance, she should do what Jamie would do. Her friend always made the opposite choice, and there were times when Mia was envious of Jamie's devil-may-care attitude.

Mia leaned back on the couch and stretched her arms out as if she was confident that she wouldn't be denied. "I'll let you know when to stop."

Caleb's eyes gleamed with amusement. Mia blushed and looked away. She wanted him to be aroused and excited. She'd bet Jamie didn't get this type of response from him. Maybe she shouldn't try to be like Jamie and follow her instincts.

Caleb bent his head down and pressed his mouth against her left breast. Her thin tank top was the only thing separating them, but she felt his warm breath and wet tongue.

She was tempted to give him orders. She'd start by telling him to bunch up the shirt. But she didn't dare. Not yet.

With her breath hitching in her throat, Mia watched Caleb kiss the top of her breasts. He took his time, leisurely exploring the gentle slope until he reached her nipple.

He swirled his tongue around the peak of her breast, instantly wetting her tank top. Her nipple poked hard against the transparent cotton. She didn't move, her fingers raking the couch cushion as he closed his mouth around her nipple.

Mia swallowed back a moan as liquid heat gushed through her. She allowed her eyelids to drift down as he latched on to her nipple. He drew the crest deeply into her mouth, and this time she couldn't hold back a moan.

She wanted to keep her eyes open and watch Caleb, but she was afraid to show how she felt. What would her eyes reveal? What would Aidan read into it? Would Jamie see how much Mia enjoyed Caleb's touch? Would Caleb?

This time Mia felt Aidan's presence strongly. It was as if he were sitting next to her. He was silent but she knew he was attuned. She felt every time he shifted or made a move.

Was he surprised? Horrified? She was becoming increasingly curious, but she didn't want to ruin this moment.

Caleb bit down on her nipple. The edge of his teeth sliced through the sensual fog enveloping her. Mia gasped as the heat spread through her breasts.

She wanted Caleb's mouth all over. She wanted him to lick and taste her skin. She longed for him to bite and leave his mark.

"Push up my shirt," she said in a whisper. Giving the sexual command felt uncomfortable against her tongue.

She felt Caleb jerk his head up in surprise. "What was that?"

She wasn't going to repeat it. Mia grabbed the hem of her tank top and yanked it up to her armpits, exposing her naked breasts. "Keep going."

She opened her eyes, ready to risk everything so she could watch Caleb take her breast into his mouth. She already made it clear that she liked his touch and wanted his mouth on her naked skin. Aidan hadn't said a word. Neither had Jamie. Could she take their silence as acceptance?

Her breath caught in her throat as she watched him lave his tongue along the underside of her breast. Her pussy tingled, and she squeezed her thighs together. When Caleb pressed her breasts together and nuzzled his face in her cleavage, Mia bit her lip, enjoying the rasp of his unshaven jaw.

In fact, she wished he weren't so gentle. She wanted him to squeeze her breasts until he left red marks streaking her pale skin. She needed him to pinch and nip and chew her nipples until she was writhing underneath him, screaming his name.

But she couldn't—wouldn't—go that far. The agreement was a kiss only, and she would follow the rules, no matter how much she wanted to break them.

Mia arched her spine when Caleb chewed her crinkled nipple. She gasped, not from the savage touch or the fire streaking through her blood. How did Caleb know exactly what she needed without her telling him? What gave her away?

Her gaze collided with Jamie. Her friend was on her knees, her face flushed as her eyes glittered. Jamie was smiling and nodding her head, silently encouraging Mia to go further.

Caleb kissed the underside of her right breast. His touch was sweet and gentle. She wasn't expecting him to suddenly suck her breast hard. She cried out as her nerve endings sparked to life. Mia felt the pull of his teeth go straight to her clit as he branded her with his mouth.

Oh, no. Caleb had marked her. What was Aidan going to think about this? She turned and looked at her boyfriend. He was rising to his feet and approaching her with a swiftness that surprised her.

What was he going to do? For once, she had no idea what would happen next. Would Aidan push Caleb away? Would he join them? Mia gasped as her pussy creamed from the thought.

She couldn't tell by his expression, but she didn't move away. Caleb's mouth felt so good, and she wanted his mouth all over her. Aidan was just going to have to wait his turn.

Mia's eyes widened. Had she said that out loud?

Aidan reached out and picked her up in one sweeping move. She suddenly didn't feel powerful anymore. More like delicate and small against Aidan's strength.

But she wasn't afraid. Not with Aidan. Even in the heat of passion, Aidan never lost control. He was, however, dangerous to her senses.

Mia looked into Aidan's eyes, and excitement twisted sharply inside her. Aidan had had enough of foreplay and was ready to claim her.

Had he gotten turned on watching her half naked with Caleb? Or was he staking his territory? If that was the case, this swapping was over before it started. But she didn't care at that moment.

She clung to his bare shoulders. Aidan wrapped an arm around her back and held her close. His body heat scorched her as her breasts pressed against his chest. She whimpered as the coarse hair scratched her hardened nipples.

"What are you doing?" Jamie asked Aidan, jumping up from the couch.

"The game is over," Aidan announced. He carried Mia out of the room. She heard Jamie's throaty laugh trailing behind her.

Aidan took Mia to her bedroom and kicked the door shut. He

didn't put her down as he pulled the scrunched up tank top from her body before tugging off her shorts and thong.

"Are you okay?" Mia asked. She hated having to pose the question, but Aidan's moves were usually graceful and thought out. Tonight he was abrupt and urgent.

"Oh, yeah," he said in a growl. He gradually lowered her to a stand, brushing her small curves against the hard planes of his body.

She stood before him, unsure what he was going to do next. She'd never seen him like this. Mia clasped her hands behind her back and obediently dipped her head, eagerly waiting for instructions.

Aidan stroked his hand along her cheek before he crooked his finger under her chin. He gently tilted her face up, but she felt the hot desire whipping through his body. She admired his ability to master his responses, but at the same time she wished she could unleash his lust just by being naked in front of him.

"Take my jeans off."

Mia did as he asked. She pulled his belt free and unzipped his jeans. Shoving the denim down his thighs, she knelt down before him, ready to serve.

He petted the top of her head, and she felt the tremor in his hand.

"Now my underwear," he said.

Mia reached for the waistband of his white briefs and slowly stripped him naked. Aidan's thick cock bobbed in front of her face. His masculine scent whetted her appetite. She had to taste him.

But first she had to wait for permission. It was a rule they had established long ago, and Mia was proud that she had never broken her word, no matter how much she wanted him.

Aidan gripped the base of his erection and fed his cock to her. Mia groaned and licked the wet crown hungrily.

As she swirled her tongue around his cock, she fought the urge to grab and fondle his balls. She wanted to lick and suck the heavy sacks.

Instead she licked the length of his cock. Every move she made got her closer to his balls. She abruptly pulled back, not sure if she could fight the temptation.

Aidan stepped back and Mia looked up in surprise. Did he know she had almost disobeyed him? Would he punish her with sensual torment? A shiver swept down her spine as her core clenched in anticipation.

"Wait," Aidan told her. He reached for his belt and stepped behind her. Mia held her breath. What was he going to do?

She almost turned her head to see, but stopped herself short. It didn't matter if she felt vulnerable. She trusted Aidan. Everything he did was for her pleasure as well as his own. She knew this and kept her gaze directly ahead.

Mia felt the leather slither against her wrist before he bound her hand with his belt behind her back. The position caused her to thrust her breasts out. Mia bit her lip as the arousal dripped down her thigh.

When Aidan stepped in front of her, he held her jaw in his hands and opened her mouth wide.

"Suck me," he ordered, guiding his cock past her lips.

Mia kept her gaze on his face as she licked and suckled his cock. She drew him deep in her mouth, but she couldn't take all of him. She wished she could wrap her fingers against the root of his cock and pump hard. She would love to squeeze his balls. But she couldn't. Her arms burned as she pulled at her bindings.

She lavished all of her attention on Aidan. She sucked hard and then brushed her tongue lightly against his cock. Aidan's hips started to buck against her face and she mixed up her tempo to keep him on edge.

When Aidan began to thrust in her mouth, he froze. Mia continued to lap his cock, feeling every twitch and pulse against her tongue. She knew he was going to pull out, and she was going to do everything to stop it.

As he reluctantly withdrew, Mia curled her tongue along the sensitive spot under his cock. Aidan shuddered and didn't move. She lunged forward and clamped her mouth around him, drawing him deep, until he touched the back of her throat.

It was too much for Aidan. He held the side of Mia's face and started to thrust, long and hard. Mia enthusiastically met his demand. Aidan tried to hold back but at the last moment he plunged forcefully past her lips, pulsing hotly in her mouth.

Mia closed her eyes and swallowed. She smiled, realizing that she had created a chink in Aidan's armor. She had made him lose control. Testing her boundaries revealed a power of hers that she didn't know she had.

She didn't want to stop exploring. It was time to see if her powers of persuasion could convince Aidan to continue the swap.

SIX

Later that night, Mia lay in bed with Aidan, her head resting against his shoulder as she stared up at the lace canopy. The heady sense of power she had enjoyed drifted away, and she now felt uncertain. She needed to know how Aidan felt about her kissing Jamie. She had to hear what he thought about the way she ordered Caleb to lick her breasts.

"Aidan," she asked softly, "are you okay with what happened during the game?"

"If I wasn't, I would have said so."

She looked at him. His eyes were closed and he appeared on the verge of sleep. What happened in the media room hadn't bothered him at all. "Then why did you pull me away?"

He opened his eyes and looked down at her, a smile playing on his mouth. "I wanted you too much."

She narrowed her eyes, not sure if that was the whole truth. There had been plenty of times when he'd wanted her, but he hadn't rushed her out of the room to have sex. "So"—she took a deep breath and plunged right in—"do you want to do it again?"

Aidan didn't move, but she felt him tense. "Do you want to?"

This was her chance. She had to tell him the truth. "Yes." She cringed at the way her voice wobbled. She really wanted this. Why couldn't she ask for it loud and clear?

"Why do you want it?" Jeez . . . why did he always ask her such tough questions? Did he know it was one way of stripping her naked, layer by layer?

Mia looked away and wished she hadn't. Why couldn't she tell him her fantasies? He was her boyfriend, after all.

But there were times she felt too much was at stake. She was invested in this relationship, and she didn't want to mess it up. Mia gave a fractured sigh. She felt very vulnerable, more exposed than when she was naked, spread-eagle, and chained to his bed.

But if she told Aidan what she wanted, then he would think he wasn't enough for her. That would lead to all sorts of questions and complicated answers. It would be best for everyone involved if she held back.

Mia gave a halfhearted shrug. "I just want to do something different and see what it's like."

"What do you want to do exactly?"

Trust Aidan to ask for the gritty details. "I want to swap with Jamie. Just once." She squeezed her eyes shut. *Don't ask me why. Please don't dig too deep, because I don't know why I want to do this. I don't know what my answer will be.*

"Okay."

She swiveled her head. Did he agree? She almost couldn't believe it. Had simply agreed without any conditions or limitations? That didn't feel right. "'Okay?'" she repeated. "Just like that?"

"Yeah, just like that." He curled her closer to his side, and she flattened her hand against his chest. "But I don't know about Jamie."

"She's okay. . . . I mean"—she grimaced as she stumbled on her explanation—"she'll be okay with the swap." No need for him to know it was a done deal.

"She might say she's okay with it, but she doesn't know what she's getting into."

Mia rubbed her palm against Aidan's chest, the crisp hair rough against her skin. "Jamie isn't naive."

"It isn't about being naive," Aidan argued. "When it comes to sex, Jamie is all about having the power. I bet she can't relinquish it."

Mia knew Jamie couldn't. She was too strong-willed, unlike Mia. "Well, you could go easy on her."

"I don't think so." Aidan placed his hand over hers. "Jamie can be greedy with power. She would do anything to be on top, and I'm not going to let that happen."

Mia raised her head. "Why won't you let a woman overpower you?"

"Because they see me as a challenge and try to break me," Aidan replied in a harsh tone.

Mia gnawed on her bottom lip. She knew Jamie would try to tame Aidan. Her friend wouldn't be able to resist teaching Aidan some manners.

"You could tie her down if you wanted to," Mia offered. "Don't worry about Jamie. She's been tied down before."

"Not by me." Aidan closed his eyes as if that were the end of the discussion.

Mia patted his chest. "She can handle you."

"Maybe you should be with us."

Mia snatched her hand away. "Excuse me?"

"I think you should be in the room when we swap," he clarified.

Mia's mouth sagged open. "You want me to watch you have sex with my best friend?"

He opened his eyes and studied her face. "I thought you were okay with it."

She was when she thought they would have private rooms. This was something entirely different. "Well, yes, but . . ."

"I'm not asking you to join in."

A vision exploded inside her head. She was in bed with Jamie and Aidan, both determined to give her pleasure. They would make it a competition. Mia would be in the middle as their hands and mouths roamed over her naked body. . . .

"Unless you want to."

Mia jerked out of the daydream. "No, thanks."

If she ever did a threesome, it would be with Aidan and Caleb. She would want all the attention and pleasure directed on her. Although if her daydream was any indication, she would find that no matter who her partners were.

"You'll need to be with Jamie," Aidan decided and burrowed his head into his pillow. "It will make her feel safer. More comfortable."

"I thought you knew Jamie," Mia teased. "She doesn't care about comfort. She's all about what's dangerous and wild."

"She might change her mind when she's with me. You can coach her through it."

"Ha! Me teaching Jamie about sex?" She had to laugh. "That'll be the day!"

Aidan rolled over and pinned Mia to the mattress. He held her arms out wide and didn't speak until she looked into his eyes.

"Mia, don't sell yourself short. You are the most sensual woman I've ever known."

Mia's heart melted a little from his words, but she knew he

would say that to her. She was his girlfriend after all. "But I've hardly done as much as she has."

"Doesn't matter," he said as he nuzzled her neck. He deeply inhaled her scent. "You know how to give and receive pleasure."

Mia smiled shyly and blushed.

Aidan traced the love bite behind her ear, which he had given her earlier in the week. "And when you and Caleb get together, I want to be there."

"Wait a second." The warmth zinging her body disappeared in an instant. "I didn't agree to that."

Was this why he was being so accommodating, and why he'd invited her to be in the room when he and Jamie got together? Was he choosing his battles? Then Aidan was in for a big surprise. She wasn't going to obey this wish so easily.

"What's the problem?" he whispered in her ear.

"I—I . . ." She tried again. "You don't have to worry about me."

"I'm not."

She closed her eyes and sighed. How was she going to explain this? "Trying something different means not having you involved."

Aidan lifted his head, and she saw the hurt flicker in his eyes. "I see."

Mia pressed her lips together. That hadn't come out right. And it wasn't like she had to have privacy to find satisfaction. The four of them had urged one another on when they'd shared a few kisses. She'd even enjoyed it when Jamie had kissed Aidan.

That had surprised her. She thought she would feel a twinge of jealousy or insecurity. Instead, the kiss got her excited.

Now she wondered if she had ruined the swap because she didn't want Aidan watching over every sexual situation in her life.

Aidan sighed. "How about a compromise?"

Compromise? Mia tilted her head, as if she didn't trust her

hearing. Did Aidan, her dominating lover, just offer a compromise when it came to sex? "What are you suggesting?"

"You let me watch the first time you and Caleb are together . . . ."

First time? Her heart gave a twist. How many times did he think Caleb could get it up in a night? "And?" she prompted.

"And we'll extend the swap to last until Jamie leaves Monday morning."

That was four days of swapping. It was more than Mia had hoped for. How could she possibly say no? She wasn't going to waste her time weighing the potential problems. "Agreed."

"I'll call in sick tomorrow."

"This isn't a done deal," Mia told him. She didn't want him to lose a day of work for nothing. "We still need to get the others to agree."

"Oh, I doubt that's going to be a problem," Aidan said as he claimed her mouth with his.

The next morning Jamie jumped up from the kitchen table and stared at Mia standing beside her before glaring at Aidan leaning against the doorway. "You both have lost your ever-lovin' minds."

Mia held up her hand. "Jamie . . ."

Jamie looked at her friend. How could Mia agree to this plan? "The way he's explaining it, he wants to dominate me."

"Well . . ." Mia's voice puttered out.

Jamie pointed at Aidan. "I'm not agreeing to be a guy's sex slave."

"You won't be," Mia promised. "I'll make sure of it."

Jamie raised her eyebrow. "You?" She adored her friend, but Mia could not stop Aidan from doing whatever he pleased.

"I'll be right there with you."

Whoa. Jamie's eyes darted from Mia to Aidan. Mia was going to be with them while they had sex? That put a different spin on things.

Jamie had been pleasantly surprised by how she felt kissing Mia. Oh, who was she kidding? Kissing Mia had rocked her world.

Mia wasn't the first girl she'd kissed, and she probably wouldn't be the last. But kissing Mia was different. It aroused Jamie, and she felt the emotional bond between them tightening.

Jamie cast a suspicious look in Aidan's direction. "What do you plan to do to me?"

"Forget it," he said. "It's not going to work if she can't trust us."

"Trust isn't the problem." She trusted Mia with her life. Aidan wouldn't cause her pain, but he would try to make her surrender. She didn't do that for any guy.

"Then what is?" Mia asked, desperate to make this work. It made Jamie feel even worse for refusing.

Jamie folded her arms across her chest and glared at Aidan. "I don't like being tied up."

"Why?" he asked.

"I have this thing about freedom." Didn't everyone? Well, everyone but Mia, but she didn't know any better. That was why she needed this swap.

"What about your lover?" Aidan asked. "Swapping isn't all about your fantasies and what you want. It's also about your partner's need."

What was he suggesting? That she was a selfish lover? To whom had he been talking? "I can do that and stay away from bindings. I'm multitalented that way."

"Maybe you need an introductory lesson," Aidan suggested.

It was difficult for Jamie to keep the outrage from bubbling to the surface. "Lesson?" she repeated. Did he know who he's talking to?

"What if Mia holds you down?"

Jamie blinked, and she looked at Mia. "How?" Mia appeared fragile and petite. She wasn't muscular, but Jamie knew Mia's strength was moving fast.

"You'll take off your clothes and lie on the table," Aidan said. "Mia will sit on the end where your head is, and she'll hold your wrists down."

Jamie's nipples tightened at his matter-of-fact explanation. "And you?"

"I'll hold on to your legs."

That wasn't the answer she was looking for. She wanted to know what he had in store for her. Was he going to tease her unmercifully or drive his cock into her without any foreplay?

"It's okay, Jamie," Mia said, resting her hands on her shoulders. "You don't have to do this. I don't want you to be uncomfortable about anything."

Okay, now the world had gone mad. When Mia was trying to soothe Jamie about sex, she had lost control of the situation completely. Jamie rubbed her tired eyes, knowing she had to regroup.

She wasn't afraid or uncomfortable with bondage, but she liked to keep it to a minimum. If a guy tied her up, he was inevitably testing this luck. Aidan was no different from any other man in Clover Bud.

But what was she worried about? Aidan wasn't smarter or stronger than she was. Jamie knew she could handle him with her hands literally tied behind her back.

"Okay, Aidan." She rubbed her hands together. "Let's do it."

"Now?" Mia asked, obviously surprised by her attitude change.

"No time like the present," Jamie said with a shrug. "Would you like to undress me?"

"No," Aidan said coolly. "Mia will."

"What?" Mia said. It was obviously news to her. "I thought . . ."

"It's no big deal, Mia," Jamie said. "You've helped me in and out of clothes in dressing rooms."

"Yeah, but . . ." Her voice trailed off. She cleared her throat and rolled her shoulder back. "Okay, sure."

Jamie felt jumpy as Mia stood behind her, and she flinched when she felt her friend's hands on her waist. Mia grabbed the hem of Jamie's T-shirt and inched it above her abdomen and ribs. Jamie kept her eyes defiantly on Aidan. Once her shirt went over her breasts, Jamie raised her arms, and Mia pulled it free.

She felt Mia hesitate. Was Mia trying to decide how to attack her front-closure bra? Rather than going around and blocking Aidan's view, Mia reached around Jamie and unhooked the bra.

Jamie shivered as Mia's arms went around her. Mia and she had hugged before, but this was different. The sight of Mia's delicate hands next to her voluptuous breasts was startling.

Mia slowly peeled the bra from Jamie's breasts and allowed the shoulder straps to drop down her arms. Jamie wished Mia would touch her breasts. She would be happy if Mia's hand brushed against her tightening nipples. But Mia was being very careful not to touch her. Jamie shrugged off the bra and heard it drop to the tile floor.

Mia was already hooking her fingers around the waistbands of Jamie's shorts and panties. She worked them down Jamie's legs. Jamie decided not to help Mia or make it easier for her friend. She stood still and continued to watch Aidan.

The man was playing it cool. There was no tension, no shifting of his feet. One would think he wasn't turned on by the sight. But what man didn't want to see his girlfriend strip her best friend naked? How often did his girlfriend prepare another woman for him to play with?

Aidan could play it anyway he liked, but she had seen his eyes. They were hot and smoky with lust. He was just as aroused as she was. Now if only she could see Mia's expression. Was her friend getting turned on? Was Mia getting excited undressing her? Jamie wanted that to be the case.

"Lie on the table," Aidan said the moment Jamie stepped out of her clothes.

She bristled at the order. "I'm getting there." She knew what was expected of her. She'd do it when she was good and ready. Did he like the sound of his voice ordering commands?

She perched on the edge of the round table, surprised at how cold it felt against her skin. Jamie slowly reclined, jerking still when she felt Mia's hand on her shoulders. Her nipples stung with anticipation, but Mia was only guiding her down gently.

Once Jamie's head touched on the wood table, Mia reached for her arms. She stretched them above Jamie's head and held her wrists firmly against the table. Jamie thought Mia was taking her job way too seriously. And shouldn't Mia be on her side and loosen her hold?

Aidan strolled toward the table, his eyes slowly going over every inch of Jamie. Her skin tingled with anticipation as her breasts felt full and heavy. Heat seeped through her body, flooding her core.

But Aidan didn't move. His gaze took in every inch of Jamie, from her puckered nipples to her glistening pussy, but he didn't touch her. He seemed content to look.

"I'll be right back." he said as he turned and walked out of the kitchen. "Don't move."

"What the hell?" Where did Aidan think he was going? She was laid out before him, and he walked away? The nerve. Jamie tried to get up, but Mia's hold tightened on her wrists.

"Don't move, Jamie," Mia whispered.

Jamie rolled her eyes. "Oh, like he's going to know."

"He will." Mia paused. "By the way, thanks for swapping."

"No need to thank me. This is going to be fun." And the moment she said it, she knew it would be. Okay, she wasn't sure about being pinned down, but she'd have Aidan pinned down before she left Clover Bud. The challenge excited her.

Aidan excited her. She wasn't sure how she felt about that. She had never thought of him that way because he was Mia's. Now that she was borrowing him, she was beginning to see what Mia saw in him.

Aidan returned. Jamie noticed he wasn't carrying anything, and nothing was different in his appearance. The man had walked away to play mind games with her. She wasn't going to tolerate that.

Not that she had much say in the matter as Aidan grasped Jamie's knees and parted legs. He stepped between her knees, cupped her face with his hands, and claimed her mouth. There was no coaxing as he immediately darted his tongue past her lips. She caught him and drew him in deeper.

Aidan pulled away and glared at her. She smirked back at him. Had he really thought she would lie there and do nothing?

"Mia," he asked as he kept his eyes firmly on Jamie, "what do you think your friend would like?"

Jamie's jaw shifted to one side. She didn't like being talked about as if she weren't in the room. "Why don't you ask me?"

"Because I'm interested in Mia's opinion."

"She really likes oral," Mia said.

"Mia!" she tried to look at her friend so she could glare at her. "I told you that in confidence."

"Thank you, Mia." He slowly kissed a path down Jamie's body, while squeezing and pinching her breasts.

Jamie twisted underneath Aidan's seductive touch. She had to admit that he was very focused on giving her pleasure. That surprised her. She thought he would take what he wanted and leave her begging for more.

But not once did he ask for anything from her. She wasn't sure if she liked that. Aidan didn't seek pleasure for himself as he stroked her body. His fingers seemed drawn to her ticklish and sensitive spots. She squealed and tried to move, but Mia held her tight.

Aidan pulled a chair behind him and sat down, his face level with her pussy. Jamie bit her lip, feeling very exposed. She was hot and aroused; the wet heat dripped from her core. And now Aidan knew it.

She wasn't embarrassed by her sexual need, but she didn't want Aidan to know how easy it had been to arouse her, especially since he wasn't panting or desperate to thrust into her. That was unusual; most of her sex partners were beyond coherent before she was this wet and ready.

Aidan hadn't moaned or growled, and it was really beginning to get on her nerves. He lowered his head and licked her dripping wet slit. Jamie gasped and bucked against his mouth. He slowly worked his way to her clit, his tongue flicking against the swollen nub until she thought her eyes were going to roll back.

Aidan's touch was light and delicate. She rocked her hips from side to side, clenching her vaginal walls, desperate for more. She whimpered when he moved away from her clit and returned to her wet slit. He stabbed his tongue into her core, and she muffled a scream.

Jamie wanted to grab his head and press him hard against her center. Flip him onto the table and ride his mouth until she shattered. But when she made the smallest move, Mia held her down hard.

Jamie arched her spine as the fiery pleasure rippled through her. She hooked her legs over Aidan's shoulders. She couldn't help squeezing her thighs against his head, determined to draw him closer.

Aidan raised his head and withdrew his tongue from her drenched pussy. She almost expected him to push her legs off, but he didn't. "Mia," he said conversationally, "do you think I should continue?"

"Oh, God, yes," Jamie replied as she twisted her hips from side to side. He couldn't stop now!

"I wasn't asking you, Jamie," he said kindly. "I'm asking Mia."

"No, you shouldn't," Mia replied.

Surprise jolted inside Jamie. "Mia!" How could her friend deny her satisfaction? She couldn't believe Mia would be so stingy.

"She's going to climax soon," Mia explained, her voice soft and husky. "She needs your cock inside her."

Jamie's womb contracted at the words. Mia was willing to share every inch of her boyfriend. And Jamie wanted to be stuffed and stretched by Aidan's cock. She knew he would be large. She licked her lips as she watched him stand up and unzip his jeans.

Her eyes widened as he shoved the denim down his hips. *Oh, wow.* He was large and thick, and she couldn't wait for him to fill her.

Mia couldn't wait, either, judging by her shallow, uneven

breaths. Jamie tilted her head to the side to get a good look at Mia. "Is this turning you on?"

"Oh, yeah." Mia leaned down and Jamie inhaled her scent. Her lips tingled, tempted to capture Mia's mouth. She looked away quickly before she followed her instincts.

"Take a deep breath when he enters you," Mia whispered in her ear.

"I know how to handle—" She gasped as he claimed her in one long thrust.

"Told you," Mia muttered.

Aidan grabbed Jamie's hips and tilted them before plunging deeper. She wrestled for a better position, wanting to take over, but Mia wouldn't let go. Aidan parted her legs as far as they would go, and held them still before he gave another thrust.

His thrusts were timed agonizingly slow. She wiggled her hips and squeezed her core, but she couldn't break Aidan's rhythm. She swore his cock was so long it was tapping her uterus. One more thrust and she would shatter. The need built inside her, pressing against her skin, ready to burst free. One more tap . . .

Aidan withdrew completely, the move costing him his control. Jamie saw the tremor sweep his body, but there was no hitch in his voice. "Mia, should I stop?"

Stop? Jamie's mouth dropped open. Was he serious? Was he going to deny her?

He would. Jamie clenched her teeth. Aidan was that kind of guy. "Please," she said in a hiss.

"One more time," Mia urged.

He tilted her hips, lifting them off the table and driving deep into her core. His thick cock rubbed against a bundle of nerves in her pussy that had her vaulting off the table. Jamie's high shriek of release echoed in the kitchen.

The world spun wildly as a wave of pleasure crashed through her hot, tingly body. She sagged against the table, conscious of nothing but Aidan's cock burrowed deep inside her and Mia's hands pinching her wrists.

"Jamie?"

Oh, sure, now Aidan says my name and includes me in the conversation. Although it didn't sound like Aidan. It sounded more like . . .

"Caleb?" She turned her head toward the door that led to the attic. Caleb stood in the doorway, his hands on his hips. He was frowning.

"Jamie, what the hell is going on here?"

SEVEN
SEVEN

Caleb rubbed his hand over his eyes. The sight before him was a hell of thing to wake up to first thing in the morning.

Jamie was naked and sprawled on the kitchen table. He saw the bites and whisker burn on her breasts, and he couldn't miss her tight nipples. Her eyes shone with desire, and he inhaled the musk of sex.

Caleb was instantly rock-hard. He wanted to pounce, push aside Aidan and Mia, and take Jamie before she drew her next breath. It was difficult not to follow his instincts.

He was surprised to see Mia playing a part in all of this. Her pink face looked so innocent and sweet, but seeing her hold down Jamie's wrists stirred something dark in his soul. He wondered what naughty things she had been whispering in Jamie's ear.

Aidan had been ramming into Jamie so hard that the table shook. Jamie had loved every minute of it, meeting each thrust with the wild buck of her hips.

And not once did they think he might have wanted to be included. Did they think, *Hey, let's wake up Caleb and see if he wants to join.* Hell, all they had to say was "group sex," and he would be wide-eyed and jumping out of bed.

But they didn't think of him. A sharp pang bloomed in his chest, and he absently rubbed it away with his knuckles. God, he hated that most of all. He knew what it was like to be invisible and ignored. Forgotten. It was what he did best.

Mia guiltily dropped her friend's wrists as if they burned to the touch. "Jamie," she said, her voice rising with concern, "I thought you told him."

"Told him what?" Aidan asked, giving one final thrust into Jamie's pussy as he looked at Caleb. "We just decided."

Normally Caleb would have enjoyed watching Mia and Jamie get caught in their own trap, but this morning was different. They hadn't included him. Did Jamie even think of him? He kept his gaze locked on hers.

"Caleb, what's the big deal?" Jamie asked. Aidan carefully withdrew from her, and she sat up.

"You're having sex with another man while I'm under the same roof."

"Oh, please," Jamie said as she rubbed her wrists. "Don't get all he-man about it. It's so not you."

Caleb glowered at her. How would she liked it if she woke up and discovered him having sex with another woman? She would have liked to have been informed. No, she would have expected to be invited.

It didn't matter if they weren't an exclusive couple; Jamie wouldn't take it too kindly. In fact, there would be lots of screaming and drama.

Jamie made a face at his brooding silence. "Don't you remember? Once we talked about swapping, in theory"—she gave Aidan a quick look—"and you agreed."

He clearly remembered that conversation. Jamie had asked if he would do it but didn't wait for an answer. A part of him was pleased that she could rely on him, but he didn't like being taken completely for granted.

When Jamie had told him that Mia had agreed, she had assumed he would go along. And, really, when had he ever refused her?

"I never agreed with you," he said softly, letting each word hit its mark. He had, however, agreed with Aidan when they came up with their strategy. But she didn't know that.

"Yes, you did. You said . . ." Her eyes widened when she mentally rewound to that morning in bed. "Oh . . . shit."

Caleb looked away and saw Aidan's smirk. The other guy knew what he was up to. This was his chance for Jamie to really think about what he wanted. But if Jamie caught on that he was putting her through the paces, he would be in big trouble. Caleb decided it was a good time to retreat and walked back up to the attic.

As he climbed the stairs, he decided that if they were going to swap, everyone had to be an equal partner. That didn't mean everyone had to dominate his or her new lover. It meant that each person got a chance to live out a fantasy.

And he wasn't going to be left on the sidelines or have his needs ignored. Jamie and Mia had come up with the plan without any thought of what Aidan or he wanted. He never thought of them as greedy or thoughtless, but it was amazing what one wild sexual encounter could do to a person.

Caleb headed straight for Jamie's bathroom and closed the door, but didn't lock it. He turned on the shower, waiting for the water to heat, and stripped off his jeans, the only piece of clothing he had put on when he had woken up, hearing Jamie's cries of pleasure.

Jamie knocked on the bathroom door, but he ignored her. He

really had made it too easy for Jamie. He gave her whatever she wanted, whenever she needed it. Did she ever stop to think what he wanted? Did she try to get it for him?

He wasn't surprised when Jamie cracked open the door. The woman couldn't handle being ignored. She stopped from swinging the door open. It was as if she realized he hadn't said she could come in. Well, she was learning. He'd give her that.

And for the next four days, he needed to learn how to be greedy. It was time to make demands, create expectations.

Jamie didn't have to agree or follow them. Knowing her, she would refuse loudly. She didn't have to do anything but listen. If she didn't like it, it was no big deal. She was leaving him soon.

He wondered if that was what bothered him so much. For the past few weeks, he had felt like he was slowly being shut out of Jamie's life. Whether she had done it intentionally or by accident didn't matter. It was her way of cutting ties.

She poked her head into the bathroom. "Caleb?"

He knew he shouldn't complain or make a scene. He had wanted to part on a positive note. No, that wasn't totally true. He had been on his best behavior so she'd invite him along.

Now he knew that was the wrong tactic. She was leaving him in four days, and there was nothing he could do to change her mind. It was time to say goodbye to her. He needed to create some memories and move on.

"Caleb!" Jamie yelled over the sound of the shower.

He turned toward the door, grabbed the doorknob, and swung it open. "What?"

She was as naked as he was. He should have been used to her voluptuous curves and golden skin, but her nudity packed a wallop every time.

His gaze traveled down her body. Jamie loved the size of her breasts, and she had every right to be proud. She was more than a handful, and her large, dark nipples pointed up.

She might curse her hips every time she tried to buy clothes, but he thought she was just right. He could clutch onto her hips when he drove into her pussy or when she rode his cock. He couldn't get enough of her lush ass.

She had a traditional hourglass figure, although he knew better than to tell her that. It was the perfect shape for a woman, but she refused to believe anything about her was old-fashioned.

"I'm sorry," she said, her eyes pleading for him to accept her apology. "I really thought you were okay with swapping."

He ushered her inside the bathroom and closed the door behind her. "I was okay with it."

"Then what's your problem?" She gave him a little push, but he didn't budge. "Damn it, you made me feel so guilty."

"You should. You left me out."

She winced when she realized her mistake. "I'm sorry about that. But I needed to prove to Mia and Aidan that I can take whatever Aidan dishes out."

"Mmmhmm." He wasn't buying that excuse.

She draped her arms around his shoulders and curled into him, her breasts rubbing his chest. "I didn't forget about you."

He didn't believe that. Caleb disentangled himself from her arms and stepped into the shower. He tilted his head up and let the warm water course down him.

"I won't leave you out again," she said as she watched him. "I promise."

"Okay." He couldn't fix the past, and the promise was all he could hope for. Caleb reached for Jamie and helped her into the shower.

She tilted her head up, allowing the water to spray on her hair and face. Jamie brushed her mouth against his. "Let me make it up to you," she offered in a purr.

"You will." He would make certain of that.

Jamie frowned at him as the water beat down her head. "What does that mean?"

"Since we're swapping, you've already told me what Mia wants. And I can tell that you want to retrain Aidan."

She stepped away and lowered her arms. "How did you know that?"

"It's obvious. To me," he hurriedly assured her. "I doubt Aidan has a clue."

"Whew." Jamie brushed her wet hair from her face and visibly relaxed.

"But no one asked what I want," Caleb emphasized.

Jamie slowly closed her eyes and shook her head with regret. "I've really messed up with you, haven't I?" she muttered.

"Not if you know how to fix it." He'd like to see what she would do to make him happy.

"I'm sorry I was so focused on seeing what Mia would get out of it. I came up with the idea for her. You know I'll do anything to help her."

"I know." Jamie didn't have many friends or people she could rely on. In fact, it was probably just Mia and him. Maybe Aidan. He wished Jamie would show him the same care and loyalty she did to Mia. Then again, Mia and Jamie had been friends for decades, while he'd known Jamie for less than year.

"Tell me what you want from this swap," Jamie said.

"You can't tell?" He wondered what her guess would be. He had a feeling she would be far off the mark.

Jamie grimaced, knowing she was not scoring any brownie points with him. "No, I can't. Why would you do it? You've swapped before, so it's not a novelty."

This was the best time to make his request. Jamie wouldn't deny him. He pressed his mouth against her ear and whispered, "I want to watch you and Mia have sex."

Jamie's shocked gasp ricocheted in the shower stall. She jerked back and stared at him. Her eyes were wide, and her mouth was parted in surprise.

She looked . . . vulnerable. He'd never seen Jamie like this before. It was as if he had ripped away a veil and exposed her deepest secret.

He gathered her closely as the water streamed down his back. "Would you do it?"

She shook her head. "Mia is never going to go for that."

Caleb noticed the way she avoided a direct answer. "But would you do it . . . if I asked?"

She closed her eyes and surrendered to the truth. "Yes . . . but don't you want something else?" she urged. "Something where all the attention is on you?"

It was a tempting offer, but would she remember how she'd rocked his world? No, because she wouldn't have risked anything to please him. Jamie might carry along the memory of doing something raunchy or difficult, but as time went by, she'd be hazy on his name and face.

But years from now she would still think of her friend. She'd remember with vivid clarity how they'd spent their last days together, and he'd be a part of those memories.

"I'm all for sharing a bed with you and Mia," she said as he slicked his hands on Jamie's hips, "but I don't think Mia would go for that. Or Aidan."

"You never know." He smiled at the gleam in her eye. "You like the idea of having sex with Mia, don't you?"

Jamie rested her head on his shoulder. "Yes."

He wrapped his arms around her. "Don't be shy about it."

"You don't understand," she said, burrowing into him as if that way he wouldn't see her face. "I can't explain how I felt when I kissed her."

"You've been with women before," he reminded her.

Jamie lifted her head. "Mia doesn't know that, okay?"

That surprised him. "I thought you two shared everything."

"Almost everything," she admitted. She reached up and wiped the water from her face.

"Wait." He tilted his head and stared into Jamie's eyes. "I know something about you that Mia doesn't?" He was too pleased by that fact.

"I told you because you asked."

"And you knew I wouldn't have a problem with it," he felt compelled to add.

"Yes," she admitted with a sigh. "Mia would have a fit if she knew I got turned on by our kiss."

"What makes you think she didn't?" He turned Jamie around until her spine was pressed against his chest. "Did you want her just now?"

Jamie nodded. "But she only held my wrists."

"You wanted her mouth on you." He pressed his lips against her neck. "Like this."

She shuddered against him. Caleb's cock twitched and hardened in response. He knew how to bring Jamie's fantasy to life.

"You wanted Mia's hands to play with your tits." He grabbed her big breasts, splaying his hands around them before he crushed them together.

"Oh, Caleb," she moaned as she slapped her hands on the tiled wall in front of her. "What are you doing?"

"Close your eyes," he told her, darting his tongue in her ear. "Pretend I'm Mia."

She gasped, and he knew she found his suggestion taboo. "I can't."

"You want to." She should let her imagination run free. It might be the only way she would have her friend.

"I want you, too," Jamie insisted.

It wasn't the same. He was a vessel for all of her fantasies. "You already have me. Now close your eyes." He looked at her face and saw that she was following his suggestion. "Tell me what you want Mia to do," he said as he roughly massaged her breasts. The shower made it easy for his hands to glide over her smooth, wet skin.

She paused and quickly said, "I don't know."

"Yes, you do." Caleb knew she didn't trust herself to say it out loud. "Would she do this?" He pinched her nipples, not letting go until he thought she would keel over from the touch.

Jamie's body shook and she thrust her breasts into his hands. "Harder."

"She would go harder? Are you sure?" he teased as he squeezed her nipples until she cried out. "She seems like such a nice, sweet girl."

"Caleb . . ."

"Mia," he corrected her. "Would she do this?" he asked against her neck as he kissed a trail down her spine. Kneeling on the shower floor, he slid his hands over her stomach and hips before he cupped her ass.

"Yes-s-s." She rested her arms on the wall in front of her, pushing her ass out so he could knead and squeeze. Jamie's moans echoed loudly in the shower stall.

He lavished kisses on her buttocks, enjoying the tremors racing through Jamie. He licked her cleft, and she rocked against his tongue.

Caleb couldn't take it anymore. He stood up and put his hands on her curvy hips. Gripping her tightly, he pressed the crown of his cock against her entrance.

Jamie groaned. "Mia wouldn't do that."

Caleb heard Jamie's smile in her voice. "Yes, she would," he whispered in her ear as if he was sharing a secret, "because you gave her your dildo."

The moment she arched her back and groaned, he knew exactly what Jamie was imagining. Little Mia wearing nothing but the black vinyl harness and a purple cock. She would climb on top of Jamie and thrust into her.

Caleb held on to Jamie's hips and slowly worked his cock into the hot, wet core. Her body shook and trembled as she tried to hold back. He barely moved, and Jamie was already coming.

Her vaginal walls gripped his cock and drew him in deep. His thrusts grew wild as he rubbed his hands over Jamie's breasts and pussy. He pressed her hard against the wall, pounding into her until his skin slapped hers.

He was worried that he was being too rough, but Jamie didn't complain. She begged for more, telling him to go faster.

Caleb felt the need inside him grow stronger and stronger. He thrust into her one last time, coming in long, thick spurts, before slumping against the wet tile.

Caleb rested his head on Jamie's shoulder. "Mia's a little rough, isn't she?" he asked.

Jamie laughed, reached up and pressed her hand against his cheek. "But you are perfect."

"I aim to please," he said, turning his head to press a kiss on her palm. She had no idea just how much he would sacrifice to give her pleasure. And if he did it right, she never would.

Mia puttered nervously around the kitchen, trying to keep busy. She went to the refrigerator and grabbed a carton of eggs, not quite sure what she was going to make for breakfast. She wasn't hungry. She couldn't think of eating as every noise and creak from the attic had her looking up toward the ceiling.

"It's going to be okay," Aidan said.

She looked at Aidan who was sitting at the table reading the morning newspaper. He had changed into an extra pair of clothes he kept at the house, and his hair was still wet from a quick shower.

How could he sit there casually like he did every morning? He'd just had sex on that table. Mia knew that she would never be able to look at that piece of furniture without thinking about Jamie, naked and panting for Aidan's touch.

Mia looked away and cleared her throat. "For all you know, they could be having a knock-down, drag-out fight." She would put her money on Jamie. No offense to Caleb, but her friend never played by the rules.

"They're not." Aidan turned the page.

Mia didn't understand how he could be so calm while she imagined all the horrible things going on up there. She knew Jamie and Caleb didn't have a monogamous relationship, but it was different when Jamie was screwing with someone right under Caleb's nose. "How do you know?"

Aidan looked over the corner of the newspaper. "They're not arguing," he simply stated.

Mia stood by the kitchen counter and listened to the silence. Aidan had a point, but she wasn't going to take it as proof. It was just as likely that Jamie had Caleb in a headlock.

Mia was tempted to check on them, but she remembered what she'd seen the last time she went up there. It would be best if she stayed in the kitchen.

"Jamie can talk her way around anything," Mia said as she grabbed a bowl from the cabinet, "but I think she has finally pushed her luck too far."

Aidan looked up from the newspaper when he heard footsteps on the attic stairs. "We'll soon find out."

Mia clenched the edge of the countertop when she heard the door to the attic open. She looked over her shoulder just in time to see Jamie and Caleb enter the kitchen.

She searched for any signs of anger or hurt feelings. She didn't see any as her gaze traveled from their toweled-dry hair to the way Jamie's T-shirt and shorts clung to her damp skin.

Caleb's hand rested on Jamie's hip, and he smiled down at her. Mia started to relax. From their body language, it looked as if Jamie had managed, once again, to talk her way out of trouble. She didn't know how her friend did it.

"Okay, you guys," Jamie said as she stepped into the kitchen. "Everyone is on the same page. We all agree to swapping, and it's going to last for four days."

"Right." Aidan said as he folded the newspaper.

"Great," Mia replied weakly. It was really happening. She wanted this, but she was so nervous she might have to throw up.

Aidan tossed the paper onto the table. "But I have a condition for when Caleb and Mia hook up."

Jamie's head snapped back, and she glared at Aidan. "What?"

"It's okay," Mia assured her. The more she thought about it, the more she wouldn't mind Aidan watching over her.

Jamie pressed her hand against Caleb's chest. "Well, it may not be okay for Caleb."

Jamie didn't see the look Caleb gave her, but Mia did and her heart melted. Caleb was pleasantly surprised that Jamie was looking out for his interest. Mia wished Jamie had seen the sweet look on his face, but it was probably for the best. Jamie didn't do sweet and adorable.

"Aidan wants to be in the room while I'm with Caleb," Mia told her friend. "Just the first time. It's no different from what we just did with you."

"Are you okay with that, Caleb?" Jamie asked, looking up at him and missing his affectionate look.

"Sure," Caleb agreed and looked at Mia. "Are you ready?"

"Now?" Her voice cracked as her body went from hot to cold.

"Yeah, now." He pulled away from Jamie and looked around the room. "Where should we do it?"

She looked wildly around the room. "I don't know." She wasn't that imaginative. Was he going to lay her out on the counter or bend her over the sink? Her knees weakened at the thought.

"Try her bed," Aidan suggested drily.

"Hey," Jamie interrupted, "no one said you could interfere."

"You won't feel weird about that?" Caleb asked Aidan.

"My ego won't be dented."

"Good to know."

Caleb walked over to Mia, and it took every ounce of her willpower not to back away. Her fingers gripped the countertop as if her life depended on it.

Caleb stood in front of her. He towered over her, surrounding her until she didn't see or think of anything else. "What do you want to do?" he asked.

"Uh." What *did* she want to do? The bed sounded like a good option, but she had no idea what she wanted after that.

Why did she think Caleb would guide her through this? She

wanted to try something different and take charge, right? She just didn't know where to start. Mia gave a panicked look at Aidan.

"I tell you what." Aidan rose from his seat. "I'll direct Mia."

Oooh . . . She kind of liked that idea. A lot. Her pussy warmed as she imagined Aidan instructing her how to suck on Caleb's cock.

"Oh, I don't think so," Jamie said, putting her hands on her hips. "This is Caleb and Mia's time."

"It's okay, Jamie," Mia assured her. She didn't want Aidan to take away his offer. "I like this idea. It's sounds interesting."

Jamie scrunched her nose in disbelief. "Really?"

Mia nodded her head and gnawed her bottom lip, slightly embarrassed. Someone as sexy and brazen as Jamie wouldn't understand. Would Caleb? Mia cast him a questioning look.

"Let's go with it," Caleb said.

"I'm not too sure about this," Jamie warned. "Aidan is going to take over like he always does."

Aidan dramatically placed his hand over his heart. "I promise I won't sweep Mia out of the room."

Jamie wasn't amused. "You're just saying that because you know her bed will already be occupied. I'm coming, too."

Mia stared at her friend. "Fabulous," she said in a croak. This was the first time she would have sex with someone other than Aidan, and she was going to have an audience. "Just fabulous."

EIGHT
EIGHT

Mia wasn't sure about leading the parade to her bedroom. She sensed Caleb right behind her, and knew Jamie and Aidan were following. No one said anything, and the silence was grating on her nerves.

Her stomach twisted and flipped. She wanted this, Mia reminded herself. She had risked her relationship for this, but now that it was time for action, she didn't think she could go through with it.

What if this was all a mistake? What if having sex with Caleb was really bad or, worse, incredibly good? Was she going to regret having sex with Caleb? Mia didn't think that would happen. She had a feeling the only thing she would regret was not following through.

Her troubled thoughts must have been noticeable, because Caleb reached for her hand. She flinched but didn't pull away. She found Caleb's hands large and comforting as his fingers slid through hers.

She stopped at the doorway to her bedroom. She wasn't sure why, but her feet wouldn't move. It was as if her body knew that once she stepped into the room, there was no turning back. She needed to make sure that she was ready for this.

But how could she be sure? Was anyone ever truly ready for having sex with her best friend's lover while her best friend and boyfriend watched? She doubted it.

Mia looked around, deciding her bedroom wasn't big enough. It had just enough space for a queen-size bed, a chest of drawers, and an overstuffed chair. She didn't think four people had ever been in here at the same time.

Caleb stepped over the threshold and led Mia into the bedroom. For some reason, it was easier for her to follow him than to invite Caleb to her bed.

Jamie strode into the room as if she owned the place. Mia envied the woman's confidence. Jamie sat down on the chair, draping her feet over the armrest. She looked comfortable and ready for a show.

"Had to get the front-row seat?" Mia asked drily, trying to hide the nervous tic in her mouth. "Want some popcorn with that?"

Jamie smiled. "At least I'm not holding you down."

Jamie had her there. Mia looked over her shoulder and saw Aidan leaning against the wall, his arms folded across his chest. She was surprised he was hanging back and was hardly in the room. Mia was sure he would be right next to her the whole time. Was he having second thoughts?

His stance was casual, but she saw the heat in his eyes. His nostrils flared as he controlled each breath. If she didn't know any better, she would have thought he was looking forward to this.

That surprised her as well. Aidan was possessive, and she

thought he would be too territorial to let her even look at another man. Just when she thought she understood him, Aidan did something unexpected. He really was a mix of contradictions.

"Are you guys ready?" Aidan asked in a clipped tone, immediately taking charge of the situation. He waited until they nodded before he continued. "Mia, I want you to kiss Caleb."

She turned to face Caleb, and placed her hands on his shoulders. The top of her head only reached to his chin. He wasn't as broad and tall as Aidan. He was, in fact, far less intimidating.

Mia pushed the thought aside. She shouldn't compare Caleb to Aidan, but the thought sprang into her mind unbidden. Mia lifted up on her tiptoes so she could reach Caleb's mouth. Tilting her face up, her lips collided with his.

His mouth was playful as he nibbled her mouth. She teased him back, swiping her tongue along his bottom lip. A warm, fizzy sensation invaded her. It was unlike the dark intensity she felt when she kissed Aidan.

"Hold his face with both hands," Aidan suggested.

Mia reached up and pressed her palms on Caleb's cheeks. The stubble on his lean face scratched her skin, just like Aidan's. She stroked his face, exploring the planes and contours with her fingers, and she continued to kiss him.

Caleb's hands rested on her back, and he slowly caressed her. The light touch tickled and she stepped closer into his embrace. He didn't hold her tightly the way she liked, but she wasn't going to ask for more. That was Aidan's job.

"Kiss him harder," Aidan told her.

She darted her tongue past Caleb's lips and into his warm mouth. Kissing Caleb was different from what she expected. He didn't swoop in and take over. Instead he allowed her to set the pace, let her explore to her heart's content.

Mia wasn't sure if she liked it. She preferred to be taken, and swept up in the swirling emotions. If he didn't claim her soon, she was going to have to ask him to suck on her tongue. She needed to tell him to grind his mouth against hers.

"Caleb," Aidan said harshly, "fuck her mouth with your tongue."

"Wait a second," Jamie said, immediately jumping in. "The agreement was telling Mia what to do."

Mia pulled away from Caleb and blinked her eyes open. She felt slightly disoriented and looked up at Caleb to find her balance. They shared a wry look as they listened to the others squabble. Mia should have known that Aidan and Jamie were going to bump heads and wrestle for control.

Mia licked her swollen lip and looked over at her friend, who was too busy glaring at Aidan. "Jamie," she said, noticing her voice sounded husky, "why don't you tell Caleb what to do while Aidan gives me instructions?"

"What are we," Caleb muttered in Mia's ear, his warm breath wafting over her long hair, "puppets?"

"Fine," Jamie said. "We'll do that."

"As long as she doesn't contradict me," Aidan said, clearly unhappy by the rule change.

"Do you ever get the feeling," Caleb said for Mia's ears only, "that this isn't to make you comfortable? I think they can't give up control."

She gave him a sharp look, realizing Caleb was right. She thought they were helping her, teaching her how to go after her fantasies. They were doing that, but that was secondary to their own goals. Aidan and Jamie couldn't stand it when they weren't in charge.

"Jamie, what do you want me to do next?" Caleb asked, his eyes never leaving Mia's face.

There was a pause. "Fuck her mouth with her tongue," she answered grudgingly.

Mia and Caleb tried not to smile. He tenderly cradled her face with his hands. It caught her off-guard when he plunged his tongue past her lips.

Mia grabbed Caleb's shirt and held on tight, her fingers twisting in the soft cotton as he claimed her mouth. She opened her mouth wider, surrendering instantly to his invasion. She rubbed her breasts and hips against him, her nipples poking against her shirt, begging for attention.

"Caleb," Jamie said, "take off her shirt."

Mia wondered how Jamie knew what she needed. Did Jamie see her nipples tightening, or the way she enjoyed the friction when she rubbed against Caleb? Or were Jamie's nipples puckering as she watched them?

"No, Mia will," Aidan contradicted Jamie's command. His tone warned Jamie not to push her luck.

Caleb reluctantly pulled his mouth away, his lips clinging onto Mia's. He was breathing hard as Mia reached for her shirt and wiggled out of it. Once she pulled it over her head, Mia tossed it onto the floor and reached for the back hooks of her bra, thrusting her breasts against Caleb.

"Did I tell you to take off your bra?" Aidan asked coldly.

Mia froze and immediately dropped her hands. She couldn't believe she did that. She always waited for Aidan's next command. He was going to punish her by making her wait. She just knew it.

Jamie huffed with disgust. "Aidan, get over it." Jamie told him. "She can take off her own bra if she wants to."

Caleb waited for the next instructions, caressing Mia's back. His gaze drifted onto her small breasts. Her nipples tingled as she remembered how he had kissed her the night before. She was eager to feel his mouth on her nipples again.

"Mia, take off your bra," Aidan said.

Thank God, Mia thought as she closed her eyes. She wasn't sure how long Aidan would have made her wait. She fumbled with the closures as Caleb helped her off with the bra.

When it fell to the floor, Aidan was ready with another command. "Turn around and press your back against Caleb."

Mia didn't know what Aidan was planning. She slowly turned and pressed her spine against Caleb's chest. He still wore a T-shirt, and it felt warm and soft against her bare skin.

"Caleb, play with her breasts," Jamie quickly inserted, refusing to let Aidan call all the shots.

Caleb's long fingers stroked her small breasts. She watched him drag his fingers from the full curve to the pointed crest, over and over. Mia pressed her lips together, holding back a moan as he pinched her nipple. She looked up, her eyes colliding with Aidan's.

She felt naughty and wicked standing topless in front of Aidan while another man fondled her. She felt everyone's eyes on her breasts, and she wanted to arch her spine and preen. Caleb's fingers captured both nipples and gave them hard twists. A moan ripped from her throat as her knees buckled.

Hunger flared in Aidan's eyes. His face tightened, and for one brief moment, Mia thought he was going to pounce. He didn't move, but she felt the tension curling inside him. He enjoyed watching Caleb fondle her and found pleasure in how Mia reacted.

"Lick her ear," Jamie said, her voice sounding far away to Mia. "She loves that."

I do? Mia didn't remember saying anything like that to Jamie, but the moment Caleb pressed his mouth against her ear, heat flooded her body. He tongued her ear and her pussy creamed. Mia arched back, raising her arms and linking them behind Caleb's head.

She turned her head and captured Caleb's mouth. She wasn't going to ask for permission or wait until Aidan came up with the idea. Mia sucked on Caleb's lower lip, waiting for Aidan to tell her to stop.

He didn't. How could that be? Did she not hear it, or was Aidan letting her follow her needs?

Caleb slicked his tongue against her upper lip. She imagined him licking her pussy the same way. She wiggled her hips in anticipation. When Caleb palmed her breasts and rubbed her nipples in a hard, circular motion, she felt it tug on her throbbing clit.

"Take off her shorts," Jamie said in a hoarse voice.

Mia glanced at her friend and froze. Jamie was sprawled on the overstuffed chair, arching her spine as she pinched her nipple through her shirt. She murmured with pleasure, her eyes drifting closed as her other hand slid under her shorts. Mia watched, fascinated, as Jamie played with her clit.

Caleb slid his hands down Mia's stomach. Her muscles bunched under his exploration. He grabbed the waistband of her shorts. Aidan gave another order. "Look at me, Mia."

It was difficult to tear her attention away from Jamie masturbating, but she slowly turned her head and met Aidan's knowing gaze.

"Play with your breasts," he told her.

She clamped her hands on her breasts and looked straight at Aidan. Massaging her breasts hard, she gritted her teeth as she squeezed and plucked. If only she could pinch harder . . . She wanted to leave red streaks on her pale skin.

Caleb unbuttoned her jean shorts and pulled down the zipper. He dipped his hand under her panties and spanned his fingers over her sex. She closed her eyes as his fingertips raked her damp curls, each stroke inflaming the hot need churning inside her.

She spread her legs apart, waiting for him to find her clit and press down hard. Instead, Caleb removed his hand and slid her shorts down her legs. She tried to hide her disappointment as he crouched behind her, helping her step out of her clothes.

"Keep playing with your breasts," Aidan reminded her.

She opened her eyes and realized she was only holding her breasts. Mia glanced in Aidan's direction, wondering if he knew how Caleb touched her. He must have seen it and her reaction. Yet he hadn't complained and hadn't told her to move away.

Mia squeezed her breasts, giving Aidan a performance. She lifted her breasts and bent her head. Watching Aidan, she licked the reddened crest. Her nipples beaded under the wet heat of her tongue.

She smiled when Aidan jerked back in surprise. Feral lust swept across his face until his eyes shuttered and he regained his composure. But it was too late; she knew he wasn't unaffected. She bet his cock was rock-hard and hitting his stomach, begging for release.

She felt Caleb smoothing his hands up and down her legs. His caresses made the back of her knees tingle. Every time his hands glided along her inner thighs, his fingers flirted with the edge of her panties.

Mia wished he would dip his fingers past the damp fabric and rub the swollen folds of her sex. She would settle for Caleb to press the heel of his hand against her mound. But she wouldn't dare voice those requests. That was a job for Aidan and Jamie.

He tugged her last item of clothing off her hips. She jumped when he placed a soft kiss on the small of her back. It was so soft and almost ticklish. She held her breath as he continued to kiss down the slope of her buttocks.

It wasn't difficult to imagine him dipping his tongue in her anus. Her pussy flooded as she envisioned him darting the tip past her rosebud. She'd never had anal sex before, but she knew she would pass out from the intense pleasure.

She should pull away before she begged Caleb to lick her puckered hole. She couldn't until Aidan told her to. She waited for Jamie to tell Caleb to stop. Her arms and legs were shaking, but her best friend didn't give any commands.

Was she the only one following the rules? Mia wondered wildly as Caleb kissed the underside of her buttock. She pressed her lips together and wobbled as a white-hot sensation forked through her.

Caleb wasn't following the directions. Instead, he was following his own instincts. Mia watched Aidan, waiting for his next command. He remained silent, watching Caleb kiss her intimately.

Aidan didn't stop Caleb. It was as if he was mesmerized by the sight before him. His eyes were glazing over with lust as he watched Mia's face. She knew he found pleasure in her responses to Caleb's kisses. That knowledge made her lose any inhibitions. She wanted to give him a taste of the ecstasy she felt.

Jamie was unusually silent, and Mia didn't dare turn to see her friend's expression. She heard Jamie's hitched breaths and grunts, and she wondered if her friend was too wrapped up in her own quest for satisfaction.

She knew Jamie had a perfect view of what Caleb was doing. What did she feel, watching her lover slathering kisses all over her best friend's ass? Jamie hadn't asked him to do it, but she didn't tell him to stop, either.

"Caleb," Jamie said, her voice breaking through the tense silence, "play with her clit."

Mia's knees buckled at Jamie's command. Finally! She wanted Caleb's large fingers teasing her clitoris and didn't think she could wait any longer. He had better not finger her lightly. She needed his touch to be forceful.

Caleb stood up swiftly, and he pressed Mia's spine against his chest. She had forgotten that he was still fully clothed. His soft T-shirt and jeans brushed against her hot skin. She swallowed roughly when his hard cock pressed between her buttocks.

He cupped her mound and the tension zoomed in her body. Parting her labia with two fingers, he exposed her hard clit. He slid his middle finger over the swollen nub. His touch was as soft as a butterfly's wing. Mia groaned and closed her eyes as the wild sensations flooded her.

"Slow and easy," Jamie told him.

Her order was meaningless. He was doing just that, damn it. It didn't matter what she thought she needed; Caleb knew exactly how to draw the most exquisite pleasure from her body.

"Pinch your nipples," Aidan reminded her again.

For once she didn't want to obey Aidan. If she did that, she might come before she got to the bed. But Mia wouldn't break the agreement, even though every one else was playing by his own rules.

Mia followed Aidan's orders and plucked her nipples. She hissed through her clenched teeth, and the fire went straight to her clit.

Caleb caressed her clit with an insistent rhythm. Her hips bucked against his hand over and over. If he moved his finger faster, she could . . .

"Don't come," Aidan said sharply.

Damn.

Aidan always knew when she was about to climax, but he usually let her ride it out, knowing he could take her to that level of pleasure again. Why did he make her stop now? Did he think Caleb wouldn't be capable of giving her multiple orgasms?

"What did you just say?" Jamie yelled at Aidan. "You can't tell her that."

"I just did." Aidan gestured proudly toward Mia. "Look, she knows how to delay her pleasure."

"Just because she can doesn't mean she should," Jamie argued.

It was hard not to rock her hips and come. Caleb's hand felt so good. Mia knew the tingling sensations would bloom inside her, filling her with heat.

"Get on the bed, Mia," Aidan said, ignoring Jamie's argument. "I want you on your hands and knees facing me."

It was difficult stepping away from Caleb. She had been leaning against him, relying on his strength. Mia felt cold once he wasn't surrounding her. She climbed onto her bed, her knees digging into her bedspread and her legs shaking.

"Get right behind her," Jamie told Caleb.

Mia slowly exhaled as her stomach flipped with excitement. She preferred the doggy style, but Aidan didn't suggest it too often. He always wanted to see her face, which was romantic in a way, but there was something to be said about this position. She always enjoyed how Aidan would thrust deep inside her while playing with her breasts and clitoris.

She lifted her head and looked straight at Aidan. He still had not moved from the bedroom doorway. Mia felt the mattress sag as Caleb climbed behind her. The metallic sound of his zipper and the rustle of his jeans were loud to her ears.

Her heart pounded fiercely, and she knew she was about to

cross a line she'd never dreamed she would. She was taking on another lover, one who would last for four days, but it was significant to her.

She closed her eyes when she felt Caleb's finger dipping into her wet core. He stroked her gently, and she started trembling, knowing she was close to coming.

"Open your eyes," Aidan demanded.

Mia forced her eyes open. Caleb pressed the tip of his cock against her entrance, and Mia clawed the bedspread with her fingers. She couldn't stand the wait. She knew Caleb's cock wasn't as thick as Aidan's, but he was still big.

"Go for one long thrust," Jamie said.

Oh, boy. Mia braced herself. She kept her gaze steady on Aidan. He was her anchor.

Her mind was whirling and her body was reacting in ways she couldn't control. Yet she felt safe and curious because Aidan was there guiding her.

Caleb grabbed her hips and entered her with one long thrust. Her eyes widened and her guttural groan echoed in the small bedroom. She tried to breathe as her body took his full length, his heavy balls slapping against her bottom.

Mia saw Aidan shudder, but he didn't move. She glanced down at his jeans and saw how aroused he was. She returned her attention to his face. His eyes glittered with lust.

She knew the truth now. Aidan liked watching her with another man. Mia knew she should be thrilled, or at least intrigued. Instead she felt confused. It didn't make sense. She was his, wasn't she?

Caleb pumped slowly, almost gently, as if Mia were made of spun glass. She didn't want that. She wanted it hard and fast. She needed a rugged lover who was ready to lose control.

Mia wasn't going to wait for Jamie or Aidan to come up with

the idea. Squeezing her vaginal walls, she gripped Caleb's cock, milking it. Caleb reared back, his fingers digging in her hips. She heard his groan before he drove deep into her.

His hips bucked against her at a breathtaking rate. She felt the pleasure draw tight in her pelvis and dipped her spine, but couldn't find the release she longed for.

"Rub her clit," Jamie told Caleb. Her tone was urgent as if she couldn't wait to see Mia come.

"No," Aidan barked out, "her nipples first."

Oh, God. Mia closed her eyes as the frustration bubbled up from the surface, pressing against her skin until she thought she would splinter. She was going to come before Aidan and Jamie reached an agreement.

"Caleb," she said in a moan.

Caleb stopped and leaned over her. "Yeah?"

She licked her lips, knowing she was breaking her agreement, but she didn't care at this point. She had to take control and to hell with the consequences.

"What is it, Mia?" Caleb asked.

"Do whatever you want to me."

NINE

Caleb was suddenly on top of her, his chest pressing down on her shoulders as he pumped his cock into her slick core. Mia liked how he surrounded her.

She kept her elbows locked, not wanting to collapse. Caleb grabbed her breasts as he thrust hard. He roughly caressed her breasts, eliciting a moan from her.

He rubbed his hands over her roughly. She liked that. A lot. Her body shook at each thrust.

Caleb sought her clit, and Mia shuddered as he caught the nub between his finger and thumb. The hot and jagged pleasure, threatened to consume her.

He rubbed his face against her neck, licking the sweat from her skin. She moaned, watching Aidan getting excited. She wanted him to join in but didn't know how to ask. She didn't know the rules for swapping.

Caleb slicked an openmouthed kiss on her shoulders. She felt the edge of his teeth. Her pussy throbbed, and she shuddered at the promise of pain.

"Do you like that?" Caleb asked.

"Harder," she whispered.

He bit down on her shoulder. She reeled back, crying out as the bite heightened her pleasure. Her eyes rolled back as the orgasm swept through her.

Dark spots danced before her eyes. Her body went from hot to cold as her limbs suddenly felt heavy. She gulped for air and blinked away the spot, keeping her eyes on Aidan, who watched her with an intensity that made her toes curl.

"Jamie, I need those pillows behind me."

She liked the authoritative, tough tone Caleb used. Jamie didn't seem to mind, either. She didn't bristle or counter his order. Instead she grabbed the pillows from the head of the bed and handed them to Caleb.

He tucked the pillows under Mia's hips, and she gratefully sank onto them. She didn't know how much longer her shaky arms and legs would have held her. Her ass was still tilted up high in the air, but Caleb was now able to thrust deep inside her.

No one stopped him or gave him advice. All she heard was Caleb's body slapping against hers, their choppy breath and moans. She didn't know how much longer she could take his demonic rhythm when Caleb's thrusts became wild. She knew he was about to come.

Caleb froze and sank deeply into Mia. He withdrew, his body shaking. Mia rocked against him, and he plunged into her one last time, shouting as he found his release. Mia sagged against the mattress and pillows as Caleb collapsed on top of her.

Aidan finally left his spot next to the door and walked to the bed, his gait slow and awkward. Mia watched him, anticipation twisting at her stomach. For a moment she thought he was going to grab her like he had the last time.

Instead Aidan helped her into a sitting position and cradled her in his arms. "You guys need to work on following orders," Aidan said.

"Seriously," Jamie agreed, crawling onto the bed and draping her arm on Caleb's shoulders.

Aidan scooped Mia up, his arms underneath her shoulders and thighs. He carried her toward the door. Was he going to whisk her off and have his wicked way with her? If so, the bed was the other way.

"Where are you taking me?" Mia asked when they left the bedroom.

He held her closely and walked down the hall toward the bathroom. "I'm going to give you a nice, long shower."

Was that a euphemism for something else? She might be sore and tired, but she could never deny Aidan. "Is that it?"

"It is for now," he promised.

Life was good, Jamie thought as she lay on Mia's lap. She inhaled her friend's scent and rubbed her cheek against Mia's soft, pale leg.

Mia stroked Jamie's hair, threading her fingers through the long brown tresses. Jamie let out a contented sigh. She was sure Mia meant nothing by the friendly touch, but Jamie didn't care. It was pure bliss.

They had finished a leisurely lunch and now she watched Aidan and Caleb play on the Xbox console. She smiled as she remembered how much the men had consumed. They obviously had worked up quite an appetite this morning.

So had she, Jamie thought with a frown. She wished this weekend could stretch out for weeks. It would be the only thing that would keep her in Clover Bud, but she wasn't going to let the promise of pleasure distract her.

Yet she was greedy when it came to sex. There was very little chance that she would be invited to take part in this type of sensual game. But if she stayed so she could keep playing, it would be a big mistake. It was best to leave when she was hungry for more.

Anyway, it wouldn't take long for the people of Clover Bud to find out. They already gossiped about her and sexual situations she had never dreamed up. All the townspeople needed was a suspicion she was swapping with Mia, and life would be unbearable.

Her neighbors wouldn't understand how emotionally close she felt right now to Mia and Caleb. Even Aidan, which she never saw coming. As much as she bickered with Aidan, she had a feeling he would back her up if she needed help.

She trusted all three. But she couldn't bring herself to reveal her sexual fantasies. She'd like to think that once she confessed her secret dreams, they would do everything in their power to make it happen for her. As much as she believed her friendships had strengthened, she didn't want to test the bonds—especially with Mia.

Jamie bit the inside of her lip as she remembered her kiss with Mia. That should have been enough for her. After all, she used to think she would never get that close to Mia. But then she had seen Mia naked and wild underneath Caleb.

Jamie couldn't remember a time she felt so envious. She wanted to be in Caleb's position, claiming Mia and giving her the most explosive climax of her life.

She wanted Mia thrashing and undulating underneath her, but this was one time she wasn't going to manipulate others to get her way. She didn't want to do anything Mia would regret. She didn't want it to hurt her friendship, the one constant relationship she'd ever had.

It was the main reason why she felt the urgent need to leave. It had more to do with things than the feeling of being confined and trapped in Clover Bud. As much as she hated leaving Mia behind, it was only a matter of time before she ruined their friendship. Whether she interfered with Mia's love life, or made a pass, Jamie knew she would ultimately do something unforgivable.

At least, Jamie wouldn't forgive herself. Mia might. Mia took the good and the bad in everyone. She defended her loved ones, even when she knew they were in the wrong, and nurtured them in her quiet way.

Mia stopped stroking her hair. Jamie opened her eyes as she felt her friend move away. Had she given off some vibe, and Mia was trying to put some distance between them?

She watched as Mia got off the couch and strolled over to Caleb. Jamie sat up, intrigued by the confident swagger of her friend. It was like she was on the prowl. She would never have associated that word with Mia before.

Mia stood next to Caleb. He and Aidan looked up, but Mia only looked at Caleb. Jamie's eyebrows rose in surprise. Why wasn't Mia looking at Aidan?

Mia reached out for Caleb. "Come with me," she said in a seductively low voice.

Although they were right in the middle of the game, neither man complained about her timing. Aidan didn't say a thing and his jaw clenched. A muscle bunched in Caleb's cheek as he put down the controller and took Mia's hand.

Caleb rose slowly from the floor, his movements like a sleepwalker's. He gripped Mia's hand tightly as if he was worried she would let go. Mia smiled, heady with power and confidence, and guided him out of the media room.

Jamie couldn't stop grinning as she watched them leave. She didn't say anything until she heard the bedroom door close.

"Sure you don't want to go watch?" Jamie asked.

"I'm sure," Aidan said as he stopped the game.

"Come on, Aidan," she urged him on. "I know you want to. Go and peek. I won't say a word."

"Are you trying to avoid being with me?" he asked as he collected the game controls.

"No, I'm all for the swap." She wasn't going to confess that it had been her idea all along, although he probably wouldn't be surprised if he found out that fact.

"Because you want to teach me some manners?"

She tried to hide her surprise. She was so caught off-guard that she couldn't think of a sassy comeback. How did Aidan know about her plans for him?

Aidan laughed and turned off the widescreen television set. "Did you think I wouldn't have figured it out?"

She wasn't going to answer that. "Your lesson can wait," she said with her nose tilted high in the air. "Go and watch them. Be my guest."

"Why do you want me to watch?" he asked as he stood up. "So you can watch, too?"

Jamie made a face. "No, that's not my hang-up. That's yours." She smiled victoriously as she saw her jab found its mark.

Aidan went very still, like a wild animal scenting danger. "What do you mean by that?"

"Oh, come on, Aidan," Jamie said as she got off the couch. "It's a small town. Word gets around."

He frowned. "I'm not following."

He was going to play dumb. It was time to lay out all her cards. "I know that you like to watch your girlfriends with other men."

"That's not true."

"Okay"—Jamie shrugged—"so it only happened with one of

your girlfriends." What was the big deal? If he wanted to watch Caleb and Mia, Jamie would make that happen.

"How do you know this?"

Was he admitting it? She wasn't sure. "I knew Lacey," she told him.

"I know you did."

She wasn't sure about his tone. She narrowed her eyes with suspicion. "What do you mean by that?"

"Like you said, it's a small town." He mimicked her casual shrug. "I know you and Lacey hooked up once."

Lacey wasn't Jamie's type, and she turned out to be the one person Jamie should never have slept with. Jamie had been drunk, and Lacey had been a sexual opportunist. "Who told you?"

"Lacey."

Figured. Jamie rolled her eyes. "And you believed her?"

"I didn't until I saw how you were watching Mia and Caleb." He folded his arms across his chest and rocked back on his feet. "Your attention was all on Mia."

She hadn't tried to hide the fact, believing that no one would be looking at her. She wondered who else knew how she felt. "Did you tell Mia about me?"

"Believe it or not, Jamie, we don't talk about you when we're together."

"Good point."

"Listen. I don't care that you like to have sex with women as much as you do with men."

"Mia might." And Mia's opinion meant a lot to her. She would rather hide her sexual orientation than have Mia turn her back on her.

"Mia might be surprised, but that's about it." Aidan paused. "Why didn't you tell her that I like to watch?"

His sexual fantasy was nothing compared to those of some other people in Clover Bud. "I figured that was something she had to find out on her own."

"Why? Don't you share everything with her?"

"Obviously not."

He smiled at her snappy answer. "Did she tell you how I like to tie down lovers?"

"That has come up on occasion." She remembered the first time Mia had been tied down. Mia described it to Jamie the next day in explicit detail. The way she went on and on about it, Jamie wondered if she had done it wrong. She never had felt that kind of bliss. She had immediately tried it with one of her lovers and was acutely disappointed.

"Then it should come as no surprise that I'm going to tie you down," Aidan said by way of warning. "How much do you know about bondage?"

"Enough to know it's not for me."

Aidan took a step closer to her. "Maybe your lover didn't know what he was doing."

"That is a possibility." It might be better if she did it with an expert, but she doubted it. She couldn't see the attraction of having her movements limited.

"I want to tie you up, Jamie."

She knew that. But he didn't tell her what he planned to do once he had her trussed up like a turkey. "Have *you* ever been tied up?"

He scoffed at the idea. "No."

That surprised her. Wouldn't he want to know how it felt being tied down? "Why not?"

"No woman has ever tried."

"Really?" Jamie found that difficult to believe. "Because that's the first thing that popped into my head."

Aidan laughed.

"You know what, Aidan? I want to tie you up. What do you think? Are you up for it?"

His smile disappeared as he studied her face. She was pleased that he was giving her suggestion consideration. "Only if I get to tie you up afterward," he finally said.

"Seriously?" Jamie really hadn't expected him to agree.

"It's the only way you're going to trust me."

She stared at him and slowly shook her head. "I swear, you have been one surprise after another. Well"—she gestured in the direction of the stairs—"let's go up to the attic."

"First you need to think this through," Aidan told her. "Do you have anything to tie me down with?"

"I'll have to improvise," she replied breezily as she left the media room, Aidan hot on her heels.

"You can't improvise when it comes to bondage."

"You can if it's Jamie style." The truth was she had no idea what she was doing, but she wasn't going to tell that to Aidan. He'd snatch the control from her, and she wasn't about to give it up.

Jamie didn't like it that Aidan was more experienced in bondage, she decided as she headed for her attic apartment. She never liked it when her lover knew more, because she felt that put her at a disadvantage.

But her lovers never figured out that she was a fast learner. As long as she kept her eyes open and her mind sharp, she would figure a way to get out of any knot Aidan tried on her.

She climbed the stairs, sensing Aidan right behind her. Jamie wondered if he was already regretting this deal. She needed to distract him in case he was changing his mind. She gave a little provocative sway to her hips and walked into the middle of the attic.

Her apartment was very different from the rest of the house. While Mia's home was filled with pastels, florals, and classic pieces of furniture, Jamie's room was more exotic. She preferred bold colors, metallic and jeweled embellishments, and lots of pillows.

The room was now very bare. She had given away almost everything. All that was left was a few boxes and suitcases. The only color in the room was the bright red curtains and the bold ethnic print of her bedsheets.

"Where do you want me?" Aidan asked. His question made her pause. Aidan was usually the one who gave orders and made commands. She knew how difficult it was for him to stand back and wait for her to make the decisions.

He stood by the bed, his arms folded across his chest and his legs braced. He was prepared for action.

He wasn't a big man, but she felt like he filled the room. She definitely needed to tie him down. But how? Her bed didn't have posts or railings.

She looked around the attic for inspiration. Her eyes flickered over the support beams over her head. She stopped, looked up, and smiled.

Aidan followed where she was looking. His eyebrows arched. "You have to be kidding."

"It'll work," Jamie said as she tugged the top sheet from her bed. She jumped on the mattress and tossed the bedding over the main support beam. The colorful cotton billowed over the thick wooden beam, and she caught the other side.

She paused and decided to tie the ends into a tight knot right under the beam. The less movement Aidan had, the better. It wasn't easy to make the knot, but she refused to ask for Aidan's help.

"Okay, give me your arm," Jamie said as she pushed the sheet farther down the beam and away from the bed. She jumped off the mattress and faced Aidan.

Aidan silently offered one of his wrists, and she tied one end around it. "Too tight?" she asked brightly.

He tested the bindings with no emotion. "It's fine."

Jamie gritted her teeth. She had been wondering if he felt the same excitement roiling through her. She guessed not.

She tied his other arm and stepped back to admire her handiwork. The sheets were short enough to keep his arms up. He held his hands together above his head. If it weren't for his casual clothing, Aidan would look like an exotic sex slave tied up with veils.

"You forgot to take my shirt off first," Aidan said.

"Oh, I'm not too worried about that." She slid her hands along his chest, admiring the sculpted muscles that lay underneath his shirt. "I can still screw you with your clothes on."

She stood in front of him, toe-to-toe, and placed her hand on the back of his head. She lowered his head, pleased that he didn't resist, and captured his mouth with hers.

Jamie kissed him ferociously until Aidan tried to take charge of the kiss. It was so typical of him. But didn't he realize she wouldn't let him have all the control?

She liked having her sex partner tied up. Jamie felt strong and powerful. She could have her way with him. But she wouldn't, she decided as she sucked his bottom lip. He had put his trust in her when he knew better. She was touched by his faith in her, and she wouldn't abuse it.

Jamie slipped her hands under his shirt. He was warm and muscular. She smoothed her palms over him until his nipples hardened under her touch.

She let her fingers get caught in the curly hair on his chest before sliding her hands down his stomach. Jamie had to run her fingertips over his washboard abs. His body was a perfect example of male beauty.

Jamie wanted to see more of him. She quickly unbuttoned his jeans and pushed the denim and underwear down his powerful thighs. His cock was huge and already erect. She grasped both hands around him and Aidan flinched, groaning deep in his throat.

Jamie would love to get her lips around his cock. Would she be able to deep-throat him? She'd like to try. She considered sucking him off, but why should he get all the pleasure?

Jamie stood up. She slowly removed her tank top, enjoying the fact that she was right next to Aidan and he couldn't touch her. Her flimsy bra was the next to come off. She brushed her breasts against his chest. He didn't say a word, but she felt the tension climbing inside him.

She wiggled out of her shorts and undies. When she had stripped off the last of her clothes, she stood proudly in front of him before turning her back. She strolled to her bed and lay down in the center. Parting her legs, she rubbed her hand over her mound.

"What are you doing?" Aidan asked in a gruff voice.

Wasn't it obvious? "Getting off."

She saw the bedsheet pull tight and then relaxed. She wondered if he was trying to break free.

"If you didn't tie me up," Aidan said, "I could have helped you with that."

"True, but I know you like to watch." She smiled at his growling reply. She splayed her legs, wondering if her pussy was as pink and juicy as it felt.

Using her fingers, she spread the folds of her sex. She slid her finger along her puffy slit. She was so wet that she could hear the sound of slippery flesh.

Jamie pinched her nipple with her other hand. She arched her back and groaned as the pleasure zipped through her. Dipping a finger into her pussy, she pumped her finger in deep. She was desperate to find satisfaction.

She heard the ominous creak of wood and glanced up. Her eyes widened when she saw Aidan tugging the sheet along the support beam. His muscles were straining as he put all of his effort in getting closer to bed.

"You're not supposed to do that," she said. She watched as he continued to inch his way closer. She hadn't considered that he would be able to move. This was why she needed to be an expert on bondage before she tried to tie up a dangerously sexy man.

He didn't respond. His foot touched the mattress and she was scuttling back. He tried to kneel down, but the sheets wouldn't let him. The most he could do was settle back on his haunches.

"You have me tied up," Aidan said in a lethally soft voice. "You might as well use me."

Use him. She liked the sound of that, and she knew that she shouldn't. But she was willing to take him up on his offer.

Jamie got up on her knees and crawled over to him. He was at her mercy, and they both knew it. She grazed her hands over his thighs before grasping his cock with both hands.

She gripped his length has hard as she could. Jamie watched his jaw tighten as he pulled one hand up, squeezing as she went, over his mushroom head. She gave a little twist of her hand and saw the muscle twitch in his cheek.

Jamie grabbed the root of his cock and let her other hand squeeze up. She did it over and over, sometimes giving his cock a good twist. Aidan felt warm, wet, and rock-hard underneath her hands. Jamie longed to have his cock burrowed deep inside her.

"Let me know if I'm too rough on you," she said sweetly as she straddled his hips.

He raised his eyebrow and was about to say something when his face went blank. She slowly sank onto him, her body gradually accepting his thick cock. By the time she took every inch of him, sweat dripped from her hot skin as she struggled for her next breath.

She rocked against him and felt them sway. Jamie yelped and held on to him, her fingernails biting in his shoulders. They moved from side to side with each buck and thrust.

Jamie felt Aidan's muscles flex. She was glad his defined physique was not for show only. Jamie wrapped her legs against him and clung to his shoulders as they rocked back and forth.

She felt like she was on a swing, swirling around and enjoying the ride. Her hair flew in her face; her breasts grazed against his shirt. She couldn't get enough of this wild ride.

One little move and fireworks crackled under her skin. If they swiveled, pleasure rippled through her pelvis. When he thrust inside her, Jamie bore down on him, gasping as his cock stretched her.

She rode him hard, feeling dizzy and light-headed. She knew she should stop, but she couldn't. The heat coiling deep in her belly was too much. She wanted it to spring free and shatter.

Jamie rocked from side to side. A jagged bolt of hot pleasure ripped through her.

"Don't let go," Aidan said between gasps. "I've got you."

She wouldn't dare let go. Instead of tossing her arms and legs out and letting the tingling fire scorch out of her, Jamie clung to him like a vine.

She closed her eyes, her body swaying as the bright stars swept through her mind. She couldn't think or breathe. All she could do was hold on tight.

Maybe she had been too hasty about refusing to be tied up, she decided as she surrendered to the sensations crashing through her. She should give this bondage thing another chance. . . .

TEN

Mia woke up suddenly, her pulse racing as her heart pounded in her ears. Her arms went rigid as she bunched her pillow in her hands. She was hot, and her skin felt too tight for her body.

She looked around her bedroom, wondering what had woken her, but everything was in place. It was quiet, and she gradually realized that the sun was setting. That was odd.

She was still feeling disoriented from her dream. Mia's mouth curled into a secretive smile. Her fantasy had been wild and scandalous, and so vivid in detail.

Mia had never dreamed about having sex with Caleb before. She'd once heard that fantasizing about another man was common for women. Now she knew why.

But in her dream she did things to Caleb she wouldn't have done with Aidan. With Caleb, she was the one giving the orders. Shyly at first, but by the end there had been no stopping her.

She hadn't cared what Caleb thought of her or her voracious needs. Mia kept asking for oral sex when she was lying underneath him or straddling his face and riding his mouth. Her core clenched as she remembered her dream. Caleb had been her fantasy lover, knowing exactly what she wanted.

She had been drunk on power, especially when Caleb had made no demands of his own in her dream. Mia remembered she had made a few requests that were now causing her to blush.

She didn't know why she had asked Caleb to lick her feet. Mia curled her toes as her feet tingled. She rubbed her thighs together as the sparkling heat coiled up her ankles and legs before it spread through her pussy.

Mia remembered that her imagination had made Caleb very talented with his mouth, especially with his tongue. In her dream, she had reclined naked on the bed and fondled her breasts while Caleb had knelt on the mattress at her feet.

She didn't know why she had made him lick her feet. Maybe she was testing her boundaries with him. Or perhaps she wanted to see what the fuss was all about with foot worship.

"Kiss my foot," she had demanded, shocked as the words spilled from her mouth.

If Caleb had been surprised, he hadn't shown it. He also didn't drop his gaze dutifully like a submissive would. Mia hadn't cared about that in her dream. She wanted him to be attentive and enthusiastic. She could tell from the gleam in his brown eyes that he was eager to serve.

Mia hadn't offered her foot. She wanted complete capitulation from Caleb. She wanted to watch him surrender, step-by-step, until he was groveling to please her. Mia's skin prickled in shock at how she had acted in her dream.

Caleb had cupped the heel of her foot with his large, rough fingers. Mia had felt a twinge of vulnerability; her foot had seemed fragile in his hand.

His fingertips had grazed her ankle, and then he boldly trailed his hand up her leg. She trembled when Caleb's scarred fingers brushed the sensitive skin behind her knee. Mia had tried to jerk away from his touch, but Caleb didn't let her go.

"I told you to lick my foot," she had said through clenched teeth.

Caleb had responded by pulling sharply at her heel. Mia slid toward him. She grabbed the bedsheets, but it hadn't stopped her. Caleb had pulled her foot up to his mouth rather than bend down to her level.

Mia's next command dissolved in her throat as Caleb licked the sole of her foot just as his other hand covered the damp curls between her legs.

She shivered with pleasure at the memory of that dream. He had stroked her mound as he slowly sucked each toe. Her climax had reached a height she hadn't known existed. She wiggled as she felt the twinges in the folds of her sex.

But that demand wasn't as taboo as when she had asked Caleb to rim her hole. In her dream he had appeared surprised and called her a naughty girl, but he hadn't refused her.

Caleb had flipped her over. She had gotten on her hands and knees as he piled the pillows under her hips. Mia hadn't known what to expect, but it was as if his touch had sent an electric current through her nervous system. She couldn't get enough of him sweeping his tongue over her rosebud, but at the same time, it was almost too much. Her orgasm had been like nothing she had ever experienced.

Mia rubbed her eyes and sat up in her bed. She looked at her alarm clock, surprised that it was Thursday evening. She looked around and her heart stopped when she saw Caleb naked and asleep in her bed.

Mia's mouth fell open. Fragments of the day bombarded her memory. The way she'd held Jamie down on the kitchen table. The agreement to swap sex partners. Aidan giving instructions while she had sex with Caleb.

Oh, my God. It wasn't a dream. She had really done all those things with Caleb! Mia's skin burned with embarrassment. She couldn't believe the way she'd ordered him around, the things she'd made him do.

Mia covered her face with her hands. What was he going to think of her? Why didn't he stop her before she went too far?

She had been out of control and that was her greatest fear. This was why she needed to be tied up when she had sex. And from now on, she would need a gag so she didn't make shocking requests.

She jumped when she heard a noise in the kitchen. Mia crawled out of the bed, willing to take any excuse to put some distance between her and Caleb. She pulled on a short cotton nightgown that barely reached her thighs. Padding barefoot, she entered the kitchen and found Jamie making sandwiches.

Jamie looked like a woman who had had a wild night. She wore nothing but a tank top and panties, and her hair was a tousled, tangled mess. Her full lips were swollen, and she had whisker burn on her chin.

Mia glanced at Jamie's wrists, wondering if she had red marks from the binding. She frowned when she noticed Jamie's skin was unmarked. That couldn't be right. Jamie would never have lain still while bound. And even if she tried, it wouldn't have worked. Aidan was a vigorous lover.

"Hey, Jamie," Mia said as she stepped into the kitchen. She noticed her voice sounded rough and tired. "How's it going?"

Jamie looked up from preparing the sandwiches and smiled. "Great. How about you?"

"Uh, great." Great? Jamie found being tied up great? Mia never would have thought of it.

"So tell me"—Jamie said as she spread mustard on the slices of bread—"what do you think of Caleb? Everything you dreamed of, right?"

Mia blushed. "Yeah, he really is a fantasy lover."

"Told you," Jamie said as she layered the meat and vegetables onto the sandwiches.

"It's as if he instinctively knows what you want," Mia continued, resting her hip against the counter.

Jamie stopped what she was doing as she considered Mia's insight. "I never thought of it that way, but you're right."

"You're lucky to have him."

Jamie frowned and slapped slices of bread on top of the sandwiches. "He's not mine."

"He would be if you just said the word." Caleb obviously adored Jamie. Mia didn't understand why her friend was pushing him away.

"I don't want anything or anyone holding me back," Jamie said irritably. "It's time for me to travel light and see what the world has to offer me."

"I know, but—"

"Well"—Jamie grabbed the plate of sandwiches and headed for the door—"I better get back before Aidan thinks I'm breaking my promise. It's my turn to get tied up."

Mia grabbed her friend's arm. "Wait. Your turn?" She blinked and stared at Jamie. "You tied *Aidan* up?"

"Yeah, it was fun." She waggled her eyebrows as a wicked gleam entered her eyes.

Mia heard the words, but she couldn't comprehend them. Jamie tied Aidan down. She hadn't thought that would happen in a million years. Jamie must have been extremely cunning to pull off that trick.

"How the hell did you tie him up?"

"Easy," Jamie said with a shrug. "He let me."

Mia's mouth sagged open. She tried to picture Aidan spread-eagle and bound on Jamie's bed, but she couldn't. He would have torn off the bindings and tackled Jamie. Now that Mia could imagine easily.

Jamie had tied Aidan down. The words buzzed around Mia's head. She wanted to know everything. "How'd he take it?"

"He was scowling at first," Jamie admitted, "but he got into it."

"Really?" Mia doubted that. Aidan would have done anything to get it over and done with. That was, if he hadn't been hatching an escape plan.

"It might take all of my persuasive skills to convince him to do it again, though," Jamie said as she headed toward the stairs. "But it's my turn."

Now that sounded like Aidan. He would volunteer first, so if Jamie had abused her power, he would have a chance at retribution. "Karma is going to bite you in the ass."

Jamie paused. "Any advice?"

Where did Mia start? Aidan was going to punish Jamie for any infraction. He would deprive Jamie of pleasure until she had earned it. By the end of the night, Jamie would learn the meaning of patience. "Be on your best behavior."

Jamie gave a crack of laughter. "I'm screwed."

Mia watched Jamie close the door and heard the stairs creaking. Jamie had tied Aidan down. Mia still couldn't believe it, but why would her best friend lie to her?

She continued to stare at the door. The world had gone topsy-turvy, and she wasn't sure if she liked it. Aidan was being tied down, and she was giving out sexual commands that shocked her to the core.

Now if only she had the same kind of sexual power Jamie possessed. Mia would also need her friend's ability to make the most of it. What was the point of having that kind of power if she was afraid to use it?

Well, she had gone crazy with power when it came to Caleb, Mia realized as she put away the food that Jamie had left out. Now if only she could not be shy about using that power. That was the real trick. She needed to go for it and not worry whether she could face Caleb the next day.

It was time to test her sexual power. She could go as far as she wanted with Caleb. He had proven that he was willing to let her do anything to him. And right now she wanted a man, naked and bound, underneath her.

She strode back to the bedroom and noticed Caleb hadn't moved since she left. She turned on the light, and he didn't stir. Mia walked to her chest and pulled open the bottom drawer. She looked at the selection of cuffs, chains, and straps. Gnawing her lip, she grabbed thick cuffs to use on Caleb's wrists and ankles.

She crawled onto the bed and straddled his hips. Shaking Caleb's bare shoulder, Mia felt a bit guilty for waking him up. The guy needed his sleep, but she only had four days to go after her fantasies.

"Caleb?" she asked softly.

He blinked open his eyes and gave her a soft smile. "Yeah, Naughty Girl?"

She blushed at the nickname, knowing she earned it. "I want to tie you up."

He yawned. "Okay."

Hmm . . . That was all he had to say? Not exactly the response she had expected. Trepidation, maybe. Possibly eagerness.

She felt his gaze on her as she stretched his arm out. He didn't resist as she expertly bound his wrist and attached the chain to the bedpost. Caleb gave an experimental tug to the cuff as she tied down his other wrist.

"These are heavy-duty."

That was why she used them. Everyone thought she was all about flowers and pastels, but there was something very erotic about the scent of leather and the metallic sound of chains. She loved how they looked on her.

"Did you expect pink Velcro ones?" she asked as she bound his other wrist.

"Something like that."

She placed her hands on either side of Caleb's head and leaned down, kissing his lips softly. She took her time exploring the shape and taste of his mouth. As he raised his head to deepen the kiss, Mia pulled away, well out of his reach.

She saw frustration flicker in Caleb's eyes. She knew how he felt. Soon his longing would blend with his arousal, giving his emotions a sharp edge. Then everything he felt would be more intense than he expected.

"Have you been tied up before?" she asked as she caressed his arms and shoulders. She glided her fingernails against his nipples and watched him flinch.

"Yeah." His tone seemed to say, *Hasn't everyone?*

"Both your wrists and ankles?"

He tilted his head and studied her expression. "You want to tie up my ankles?"

She did. She wanted to make him completely immobile. "Unless you don't want me to."

He shrugged, and the metal chains on the bedposts jingled. "Go for it."

He was too relaxed, too cavalier about it. Whenever Aidan bound her, she was so excited that she could barely breathe. But then, she could always predict what Aidan would do. She trusted her boyfriend, but he knew how to tease and torment her before giving her pleasure.

Caleb seemed to know exactly what was in store for him. Was she that predictable? Didn't he worry that she might abuse her power? Or that she would deny him pleasure? For all he knew, she might walk out of the room and leave him there.

But she wouldn't. And somehow Caleb knew it. He knew her plan was to treat his body as a sensual feast. The way he could read her was unsettling.

She grabbed a cuff and wrapped it tightly around his ankle before chaining it to the post. Testing that it wasn't too tight, she worked on the other leg. When she was done, Mia crawled between his legs.

Caleb looked like a captive warrior. The cuffs emphasized his lean, muscular arms and legs. Rather than seeming weak and defeated, Caleb looked more like a barely leashed animal. Mia's body responded to the primitive sight before her.

She kissed Caleb's leg, tasting his skin. She nibbled and bit a trail along his thigh, but he didn't move. Mia didn't like that. She wanted to make him go wild. Then she would see the full extent of her power.

It was time to tease him. She kissed a circle around the root of his cock. When she inhaled his scent, it was tempting to lick him. She almost caved in, but held back at the last moment.

Mia blew a gust of air against his heavy balls. She saw him tense, but that was it. What did it take to torture this guy?

She needed to tease him with more than her mouth. Mia placed her fingertips on his inner thighs and gently massaged him. She rubbed her hands in a circular pattern, moving toward his cock. When she almost met her destination, she lifted her hands and returned them to the original spot on his inner thighs and started all over again.

She heard the clink of the metal and smiled. No matter how cool he tried to play it, the chains would give him away.

When her hair accidentally brushed his cock, he flinched. The sound of metal against wood screeched in the air. Hmm . . . He wasn't as casual and unaffected as he was pretending.

She moved on to kiss his stomach. Reaching up, she captured his nipples between her fingers. She pinched and tweaked them, enjoying how Caleb squirmed. Mia smiled at the sound of the clatter of chains, and she felt the tensing of his body.

It was a nice change of pace to have a naked, willing man underneath her. She should enjoy this moment and make the most of it. But she wasn't sure if she liked this position.

She liked being cocooned by her bed and lover. As wild as she wanted to be, she needed an anchor, or she was afraid that she would shatter and no one could put her back together again. That was one thing Caleb couldn't provide for her.

Mia also liked having everything taken care of for her. She wanted someone else to make the decisions. It was blissful when her mind went blank as she rode the sensations and emotions storming her.

Now her mind was crowded with indecision. She realized she didn't like to be in charge. It wasn't as fun as she thought it would be.

Okay, don't give up yet. It's simply something new. Give it a try.

She sat back on her knees. Caleb was breathing hard, the tension shimmering off him. She wanted to send him over the edge.

Mia reached for his cock. Grasping his length with both hands, she pumped him hard. The friction made her palms hot, but she didn't stop. She enjoyed watching Caleb's mouth sag open, his eyes squeezed shut, as the extreme pleasure ripped through him.

Mia wanted to taste him. She lowered herself between Caleb's legs and took the weeping crown of his cock between her lips. He tasted good. Different from Aidan. Not better, not worse. Just different.

She gave short, quick licks around his cock, watching how he reacted. He liked it when she licked the underside of his cock. He hissed between his teeth when she licked his balls. When she drew him deep in her mouth, his groan was loud and long.

"Take off your nightgown," Caleb said in a raspy voice. "I want to see you naked."

She was willing to honor this request. Mia wrenched her nightgown off her body, before arching her spine and tossing her hair back. She was surprised by how much she enjoyed showing off her curves.

Mia knew her breasts were small and her hips were without curves, but the way Caleb looked at her made her feel like she was the most beautiful woman in the world. The sexiest, she amended, as she saw his eyes darken with arousal.

"I want to taste those nipples," he confessed in a hoarse whisper.

Her nipples stung at his words. She wanted to fulfill his wish.

Mia slowly crawled up his lean, wiry body and placed her hands on either side of his head. She dipped her spine until the tip of her breast hovered above his mouth.

Caleb darted his tongue to lick her hard nipple. The simple, delicate touch sizzled through her. She gasped and moved away instinctively.

"More," Caleb urged. "Give me more."

She lowered herself again; this time Caleb caught her nipple between his lips and urgently suckled her. She groaned as the pleasure whipped through her.

Mia teased him with her breasts. Dangling the possibility for more only to rip them away. She pressed her breasts together and rubbed her nipples against his lips, moving quickly before he could get her.

"Ride my cock."

She immediately obeyed. She didn't care if he wasn't supposed to be in charge. It was what she wanted, too. Her core was hot, swollen, and clenching for his cock.

She gripped it with both hands and slowly lowered herself onto him. Her flesh clung to him, drawing him in deeper. Clenching her teeth, she rotated her hips until she could get all of him inside her.

"Ride me hard," Caleb said in a gasp.

She bucked and swiveled her hips, watching Caleb toss his head from side to side. His hands clenched into fists, and he couldn't stay still. Mia was tempted to let him free so he could grab her and toss her down onto the bed. The thought alone sent a ripple through her pelvis.

Caleb's hips vaulted off the bed as the sounds of the chain screeched in the air. He thrashed against his bindings, his muscles bulging. No matter how much he tossed and pulled, he wasn't going to get free.

He didn't give up. He fought the chains with all his might, and Mia knew his captivity was feeding his lust. The consuming desire was building inside him until it would burst. Caleb squeezed his eyes shut and roared as he came.

Mia rode him hard, enthralled by his savage beauty. He kept pumping into her, and she was desperate for her release. She wanted to feel the intensity Caleb had experienced.

She rode him harder, faster until she was dizzy. There was a roaring in her ears as her breath caught in her throat. Her muscles shook as the urgent desire coiled deep in her belly.

But nothing happened, and she knew it wouldn't. She couldn't find the release she so desperately needed. Not like this. She liked having the power to tie a man down, but it wasn't her fantasy.

Mia slowed her pace until she eventually stopped riding his cock. She looked down at him with regret. "I'm sorry, Caleb. This isn't working for me."

Caleb looked bewildered by her admission. "What's wrong?"

"I don't know." Why couldn't she find the same satisfaction no matter who was tied up?

She heard his hiss when she withdrew from him. "You can tell me," he said.

She knew that. Caleb wouldn't judge her, which was probably why she had gone wild with him.

She got off him and immediately removed the cuff from one of his wrists. "I like being tied up, but I wanted to try something different."

"There must have been a reason why you picked this," Caleb said as he worked the other handcuff with his free hand.

"It was important to me to see how it felt on the other side," Mia told him as she freed his ankles.

Caleb sat up. "And how did it feel?"

"Strange." She didn't hate it, but it didn't give her the same hot, addictive buzz as when she was the one tied up.

"You don't want to be in charge."

"It's true." She tossed the cuffs onto the overstuffed chair and looked at Caleb. "Kind of embarrassing, if you think about it. Men think it's hot when the women take over in bed."

"Men also like pursuing women."

"Yeah." And thank God for that. Women like Jamie got off going after any man they wanted, but Mia wanted to be seduced. She looked away, knowing that her fantasies weren't politically correct.

"Do you want to be hunted?"

Her stomach did a funny flip as she blushed. It was a struggle to look at his face. She found Caleb watching her, his expression fierce.

She swallowed hard. "Yes."

Caleb didn't say anything. He surveyed the room before looking out the bedroom door. Mia was fascinated by the change that came over him. In his eyes there was a predatory gleam that took her breath away.

"Are all the lights off in the house?" he asked.

She frowned at the question. "Yes. Why?"

"Because I'm going to hunt you."

Mia tensed, her muscles locking as heat washed over her. Her nipples immediately tightened, and excitement twisted around her chest. She was already wet as Caleb reached for the lamp next to the bed and turned it off, plunging them into darkness.

Her gaze darted from side to side, but she couldn't see a thing. The air-conditioned temperature suddenly felt very cold. She listened intently, but she didn't hear Caleb move. The only thing she heard was her heartbeat.

"Mia?" Caleb said softly.

She took a deep breath. "Yes?"

"Run."

ELEVEN

ELEVEN

Mia bolted from the bed, her feet hitting the rug. Her heart pounded in her chest, and her blood raced through her veins. She wasn't afraid. She was excited more than she could remember.

Unable to see, Mia reached her hands out in front of her, feeling her way. The door should have been in front of her, but her hands touched nothing. She spread her arms out, and her hands slapped the wall.

She snatched back her hand. Now Caleb knew where she was. She tilted her head and heard him leaping off the bed.

Mia swung her hands in front of her and found the doorway. She plunged straight ahead, hoping her bare feet wouldn't echo in the small hallway. She passed the bathroom and ran headlong, not sure where she should hide.

She stubbed her toe when the wooden floor gave way to cold tile. Mia hopped and muffled a yelp. At least she knew she was now in the mudroom.

She heard Caleb's footsteps, and it was clear he was gaining on her. She didn't want to be caught right away. She wanted him to chase her until she had nowhere else to go.

Knowing she couldn't pause, Mia took a sharp left and went into the kitchen. There was no moonlight filtering through the lace curtains. No shadows or even a faint gleam on metal. She couldn't see anything.

How far was she going to get in this darkness? She reached out and her fingers brushed against something wooden. The table? A chair?

She tried to remember where everything was in the kitchen. There had to be a good, quick hiding place, but all she could think of was the kitchen table. If she tried to crawl under the table, she would knock into something.

Mia stepped back and felt the built-in wooden cabinets behind her. She remembered there was wall space between the cabinets and the refrigerator. There should be enough room for her to hide in that small gap.

She took sidesteps toward the refrigerator just as she heard Caleb enter the kitchen. The quiet room suddenly pulsed to life.

She stopped moving when every instinct told her to run. But, more than anything, she wanted to get caught. She was wet just thinking about it.

She heard his harsh breath. He was getting as excited as she was. She tried to calm her own breathing so as not to give herself away. She took another step, her heart in her throat. She hoped she wasn't making any noise.

Caleb paused. The tension in the room was unbearable. Her nipples tightened as she wondered what he was doing. Was he squinting in the darkness, looking for any sign of movement? Listening for the sound of her breathing? Or were his arms spread out, his fingers almost touching her?

The possibility made her shiver. She held her breath as he remained there. It seemed like it was minutes, but it was probably just a few seconds before he moved forward and bumped into the chair.

The sound of the chair skittering across the tile was loud to her ears. She pressed herself against the built-in cabinets as she heard Caleb move forward. He was so close she could feel the air move between them.

Mia listened to his feet hitting the tile as he made his away across the room to reach the dining room. She inched closer and closer to the wall. She reached out and touched something cold and smooth.

She jumped back, unsure where she was. She heard something metallic sliding along the wall. She tried to reach out and stop, whatever it was, but it clattered on the floor.

Oh, damn. Mia winced. She had forgotten about the broom.

She had to get away from that area, but which way should she go? She looked in the direction of the mudroom. She wouldn't get there fast enough. If she made a run for it, he would hear her.

She heard Caleb's steps coming closer to investigate. Her only choice was to stay in the corner.

Just as she pressed her back against the wall, the rough texture prickling her skin, she felt Caleb's presence. He'd moved faster than she'd expected.

The sound of his breathing was right next to her. She pressed all the way back, knowing that it was a matter of seconds before the game was up. But she wasn't going to make it easy for him. She wanted him to work for his prize. Mia grew warm thinking about how he'd celebrate his victory.

His fingers brushed against her hair, and then she felt nothing. She remained perfectly still as Caleb moved his hand back and brushed it again.

Caleb wrapped his fingers around her hair. "Gotcha," he whispered.

He moved swiftly, pinning her against the wall, before she could say anything. His cock nestled against her stomach as his chest pressed against her breasts. He grabbed her arms and held them above her head.

"I surrender," she said.

Caleb crashed his mouth onto hers. His aggression aroused a frisson of dark excitement. She knew he was going to claim his prize in the most basic way.

He held her wrists with one hand and moved his other hand down to her breasts. His touch was possessive. Caleb held her breast up so he could suck her nipple hard. Her keening cry echoed in the room.

It wasn't enough for Caleb. He bit down, branding her flesh. The bite was just hard enough to make her jump. Crescent-shaped marks would bloom on her skin later, and she would wear them with pride.

Caleb let his hand wander over her naked body. It was one more way of showing that she was his now, and he could do whatever he liked. From the appreciative hums and growls, Mia knew that he couldn't wait much longer to enjoy her.

He covered her sex with his hand and paused. "You're so wet," he said. Mia could hear the smile in his voice. "You like playing hide-and-seek?"

"Yes." Powerful emotions whipped through her when she was being hunted and claimed. It was primitive and thrilling. It was chaos in her otherwise safe existence.

She tilted her hips toward him as he dipped one finger inside her. Mia wished that she could see him, or that he could watch the passion flickering across her face.

Pressing the palm of his hand against her mound, he curled his finger inside, immediately finding her G-spot. He moved his finger in a small circular motion. Mia rocked her hips wildly, amazed by the gentle touch.

Mia started to shake. The pleasure was so intense she couldn't stand up straight. Her knees gave out, but Caleb caught her before she fell.

"Wrap your legs around my waist," Caleb said urgently.

She hooked her legs, her back sliding up the wall. She crossed her bare feet at the small of his back and squeezed her thighs around him. As she swayed and bucked her hips, she felt Caleb's hard cock pressing against the slick folds of her sex.

Both Caleb and Mia groaned as he slid deep into her wet heat. He still held her arms as he thrust deep inside her. There was no finesse or rhythm. He took her in the most elemental way.

And she loved it. She was pinned to the wall, unable to move or see. Her world was focused on the feel of his cock and the pulsating throb in her pussy. Caleb hammered inside her, and stars danced before her eyes. She came violently, screaming his name. Her flesh gripped him like a vise, triggering his own release.

Mia clung to Caleb, their skin sticky with sweat. Her breasts bumped against him with every gulp of air. Her legs ached but she didn't move.

Caleb nuzzled his face into her neck. "You want to play again?"

Her core clenched at the suggestion, squeezing Caleb's spent cock.

He gave a half groan, half laugh. "I guess you do."

"Only this time," she said as she unwrapped her legs from his hips, "give me a head start."

———

"You can't hold off any longer," Aidan said to Jamie as he lounged naked on her bed, the colorful sheet covering him from the waist down. He took the plate of sandwiches and set it on the bedside table. "It's my turn to tie you up."

The last bite of her sandwich stuck in her throat. "I'm not avoiding it," she insisted, but he didn't have to sound so gleeful. She half expected him to rub his palms together and give an evil cackle.

It had been a while since she had been tied down. An old boyfriend had handcuffed her to his bed, and the power had gone to his head. When he had finally released the cuffs, she had punched him in the jaw and walked out on him.

She'd like to think that Aidan would be more mature than her ex-boyfriend. When he had taken her on the kitchen table, Aidan's priority had been her pleasure. And tonight he had allowed her to tie him up first.

Aidan had shown a pattern of taking care of her. Jamie had to trust that he would continue. No amount of proof or instinct was going to erase her nervousness, she realized as her heart pounded against her ribs.

"Get on your knees."

Jamie gritted her teeth. Damn, his commanding tone rankled. But she knew better than to comment or fight it. She would not give him an excuse to demonstrate his dominance.

She silently knelt down on the mattress next to Aidan and looked into his eyes. She wasn't trying to glare at him or have a showdown, but she wouldn't lower her eyes. That was asking too much.

Her pulse skipped a beat as Aidan reached for her. His fingers skimmed along the scooped neck of her tank top. The touch was light, but it sent shivers down her spine.

Aidan skimmed his hands down her sides and grabbed the hem of her top. "Raise your arms," he told her.

Jamie followed his command, and he took off her shirt. She lowered her arms, her hands clenched, as she waited for his next instruction. She had a feeling that the first one was the easiest she would receive that night.

Aidan slid his hands along her collarbone. She felt the pulse at the base of her neck twitch under her skin. Jamie hoped he hadn't seen the telltale sign. She wanted him to think being tied up was no big deal to her.

He played with her breasts and smiled as they jiggled and swayed. When he swiped the pad of his thumb against the tip of her breast, she couldn't stop her nipple from tightening. Aidan lowered his head and sucked it in his mouth.

Jamie gasped at the strong pull. She felt it tugging straight to her clit, and she wanted more. She clasped her hands on Aidan's head, her fingers spearing through his short black hair. She wanted to press him closer, have him take more of her breast in his mouth, but he stopped suckling altogether.

"I didn't tell you to do that," he said, his mouth pressed against her breast.

"Because you hadn't thought of it yet."

He encircled her wrists with his fingers and pulled her hands down. "Don't do anything until I tell you to."

Jamie sighed. "If that's what you want . . ." But she wasn't sure if she could keep her hands to herself. It was going to be a very long night.

"Since you're new at this," he said as he reached for her discarded tank top, "I'm going to tie you up now."

She dug her fingernails into her palms as the panic flashed in her chest. "Already?"

Aidan stretched the shirt and twisted it into a thick cotton rope. "Are you okay with that?"

"Yeah," she said, staring at the tank top. She blinked and looked at Aidan. "Of course."

"Hold out your hands."

She defiantly offered him her hands and watched him bind her wrists together. She had expected something elaborate that only Houdini could escape. If not that, she thought he would twist her arms and legs in some exotic configuration.

Instead, he kept her hands in front of her body, tied together in a simple knot. He didn't even give her the respect of using a top-of-the-line leather cuff.

"I'm not a beginner when it comes to bondage," she muttered.

Aidan smiled. "You are compared to me."

This must be some psychological strategy, Jamie decided, as if she couldn't handle someone strong and experienced like him. He was wrong; she could handle anything he dished out.

Aidan's hands roamed over her chest and stomach. She flinched when he found her ticklish spot, just under her breasts. She squealed and dodged his hand, wishing she could block him with her hands.

"Get off the bed and kneel on the floor," Aidan told her.

Jamie wavered, unsure if she wanted to follow that order. She would be in a submissive position, and would have to look up to him. She was already feeling vulnerable.

"Jamie . . ." Aidan warned.

"Okay, okay. I'm getting on the floor." She scooted off the bed and knelt down.

Aidan got of the bed and stood before her. "Don't question my commands. The quicker you do them, the easier it will be for you."

"Ha!" She pressed her lips together before she said anything else.

Her eyes traveled along his naked body. His physique was amazing. He looked like a powerful conquering hero.

She, on the other hand, got the role of a handmaiden. A naked one, at that.

She couldn't believe she'd agreed to this! Jamie wiggled her fingers, but the twisted T-shirt didn't give. She wrestled with the constraints. Aidan knew exactly how to bind her where she couldn't complain about it being too tight, but she couldn't work her hands free.

Aidan gently cradled her jaw with both hands and tilted her face up. Threading his fingers in her hair, he massaged her scalp until he held the back of her head with one hand. He reached for his cock with the other and rubbed the wet tip along her mouth, outlining her lips.

Jamie opened and darted her tongue against his cock. She liked how he shivered from the flirty touch. *There's a lot more where that came from.*

"Not until I tell you," Aidan reminded her, his face stern. "If you can't follow this rule, you'll be punished."

Oooh . . . Heat flooded her pelvis. No, wait. What was she thinking? That wasn't supposed to be a promise. If Aidan tried bending her over his knee, he was in big trouble.

Aidan pressed his thumb against her chin and opened her mouth before guiding his cock past her lips. "Now lick me."

She swirled her tongue along the crown, enjoying the taste of his cock. She licked and slurped with abandon, but it wasn't enough. She wanted to fondle his balls and draw him deep into her mouth. She gently sucked against the tip, and he lurched forward, ramming his cock into her mouth.

"Suck me hard," he told her roughly.

Jamie noticed he didn't say a word about sucking his cock before he told her. She opened her mouth wider, accommodating his thickness. She drew him in, the muscles in her cheeks pulling hard. The tip pressed at the back of her throat, and she relaxed her muscles.

Aidan groaned when he realized she could deep-throat him. His fingers tightened against her jaw and began thrusting in her mouth. Jamie felt an intense rush of power coiling around her and sucked harder.

When had she ever been so intent to pleasure a man? She couldn't remember. She watched Aidan's expression as he thrust in her mouth. He bucked against her face, her nose pressed against the dark thatch of hair.

She couldn't ignore the aching throb in her pussy anymore. Pressing her bound hands against her mound, Jamie stroked her clit. She closed her eyes and moaned. She pressed harder just as Aidan stopped and pulled away from her.

He took a deep breath before he spoke. "What are you doing?"

"What does it look like?" She hummed with pleasure as she continued to stroke her clit.

The corner of his mouth slanted up. "I didn't give you permission," he said softly.

Jamie's hand froze. *Uh-oh.*

"I have to punish you now." He paused, letting the words sink in. "Stand up."

She slowly got to her feet, her ass tingling, knowing that a good hard spanking was in her near future. She wouldn't tolerate it. If he so much as tried, she was walking out.

He walked behind her. Jamie shifted from one foot to the

other. She didn't like not being able to see him. It put her at a disadvantage.

Aidan brushed his fingers along her panties. He tugged them off her hips and dragged them down her legs. "Don't move," he whispered in her ear.

She took a deep breath and closed her eyes. She wouldn't move—unless he spanked her. Then all bets were off.

Aidan swept his hands along her back and waist. She tried so hard not to move, but his touch tickled. He smoothed his hands on her ass and squeezed hard.

Jamie flexed her buttocks and froze. Was that considered a move? She hoped not because she really liked how he was kneading her curves. She was tempted to jut her ass into his hands, but she didn't want to press her luck.

Aidan curved his hands over her hips and then moved down to cup her sex. Jamie's knees buckled and slumped against his strong chest.

She was so wet that she heard his finger sliding along her slit. Jamie wanted to buck against his hand, but she had to stay still. She tried to focus on not moving, but her whole world was centered on his hand. She gritted her teeth as a small wave of pleasure crashed through her.

This was the way he punished? By making her come? If she had given him more trouble, would he have given her multiple orgasms?

"Put your foot on the bed."

Her foot? "Uh, okay . . ." She lifted her foot and stepped on the mattress.

"Turn to the side."

She did as he requested without asking a question. All she wanted was for him to keep playing with her clit.

Aidan stepped aside and knelt down on the floor in front of

her. That made her suspicious. She couldn't imagine Aidan taking the subservient role.

His head was right next to her bound hands. He glided his hand up her leg before reaching her wet curls between her thighs. He spread her labia with her fingers and pressed his mouth against her clit.

She stiffened as the white-hot energy pulsed through her. Her bindings tightened as her arms jerked. She wanted to break free of her constraints and let the pleasure spread through her.

Jamie also wished she could grab his head and press him closer to her, guide his tongue to touch her just right. All she could do was instruct him and hope he was in a cooperative mood.

"Flick your tongue over my clit," she said between short, choppy breaths. She frowned when he acted like he hadn't heard her. She closed her eyes. "Please?"

He gave a wicked flip of his tongue, and she shuddered. Her moan turned into a squeal as she felt like she was falling. Aidan's fingers tightened on her hips. He looked up at her and said, "I won't let you fall."

And she believed him. She knew that she could sway and wobble all she wanted and not worry. Aidan would catch her. Sometime during the night, she had put her trust in him. She had stopped looking out for herself and started relying on him.

She wasn't sure how she knew she could. Most of the men in her life weren't all that reliable. What made Aidan so different?

He did wicked things with his tongue, Jamie admitted as her hips started to buck. Aidan dragged his tongue along her slit and stabbed it into her channel. She bunched her fingers into fists and rode his tongue. She was so close to—

Aidan pulled away and Jamie whimpered. "Don't stop," she told him in a high whisper.

"I have to." He clasped his hand around her ankle and lowered her foot onto the floor.

"What?" She stared at him, her eyes wide. "Why?"

He stood up and smiled. "That's your punishment."

"What?" The question lashed out of her mouth. "Are you kidding? Why, I oughta—"

"Don't worry, Jamie," he said as he guided her back onto the bed. "You can earn some brownie points."

The man was out of his mind, she decided as she fought with the bindings on her wrists. She wasn't going to try to gain his favor.

"There are a few rules," he informed her.

He could forget it. She wasn't playing anymore. She gritted her teeth and tried to ignore the pulsing between her legs. Besides, she probably wouldn't be able to follow those damn rules.

Aidan stroked his finger along her wet, swollen clit. Her breath snagged in her throat as her pussy clung to his finger.

She wasn't going to . . . Jamie moaned and closed her eyes, surrendering to the inevitable. "What are the rules?"

TWELVE

Mia, wrapped in her thin robe, walked down the hall to her bathroom. A yawn caught her by surprise. As she lifted her hand over her mouth, Mia saw her friend heading out the back door. "Morning, Jamie."

Jamie stopped and looked down the hall. "What are you doing up so early?"

"I'm going to take a nice, long bubble bath." The idea alone made her muscles relax. A sweet ache permeated her body. "I thought I should do it before the guys get up. I don't want to waste a minute of this weekend."

"I'm going to run out and get some food to make breakfast," Jamie told her. "I think the guys need something more than cereal and milk."

"Sounds great." Mia rubbed her eyes and yawned again. "They definitely need to keep up their energy. I'll help cook when you get back."

"You want me to cook?" Jamie looked horrified at the thought.

"Maybe you need to get some more sleep. I don't cook for anyone—and that includes me."

"This weekend is about new experiences," Mia teased.

"I'm still not cooking," Jamie said as she escaped before Mia came up with any more ideas.

Mia shuffled into the bathroom and went straight to the old-fashioned porcelain tub. It was large and deep, perfect for lying back and relaxing. She plugged the drain and turned on the faucet. The sound of rushing water seemed to echo in the small bathroom.

Mia rose to her full height and shed her robe. Turning to grab the container of bath gel, she caught a glimpse of herself in the mirror. There was an interesting mix of bites and bruises covering her skin. She smiled, remembering how she earned every one of them.

Being chased in the dark had been an incredibly sexy adventure. Caleb was a fierce, often ferocious, lover. Each time he had told her to run, her senses had gone into overdrive. Getting caught was almost as pleasurable as Caleb claiming her as his prize. She loved being hunted. Would she like it just as much if Aidan was the hunter?

Probably, Mia thought as she grabbed the bottle and poured the thick pink gel into the gushing stream of water. But then, she didn't have that edge of the unknown with her boyfriend. She wouldn't feel hunted. Aidan was more of a protector than predator.

She watched the bubbles form and bent down to test the water's temperature. A pair of hands fell on her shoulders. Mia yelped, her pulse missing a beat. She tried to turn, but the person wouldn't let her, holding her still. Why wouldn't the person let her turn around?

A dark, icy, and unfamiliar sensation trickled down her spine. It wasn't panic, but something much more dangerous and seductive. "What's going on?" she asked, trying to hide her nervousness.

The person didn't answer, but kept pressing his hands onto her bare shoulders until she was on her knees in front of the bathtub. Mia gripped the porcelain edge, finding it cool under her touch.

The hands on her shoulders and throat were definitely masculine. Was it Aidan or Caleb? She wasn't sure, and that bothered her. She should be able to tell them apart.

"Why aren't you answering me?" she asked, very carefully avoiding the use of names. She didn't want to say the wrong one!

She felt his hand span her back. He pushed her forward, and she almost lost her balance. Mia reached out, and her hands went into the bubbles, smacking her palms on the tub.

The man roamed his hands over her hips and thighs. He squeezed her ass, and Mia felt him lean over her. Surrounding her. Trapping her. Her pussy grew warm when she realized she was cornered. She heard the man's harsh breath, her only warning, before he bit her earlobe.

Mia closed her eyes and shivered. Caleb. Her lover was definitely Caleb. He had bit down hard on her earlobe last night, and she had felt the burn go straight to her nipples.

The man let go and pressed a soft kiss on the ticklish spot behind her ear. She inhaled sharply as her skin tingled.

Or maybe the lover was Aidan? She opened her eyes and looked to the side, but couldn't see him. It must be Aidan because he knew every sensitive spot on her body.

The man caressed her ribs and gathered her breasts in his hands. Her eyes widened when she realized that she couldn't tell whose hands were on her. The man tweaked her nipples just like Aidan would. She breathed a sigh of relief, thinking she had solved the mystery when the man licked down the length of her spine just like Caleb had done the night before.

She tried to turn around, but he quickly placed his hand on the back of her head. He kept her head down as he continued to taste and play with her body. She wiggled her hips as lust coiled in the pit of her belly.

Why wasn't he talking? Was it Aidan, arrogantly believing she would know him by his touch? Or was it Caleb, improvising on their game during daylight hours? Or perhaps this was all part of the seduction where she had to guess.

He let go of her, and suddenly he was squeezing and kneading her buttocks. Mia whimpered, pressing her lips. She stared at the rising mountain of bubbles as the man rubbed his fingers along her wet slit.

Mia tried to concentrate so she could identify her lover, but it was no use. All she wanted right now was for him to touch her just right. "Faster," she gasped.

The man obeyed. *It must be Caleb then,* she thought absently as his hands glided over the folds of her sex. She groaned, her voice echoing in her ears, as she rocked against him. He stabbed two fingers inside her wet core and Mia pitched forward, the water splashing at her elbows.

Aidan? The man pumped his finger into her pussy hard and fast. Why did she think it was Aidan? Instinct or wishful thinking?

The man teased her with his fingers. Deep thrusts were followed by a series of shallow pumps, designed to tease her. Her vaginal walls gripped his fingers and drew him in deeper, but he resisted.

Mia couldn't take it anymore. She didn't care who it was, she only wanted to find release. "Please!" she begged, her voice reverberating. "In me now."

The man withdrew and clamped his hands on her hips. Mia dipped her head—in prayer or surrender, she wasn't sure. Her long blond hair fell in front of her face like a curtain. It didn't matter; she couldn't see anything other than the bubbles building in the bathtub.

She felt the man position himself behind her. Mia was really hoping it was Caleb. Aidan might deny her or make her wait. Caleb would give in to her, again and again. He wanted her to lose control while Aidan wanted her to master it.

Mia felt the press of his cock at her entrance. She took a deep breath as he slowly entered her wet channel.

Aidan, she thought as she bucked her hips and slowly released her breath. Whoever was behind her was thick, just like Aidan.

He slid into her, stretching and filling her until the tip of his cock tapped her womb. Was Aidan's cock this long? She didn't think so.

Caleb. Her lover must be Caleb.

Oh, my God. Mia squeezed her eyes shut with shame. Who was it? She couldn't tell. She had no idea who was behind her, ramming his cock inside her.

It was exciting. Shocking. She really didn't know . . . and she didn't care. It didn't matter as long as he was pleasuring her.

She heard the catch in his breath and felt the pinch of his fingers on her hips as he drove into her. Mia's hands slid in the frothy water, and she struggled not to fall.

What if her lover was neither Aidan nor Caleb? A dark thrill sprung free from deep within. The hot, jagged climax forked through her, catching her unawares. It was sharp and violent, like the lash of a whip. She arched her spine and screamed as it crashed through her.

She heard the man's hoarse cry as he pulsed into her. *Aidan?* He bucked wildly, her small breasts jiggling from the impact, before he shuddered and sagged against her. She felt the thick curls of hair on his sweat-slick chest.

It had been Aidan all along.

Mia's body started to shake, as if she had experienced a shock to the system. Why hadn't she known? Aidan had been her first and only lover until this weekend. She should have known right away.

Aidan held her closely, offering his body heat to ward off the trembles. Gently stroking her hair, he murmured in her ear. She didn't catch what he was saying, but it didn't matter. The soft, comforting tone soothed her troubled mind.

He reached out and turned off the faucet. Lifting her easily, he placed her carefully in the tub. She sank into the sea of bubbles and sighed as the warm water lapped against her shaky limbs.

She was waiting for Aidan to stand up and leave. Then she could figure out what was going on. But when Aidan reached for a washcloth, Mia realized he was going to tend to her.

"You don't have to stay," she said with a weak smile. "I can do it on my own."

"I know," he said as he dipped the washcloth into the water, disappearing in the bubbles. "But I want to stay."

He liked to take care of her. She knew that on some level, but at that moment, she understood it went beyond what they shared in the bedroom. He looked after her, not because he thought she was incapable, but because it was how he expressed how important she was to him.

"Will you join me?" she invited.

"In a *bubble bath*?" He arched his eyebrows. "That smells like *roses*?"

"Mmm-hmm." She scooted closer to the front of the bathtub to show that there was plenty of space for him.

He shrugged. "Okay, sure." Aidan carefully got into the tub and settled behind Mia. He pulled her toward him, his body cradled hers. "Just lean back and let me take care of you," he ordered as he guided her to lie on his chest.

She curled into him and rested her head against his shoulder. "You do that well, taking care of me."

He didn't respond as he dragged the washcloth along her arms. When he moved it along her collarbone, swirling it against her skin, he asked, "Are you enjoying the swap?"

Mia swallowed roughly and stared straight ahead at the chrome faucet. She wasn't sure if it was wise to answer. Was it a bad thing that she enjoyed swapping sex partners? Would Aidan figure out that she had been looking for something more?

"Yes," she answered carefully. "I can't imagine doing it with anyone other than Caleb and Jamie."

"I know what you mean," Aidan said as he stroked her arched neck with the sodden cloth. "I trust Caleb with you. He wouldn't try anything you were uncomfortable with."

"Do you trust Jamie?"

Aidan hesitated. "I trust I know how to handle her."

Mia's laugh echoed in the bathroom. "That's okay, Aidan," she said as she patted his knee. "You don't have to put your faith in her completely. I trust her with you."

But she trusted Jamie in an entirely different way. She knew her friend wouldn't try to steal away Aidan. There was no competition between Mia and Jamie. If anything, Jamie would make it clear how lucky Aidan was to have Mia.

"What do you like the most about the swap?" he asked.

Mia tensed, knowing that if the first question had been dangerous, this one was a minefield. She needed to answer this as generally as possible. "I pretty much like everything. Nothing stands out."

She cringed as the last three words slipped out. That wasn't true, and she didn't want to lie to Aidan. Why couldn't she tell him how hot it was to be pursued in the dark? She wished she could share the fact that every time Caleb caught her, she reached a height of pleasure so exquisite that the powerful orgasm that followed was anticlimactic.

"Is there anything you don't like?"

She could play it safe and pump his ego by saying she wasn't spending as much time with him as she wished. As much as she enjoyed Aidan's company, the swap was fascinating to her. She was learning a lot about herself, whether she liked it or not.

"The swap is raising a lot of questions," she admitted out loud. Like why couldn't she tell the difference between Aidan and Caleb? Or why, when she could have Caleb do anything Aidan would never do with her, she returned to her submissive role? Wasn't the point of the weekend to try different things?

"What kind of questions?"

There was something she wanted to ask Aidan. Normally she would keep it to herself, not wanting to stir up trouble. But Aidan seemed to be in a talkative mood. He was tired, comfortable, and sated. More important, he was trapped in a bathtub with her and couldn't easily walk away without looking like he was hiding something. Now was the best time to ask him.

She tilted her head up to look at him. "Do you like watching me with another man?"

His expression darkened. Aidan's eyes narrowed as the angles of his face became more pronounced. His nostrils flared as he controlled what was roiling underneath the surface.

"Forget I asked." Mia quickly looked away. "Purge it from your memory."

"Yes," he said in raspy voice. "It turns me on watching you with another man."

Whoa! She couldn't believe he'd confessed that to her. She knew that was difficult for him to take such a risk. He must really trust her.

Mia curled up against his chest, feeling closer to him than ever before. "Why?"

"Everything is new and exciting for you," he said as he wrapped his arm around her and held her close. "This past year has been a sensual awakening for you, and I like watching each minute of it."

She had already felt that when she was with Aidan. It was as if her pleasure was his pleasure. But how far could that possibly go? "Even if I'm with another man?"

Aidan's arms tightened around her. "Don't think you can go screw anyone," he said with a lethally soft tone.

"It's okay, Aidan. I'm not going to. I know this is a onetime deal." And she might only need this one time. Because of this swap, she was appreciating what she had even more.

"Did you like watching your other girlfriends?" Mia asked.

Aidan shifted underneath her, and Mia knew she was stepping into unknown territory. "You've never asked me about my past sex life before," he said, his words clipped with impatience.

"You don't have to discuss every detail about your exes," she assured him. "But you met me when I was a virgin, and there will be a time when I'm no longer learning how to find pleasure. Would you still want to watch me?"

"Absolutely," he replied softly. "I watch you when we're not in bed. You have a very sensual, passionate nature. I love it when you find something that pleases you, and I will never get tired of watching you.

"I'm glad to hear that, because I get turned on when you watch me." But she hadn't known he watched her all the time. Mia felt tingly realizing she was the center of his attention. "I'm going to let you in on a little secret."

"What's that?" Aidan playfully covered Mia's chest with a mound of fragrant bubbles he had gathered.

"Don't let Jamie know," she said in a whisper. "She'll tease me forever."

"Now I'm intrigued."

"I think I liked being watched," she revealed. "When you watched me having sex with Caleb, I loved how you gave me directions."

"Is that right?" he asked as he scooped up the warm, soapy water and spilled it over her breasts.

"I felt like I was on a stage and I could do no wrong." She usually stayed out of the spotlight, but this was different. That night she had felt powerful and alive. "Do you think I'm an exhibitionist?"

"Only with me, though," Aidan said gruffly. "Right?"

"Right," she agreed. She felt both safe and wild when she was with Aidan. He really was her anchor.

Aidan placed his hands on her waist. She tensed as he lifted her up and turned her around, water splashing everywhere. She barely had time to ask what he was doing before she was facing him, straddling his waist.

"I want you to give me a lap dance," he said as he held her hips. "Show me your moves, Mia."

"Okay," she agreed. She bit down on her lower lip, suddenly feeling shy. She didn't know what would turn him on the most.

"Listen carefully," he continued as he ground her hips against him. "I am going to give you very specific directions."

Mia smiled boldly as a naughty sensation warmed her belly. "I'm listening."

Jamie wrestled with the stuffed plastic grocery bags dangling from her arms as she unlocked the back door to Mia's bungalow. She was about to turn the lock when the door suddenly swung open. Mia stood in front of her wearing a thin bathrobe plastered to her wet body.

"Jamie!" Mia exclaimed as her face, lit up with relief. "I'm so glad you're here."

"What happened?" she asked as she handed Mia some of the grocery bags. She hadn't been gone that long, so it couldn't be too bad.

Mia opened her mouth and stopped. She quickly looked over her shoulder to make sure no one was listening. Peering into the hallway and finding it empty, she returned her attention to Jamie. "I need your help," she whispered.

"What's up?" Jamie asked, kicking the door shut behind her. There was no question that she would offer assistance.

"You're not going to believe this," Mia said as she followed Jamie into the kitchen. "I was getting the bathtub ready, and one of the guys came from behind me."

"Okay." Jamie set down the grocery bags.

"He grabbed me without saying a word." Mia tossed the remaining grocery bags on the table. "I was on my hands and knees, I couldn't see him, and he took me right there over the bathtub. It was so hot."

"Sounds like it." Jamie wondered where this was leading.

"Don't you get it? I had sex with him!"

"Uh-huh?" Jamie turned to her friend and waited. That was it? Mia's eyes were filled with panic, and she was gnawing her lip over that? Why was that so shocking, and why was Mia now asking for her help?

"Don't you see?" Mia asked, flailing her arms in the air. "The entire time I was having sex with him, I couldn't tell which guy it was!"

Ohhhh . . . Jamie's eyes widened. Well, Mia had forgotten to mention that little tidbit! *Gee, what a problem,* Jamie thought with a little smile. How many women had difficulty telling their lovers apart?

"This isn't funny!" Mia insisted.

Jamie struggled to turn her smile into a straight line. "You're right," she said, offering a comforting pat on Mia's arm, "but how is this possible? Caleb and Aidan are nothing alike."

"You tell me. Aidan was my first and only lover. I had sex with Caleb like"—she flicked her fingers as she counted hurriedly—"five or six times?"

"Five or six times?" Jamie echoed. Caleb had amazing recuperating skills.

"And I couldn't tell them apart," Mia wailed, covering her face with her hands.

"Who'd it turn out to be?"

"Aidan," Mia said with a sigh and dragged her hands down her face. "I had to turn around to find out!"

"But Caleb doesn't just grab a woman and dominate her," Jamie explained. "He follows your directions."

"Um, yeah. About that . . ." Mia looked away and twirled her hair around her finger. "I tried to dominate Caleb, and it didn't work."

"What are you talking about?" Jamie asked. "He'll do whatever you want, no questions asked."

"That's true," Mia said and started unpacking the grocery bags. "He figured out that I wanted to be . . . hunted."

Jamie's mouth dropped open. *Hunted?* She couldn't imagine Caleb in the role of the predator. "How does that work?"

"All the lights are off in the house, and he chases me. You wouldn't believe the intense rush you feel when you know you're going to get caught. And when Caleb finds me, the sex is rough, almost brutal!"

"Seriously?" Predatory, rough, and brutal were not the words she'd used to describe Caleb. If asked, Jamie would have said laid-back.

Mia gave a shrug as she grabbed the empty grocery bags. "It turns out that I'm not really happy being in charge."

"You are so weird," Jamie teased.

"I tried it and I like it," Mia admitted. "It's fun, but I really want the guy to take over. I know, I know, I shouldn't like it. . . ."

"Says who?" Jamie asked, realizing that she had been pushing her personal preference on her friend. "If that's what you want, then don't let anyone else talk you out of it."

Mia nodded. "You know, Caleb is really good at dominating. Why didn't you tell me?"

"Because I had no idea! He doesn't do that with me." The guy could transform himself into any kind of lover. Jamie should have been thrilled to discover this, but she found it unsettling.

"Enough on Caleb," Mia decided. "I've got a bigger problem here. If I can't tell my lovers apart, what does this say about me?"

"Nothing," Jamie replied. "It only shows something I suspected long ago. Men are interchangeable."

"Jamie!" Mia gave her one of those I-don't-believe-you-said-that looks that Jamie knew so well. "That isn't true."

"You've just proven it."

"I was caught off-guard," Mia insisted. "He didn't say anything, and I couldn't see him."

"Fine, let's look at the problem this way." Jamie wanted to give some practical advice before Mia blew it all out of proportion. "You are placing too much emphasis on one of the senses. You should have noticed the way he breathed or his scent. Did Aidan touch you in a way that Caleb didn't? Or what about the way he thrusts, or the way he comes?"

"Why didn't I notice any of those things?" Mia asked as she sat down on one of the chairs. "Maybe I didn't want to. Oh, God, that can't be good."

Jamie rolled her eyes. It was time to take action. "You know what you need to do?"

"Oh, no." Mia flopped her arms on the table and put her head down. "I'm not sure if I can handle any more of your ideas."

"What are talking about? This swapping idea is my best yet. Admit it. You're having the time of your life." Jamie knew she was, and she bet the guys couldn't believe their luck.

Mia lifted her head. "What's your idea?"

"You need to do some one-on-one comparison." The idea was great. Why hadn't she thought of this before?

Mia frowned at Jamie. "Isn't that what I'm doing?"

"No," Jamie said patiently. "I'm talking about making the comparison at the same time."

Mia's eyes widened. "Are you talking about . . . ?"

Did Jamie have to spell it out? "Aidan on one side of you, Caleb on the other. Both of them hot, sweaty, and ready for action," she said, the image giving her a little shiver of excitement. "Think of it as a Mia sandwich."

"Both guys?" Mia asked slowly. "At the same time?"

"It's called a ménage à trois," Jamie said, trying to sound knowledgeable. She was probably pronouncing it wrong, but Mia wouldn't know that.

"I can't do both guys at the same time," Mia said in a scandalized whisper.

"Sure you can," Jamie insisted. "Don't you remember me telling you all about the time I did it on graduation night?"

"Yeah, but that's you. I'm not sure if I can take two men at once."

"It's the best way to compare their techniques. You'll notice the differences between the two right away."

Mia continued to stare at her. Had she gone too far this time? Jamie couldn't tell. Personally, she thought it was a fantastic idea and couldn't wait to see Mia in a threesome.

"So what do you say?" Jamie prompted Mia. "Are you in?"

Mia's mouth slowly curved into a wicked smile. "Totally."

THIRTEEN

"Eat up!" Mia encouraged Aidan as she poured hot coffee in his mug. She then turned to serve Caleb. Aidan noticed the way she placed her hand on his shoulder as she leaned over him to fill his cup.

He liked seeing the intimate touch. Aidan felt the sexual awareness zinging between Mia and Caleb. The unspoken communication between them heightened his longing. He wanted to watch them again, and it was a struggle to remain patient.

Caleb grabbed his coffee cup and took a big sip. Aidan's gaze narrowed on the man's wrist. The reddened skin had been rubbed raw. Had Mia tied Aidan down to the bed?

Aidan gripped the handle of his coffee mug so hard that he was surprised it didn't shatter in his hands. How had she teased him? Did she lick every part of Caleb's body, or did she ride his cock like a demon? Damn, he would have loved to see Mia in action.

"Breakfast is really good," Caleb said as he put the coffee mug down and tackled the mountain of food on his plate.

"Thank you!" Mia said with obvious delight as Jamie smiled at him from the stove.

The sit-down breakfast was a nice surprise, Aidan thought, but he wasn't going to enjoy it with the same enthusiasm as Caleb. He sensed there was a price attached to this rare event.

When the scents of butter and cinnamon had permeated the air, Aidan was drawn to the kitchen. Once he had entered, he noticed that the table had been set with Mia's best china and glassware. She had even used the tablecloth that she reserved for special occasions.

At first he thought the breakfast was a festive celebration for their wild weekend. But Mia and Jamie had gone overboard with the food. There were stacks of fluffy pancakes and a plate of crisp bacon. The toast with jam was a nice touch, but when Mia made sunny-side-up *and* scrambled eggs, Aidan knew there was more to this breakfast that met the eye.

"There's enough here to feed an army," Aidan said.

"You need your strength," Mia said with a saucy wink. She walked away, her hips sashaying, as she returned the carafe to the coffee machine.

Aidan took a sip of the coffee, watching Mia over the rim of the mug. Mia was always bright and cheerful, but her mood was amped up today. Considering how he had just roughly claimed her in the bathroom, she should have been exhausted, begging for sleep instead of clean plates.

Mia and Jamie were up to something. He just knew it. Either they wanted something, or they were about to drop a bombshell on Caleb and him. Whatever it was, it had to be big. Nothing else would have prompted Jamie to put on an apron and make pancakes.

He glanced over at Jamie. Her feet were bare, and her long

brown hair was now tamed back into a ponytail. Her tongue was tucked in the corner of her wide mouth as she concentrated on flipping a pancake.

Jamie's camisole top and shorts were almost hidden underneath the pink apron she had on. When he had first stepped into the kitchen, he had done a double take because it looked like Jamie only wore the apron. The teasing sight had inspired one or two fantasies on the spot.

But then he realized that Jamie at the stove could only mean trouble. Cooking was something Mia enjoyed, but Jamie slaving over a hot stove? No way. And she definitely would not go to the trouble of catering to men unless she expected something great in return.

He watched Mia pour orange juice in a fancy pitcher. She placed it on the table and sat down to eat. Jamie turned off the stove and removed the attention-getting apron. As she carried over the last batch of pancakes, he noticed something obvious missing: the fact that Jamie didn't make one comment about cooking while the men ate was very telling.

The easy conversation wafted over him as he watched Mia and Jamie. They were attentive, offering Aidan more food and drawing the usually silent Caleb to give his opinions about what they were discussing.

Something was seriously wrong.

What were they conspiring to do? He couldn't figure it out. Or was he being paranoid? This could simply be a show of gratitude for agreeing to the swap.

He then caught a look Mia exchanged with Jamie. He didn't know what it meant, but the Cheshire cat smile on Jamie's mouth made his blood run cold. They were definitely up to something.

Aidan dropped his napkin on his plate and leaned back in his chair. He groaned and spanned over his stomach. This was really the life: great company, great food, and great sex. He wished every weekend was like this, minus the secret alliances and underhanded strategies.

"What do you girls have planned for today?" he asked as he languidly stretched.

"Planned?" Mia echoed. She gave a little shrug. "Nothing."

Aidan looked at Caleb. The guy didn't say anything but his eyebrow went up. Yeah, he wasn't buying that either.

"We're just going with the flow," Jamie announced.

Aidan watched her pour the maple syrup on her pancakes. Either she really had a thing about syrup, or she was distracted about an upcoming plan. He was going to bet it was the latter.

He didn't know why he felt dread snaking around his gut. Whatever Mia and Jamie had planned, he could control it. He always did.

Half the fun was when Jamie threw a wrench in the works. He didn't think she actively sought trouble. Rather, it found her. Jamie's tendency to come up with outrageous ideas didn't help, but that was who she was. Nothing was going to change that, and he wasn't going to try.

He'd rather spend his energy working around whatever havoc Jamie and Mia wreaked. If he couldn't, he simply ignored what was going on. But this time it was different. He could sense it.

"Mia," he asked softly, "what would you like to do?"

"Anything is fine with me." Mia quickly picked up her frosty glass of orange juice and chugged it down.

"Anything?" Caleb asked.

An unholy gleam entered Caleb's eyes. Aidan could only imagine what the man was thinking. He wished Mia had added a disclaimer to that statement. Things like "It has to be legal and cause no mental anguish or permanent scars" would have been a good place to start.

"Anything at all?" Jamie asked Mia. She placed her fork down and rested her elbows on the table. "What do you think of a ménage à trois?"

Ménage à trois? Aidan's body clenched so hard he couldn't move. His breath snagged in his throat as he imagined a threesome with Mia and Jamie. He would want Jamie lying on the floor. Mia would ride her friend's mouth as he thrust inside Jamie's wet pussy. He would get to watch the pleasure chasing through Mia's face while he brought Jamie to a climax.

He slowly exhaled, but the tension lingered in his body. As much as he wanted a ménage à trois, he wasn't going to give in to the longing. It would be a mistake.

He was beginning to think the swap had been his first mistake, and there was no going back. Aidan had wanted to give Mia anything she wanted, but her sensual awakening was blossoming out of control.

If he allowed her to participate in a threesome, what would she go for next? How long would it take before she didn't need him anymore? But if he stood in the way of fulfilling her sexual fantasies, he ran the risk of losing her altogether.

He didn't know what to do. He felt like he was facing a crossroad, and whatever he chose would determine the future of his relationship with Mia. He wished they hadn't brought up the idea of a ménage à trois or a swap. He should have nipped it in the bud when he'd had the chance.

Aidan didn't look at Jamie or Caleb. He kept his eyes on Mia, attuned to her every move. She scraped her fork around her plate, nervously playing with her food. He noticed she was carefully avoiding eye contact.

"Ménage à trois? I haven't tried that before. What's it like?" Mia asked so innocently Aidan was surprised she hadn't punctuated her question with the bat of her eyelashes.

"Fabulous. How could it not be?" Jamie answered.

Aidan darted his gaze from Mia to Jamie. This conversation sounded rehearsed. Had they practiced it while making breakfast?

"I highly recommend it," Jamie continued. "Everyone should do it at least once in their lives. Don't you agree, Caleb?"

"It depends on who you're with," he replied without looking up from his plate. Caleb seemed more interested in food than in a threesome.

Jamie rolled her eyes. "With us, silly. We're all friends and we trust each other."

Aidan didn't like the way Jamie talked about it as if it was already agreed upon. "But doesn't trois mean three?" Aidan asked. "There are four of us."

Jamie dismissed his point with the wave of her hand. "Okay, so one of us has to sit out. I think that should be you, Aidan."

"What?" Mia's fork clattered onto her plate. She sat up straight and risked a glance at him before she spoke to Jamie. "I don't think that's a good idea."

"He can watch," Jamie said with a sly smile. "I'm sure he would enjoy that the most."

"But that means you and me . . ." Mia's voice trailed off as she blushed fiercely.

Jamie faced Aidan, propping her chin on her hand. "What do you think, Aidan?"

"No." He didn't raise his voice, but something in his tone alerted Caleb. The guy stopped eating and looked at him, waiting for the explosion to happen.

"Oh, you want in?" Jamie asked. "I don't blame you. I guess we could draw straws and see who will be out."

"You are not listening," he told Jamie. "I'm saying there is going to be no ménage à trois."

"Why not?" Jamie glared at him. Her sweet disposition had dissolved at the first sign of resistance. "What's so different from what we've been doing?"

"Everything." It was another step Mia was taking away from him. Had this been Jamie's plan all along?

"How is it different from the time Mia held me down here"— she smacked the table so hard that the plates shook—"when you fucked me?"

He wasn't going to split hairs to make his point. He didn't need to explain himself. What he said went.

"I said no." Aidan rose from the table and walked out of the kitchen.

He heard Jamie yell something after him, only to stop abruptly. Aidan had no doubt that Caleb had something to do with that. The guy might let Jamie run all over him, but Caleb had the sense to stop her when she was going to cause more damage than good.

As Aidan marched through the hallway toward the bedroom, he heard a chair dragging across the kitchen tile floor. He knew Mia was following him. She was either going to placate him or argue. He didn't want to deal with her right now.

Aidan was tempted to get out of the house. Only two reasons stopped him. First, he wasn't going to run away from the conflict. It would only drag out the argument. He needed Mia to understand that a threesome wasn't going to happen for her.

Second, he didn't want to hold this conversation out in the yard. There was no telling how many neighbors would be able to overhear them. He wasn't ashamed of what they'd done so far this weekend, but he needed to protect Mia from those who did not share their views.

Mia caught up with him when he stepped into the bedroom. He immediately felt cornered, which was ridiculous. He was in control of this situation.

"Aidan"—she whispered fiercely as she closed the bedroom door behind her—"what's wrong?"

"Nothing's wrong," he said. He folded his arms across his chest and braced his feet. He knew his stance showed aggression and hoped Mia picked up on that. "You are not participating in a ménage à trois."

"I don't understand." She closed the distance between them and placed her hands on his locked arms. "Why don't you want me in a threesome? I thought you liked to watch."

"So you're going to fuck every person who comes your way and excuse it because I get to watch?" It was what Lacey had done when she had found out he liked being a voyeur.

This was why he kept his fantasies secret. Lacey had exploited his needs for her gain. Mia wasn't anything like Lacey, but he found himself in a similar position as last time. He wasn't going to risk making the same mistake.

Mia dropped her hands and stared at him, hurt shimmering in her eyes. "I'm not planning to sleep with everyone I meet," she told him, her voice wobbly. "This is a special circumstance. I want to try something different—"

"Because you're not sure if I'm enough," he finished for her. He didn't try to hide his bitterness.

Mia's face paled, and she took a step back. "Who told you that?" she asked in a shocked whisper.

He saw no reason to hide the truth anymore. The swapping was over, and he was living on borrowed time with Mia. "I had over-heard you when Jamie first mentioned swapping."

"And you didn't tell me?" She clapped her hands over her fore-head. "Ai-yi-yi."

"I wanted to see how you were going to trick me into this." He shook his head and took a deep breath. "No, that's not true. I wanted you to ask for a swap. That way I could watch you with Caleb, and you wouldn't know that I enjoy being a voyeur."

"You could have told me that without the swapping."

"No, I couldn't." In his experience, women didn't understand his need to watch them have sex. He didn't fully understand it himself. It was better—easier—if the focus wasn't on his voyeur-ism but on the woman having sex with another man.

"You could, but you didn't trust me. You didn't think I could handle something like that? No, that can't be it," she said as the anger flared in her eyes. "You thought I'd take advantage of it."

"I trust you," Aidan insisted. Mia was probably the only person he did trust these days. "Even though you're the one who couldn't tell me that I wasn't enough."

"I didn't say anything because I didn't want to hurt you!" She dug her fingers in her hair and took a deep breath. "And I would have been fine if I knew you liked to watch," she said in a calm voice. "I would have done everything in my power to make your fantasies come true."

"Like the swapping?" Wouldn't that have been convenient for her? "And now the ménage à trois?"

"Yes!"

"Do us both a favor and don't say you'd do it for me. You want those things for yourself. The fact that I would benefit from it makes it easier for you to argue for it."

"That's not true."

He felt like they were going round and round in circles. "I need to get out of here." He moved toward the door.

"Are you sure that you want to?" she asked. "Do you trust me in this house alone with Jamie and Caleb?"

"Stop it. Of course, I do." It didn't enter his mind that she would do something behind his back.

"I can't believe you're doing this," she said as she turned away from him. "Why are you stopping now? We have today and to-morrow left. Why couldn't you have given me at least that?"

"It's too much, too fast," Aidan answered.

"And you feel the need to set boundaries because . . . ?"

"I'm trying to protect you," he said, the frustration making his voice gruff. "To protect *us*."

Mia jerked her head up. Had she heard the underlying fear in his voice? Did she finally recognize that as much as he wanted to give her everything, his first priority was to protect what they had?

"You know," she said as she slowly turned to face him, "I like it when you tie me to the bed. I always think of you as my anchor. I know I'm safe no matter what's going on."

Aidan wasn't sure where this was leading. Was she going to tell him that he went too far in his duties? That he was putting too many limits on her?

"I have no problem when you make the decisions when we're in bed together," Mia continued. "Sometimes it annoys me, but in the end, I'm grateful. It's your way of protecting me."

If she was trying to make him feel guilty, then she was doing a damn good job. Those decisions in bed were not based on the fear of losing Mia. They were made to create a glorious sensual awak-ening for her.

She stepped closer to him. "I know that you're making this decision because you are placing the boundaries that I need.

You want to make sure that I don't have to deal with my greatest fear."

"Going out of control," he murmured. He had a feeling that Mia was scared of her wild responses, and that she didn't know how to handle the intense passion.

She nodded and placed her hands on his chest. "So, if you don't want me to take part in a ménage à trois, then I won't."

It wasn't as easy as that. "You're going to resent me. I know you will."

"No, because you make me feel safe." She raised her hands and linked them behind his neck. "You'll know when I'm ready. There are a lot of things I wanted to do when we first met, but you made me wait. I want to try something different when you say I'm ready. Otherwise, I'm not going to do it."

He believed her, but he wasn't sure if he wanted that kind of responsibility. How would he know if he was holding her back for her good or for his?

"You're not disappointed?" he asked as he wrapped his arms around her waist.

"I am," she admitted wryly, "but watching you in a threesome will make me feel better."

"Whoa!" He stepped away and stared at Mia. Where had that come from? "What are you talking about?"

"I may not be ready," she said with a pout, "but that doesn't mean you guys shouldn't do it."

He was stunned by her generosity and selflessness. He knew that she had nothing to gain by the offer. "You would be okay with that?"

"I can't wait to watch you with Jamie and Caleb," she confessed, her eyes sparkling with anticipation. "But I better warn you," she dropped her voice to a whisper, "I think Caleb swings both ways."

Aidan laughed. "No, it's not Caleb."

She looked confused, her eyebrows dipping down. "Wait a second. What do you mean by that? If 'It's not Caleb,' and I know it's not you . . . " Comprehension dawned on her. "Are you saying *Jamie* is bisexual?"

Caleb winced. He hadn't mean to let that slip. If Jamie found out, she was going to kill him.

"She's not," Mia said in a weary tone, as if she had to say that a lot. "Yeah, there have been rumors, but people have said so many things about her."

He didn't say anything. He wasn't going to lie to Mia, but he wasn't going to dig a deeper hole, either. Aidan kept his mouth shut, like he should have done.

"She's bisexual?" she asked, taking his silence as confirmation. "Why didn't she tell me? Why didn't anyone tell me?"

"Because it didn't matter." And he had a feeling that Mia was upset over the fact that Jamie didn't share this information with her.

"Well, yeah. *Then.*" She motioned to the door. "But we're . . . when we were kissing . . ."

"I'd better warn you," he said, cutting her ramblings short. "Caleb is hoping for some girl-on-girl action. Jamie isn't going to push her luck."

Mia's mouth dropped open in surprise. Her eyes were big as a blush seeped up her neck and flooded her face. "But she wants to," she said softly.

"Do you?" If she did, he would make it happen. If not, he'd tell Caleb not to force the situation. He shouldn't have tried to make it happen without Mia's knowledge. He was ashamed for doing that.

"I don't know. I never thought . . ." She paused. "What are you hoping for?"

Aidan smiled. "I want to watch the two of you together, but I don't think you're ready."

"I don't know, Aidan," Mia bit her bottom lip and ducked her head. "This time, you might be wrong."

Aidan stood on the bungalow's porch, his mind chaotically whirling. He leaned against the brick column and looked out onto the street. It was easier to look outside than to analyze what was going on inside him.

It was one of those lazy summer days in Clover Bud. Everything was bright and cheerful. Homey. Men and women had specific roles, and they followed the double standards without question.

Aidan sighed and slid his hands in his jeans pockets. He used to think that he was different from those who lived here. He thought he was better. At least evolved.

Turned out he was just like every other guy in Clover Bud. He looked after his own—protected them and provided anything they needed. In return, he felt his word was law.

It was no wonder Jamie was fed up with the men in town. And now he understood why Mia didn't want to live with him. It didn't matter that he practically lived in her house. He saw his influence, as well as his stuff, but it wasn't the same.

He wanted to live with Mia. He had thought it was in his reach once Jamie left. Now he knew that his goal was much further away than he had ever imagined.

All this time he had thought Mia was under Jamie's thumb, believing in total independence and freedom. Now he realized Mia resisted living with him because he was a jerk. It hadn't mattered how much he had tried to convince her that doing so was the next step in their relationship. She knew that if she took that next step, she would deal with the double standards in every aspect of her life.

Aidan heard the squeak of the screen door and looked over his shoulder to see Caleb stepping onto the porch. "What are you doing out here?" Caleb asked.

Aidan sighed and returned his attention to the quiet street. "Figuring out that I'm a hypocrite."

"You needed to come out here to figure it out?" Caleb teased as he stood next to Aidan. "I could have told you."

"I don't want Mia in a threesome, but she suggested I participate instead."

Caleb nodded. Either Jamie had already told him, or nothing shocked the man. "That sounds like Mia," Caleb said. "Are you thinking about it?"

Aidan was, and he wasn't proud of it. He felt damn guilty. Aidan knew he should have refused the offer and instantly purge it from his memory. How could he tell Mia she wasn't ready and then turn around and jump into a threesome?

"Mia is all about sharing right now," Caleb said as if he could read Aidan's mind. "She wants to give everyone their fantasies and doesn't expect anything in return. Right now your fantasy is the ménage à trois. She knows this, and she doesn't want to stand in your way."

"But I stood in her way," Aidan admitted. It sounded worse when he said it out loud.

"I'm sure you have your reasons," Caleb said as he looked out in the yard.

"She's not ready for a threesome," Aidan explained. But was she? What if it had more to do with him? Maybe he wasn't ready for her to be in a threesome.

"You're probably right," Caleb said. "You would know better than me."

That was true. Aidan had been with Mia for a year and had

guided her through her sensual awakening. Now her curiosity and appetite were stronger than ever. He wanted to give her every opportunity, but only if she was ready.

Oh, who was he kidding? Mia was ready now. He knew it, and worse, she knew it, too. He couldn't abuse his power over Mia.

"I think I'm going for the threesome," Aidan said. He would do it first and have Mia watch. If it wasn't to her taste, then they had risked nothing. If she was eager, then she would be primed for her turn.

Caleb nodded. "Why?"

The question surprised him. "To show Mia what it's all about."

Caleb glanced at him. "If you say so."

Aidan didn't like Caleb's tone. "Why do you think I'm doing it?" Aidan asked.

"Because you can."

Aidan bristled at the accurate assessment. "I'm trying to make this a weekend to remember for Mia. I want it to be the time of her life."

"And yours," Caleb added.

"And mine," he admitted. Was that a crime?

Probably, since he was fulfilling his fantasies while saying it was for Mia. The very thing he'd accused her of doing. There was probably a spot in hell reserved for him because of this.

"Are you in or not?" Caleb finally asked.

"I'm in," Aidan announced. His nerves were jittery. "How are we going to do it?"

"Do you need step-by-step instructions?"

Aidan didn't find that funny. "Caleb, this is Jamie we're talking about. You don't think she has a strategy?"

Caleb turned and looked at the bungalow's front door. "Shit. You're right."

"And knowing her, she'll try to get some male-on-male action." That was one boundary he didn't want to explore, although he had no problems imagining Mia with Jamie. Aidan gave a deep sigh. It was yet another example of his hypocrisy.

"I got it." Caleb splayed his arms out like a magician revealing a trick. "We use the element of surprise."

Aidan waited for more details, but it soon became obvious that Caleb had given him the full plan. "That's it? I think we need something more."

"Do you have a plan?"

"Does 'follow our instincts' count?"

Caleb clapped his hand on Aidan's back. "Now you're talking."

FOURTEEN
FOURTEEN

"What are they saying?" Mia asked.

"Hush," Jamie said as she lifted the lace curtain and looked out the window. "I can't hear a word."

She saw Aidan and Caleb standing on the porch. Their heads were down as they talked quietly. It didn't look like Caleb was giving a pep talk. If anything, it looked like they were in a huddle making a game plan.

"I think Aidan is going to go for it," Mia confided in her. "Just give him some time."

"Of course he's going to go for it. He's a guy," Jamie said, rolling her eyes. It was a matter of fact, but when? Unfortunately, they were running out of time. "I'm pissed that he's not going to let you go for it."

"It's okay, Jamie."

"How can it be okay?" It was just another sign of Mia's inexperience if she couldn't understand what she was missing. "You may never have this chance again."

Mia shrugged and leaned back on the sofa. "I'm not worried about that."

Jamie looked away from the window. "You don't want to do it?"

"I don't need to do it," Mia clarified.

"Yes, you do," Jamie insisted. "Today or tomorrow. This weekend is finding out what you need."

"And I'm finding out more and more that I need Aidan," Mia said with a happy sigh.

"Oh, God." The dreamy look on her friend's face was going to make her ill. Of all the things Mia could learn this weekend, *that* was her big epiphany? "You're worse off than I thought."

Mia gave her a sidelong glance. "Did you think I was going to have such a fabulous time with Caleb during the swap that I would wonder what else was out there for me? You thought I would dump Aidan after this weekend, didn't you?"

Busted! It was true that Jamie hoped Mia would find someone else—someone who didn't have double standards or who didn't sexually dominate her friend. But, as much as she didn't like those things about Aidan, he wasn't a bad guy. Mia could have done a lot worse.

"No . . . not exactly," Jamie said, trying not to look sheepish. Maybe Caleb was right that she shouldn't interfere in Mia's business.

She thought Mia would realize she didn't have to hang on to her first lover. Jamie didn't think Mia would cling to Aidan stronger than before.

"You don't have to worry about me anymore."

"Because Aidan is there to protect you?" Jamie didn't know how she felt having him usurp her role as protector. She guessed he was the best man around to take on the job.

"There is that," Mia agreed. "But this weekend I'm learning how to ask for what I want."

"I'm glad to hear it," Jamie said with feeling. So what if it took this long for Mia? The girl had always been a late bloomer.

"Now we just need to figure out what *you* want."

Jamie frowned and looked at Mia. "What are you talking about? I know what I want: out of Clover Bud as fast as I can."

"Why now?"

"I saved up enough money." That didn't sound like a good reason. "And I feel claustrophobic in this town. I need to get out, and it's as good a time as any."

"But you've been acting like it's urgent to move right away. Are you sure there's not another reason?"

That was one question Jamie didn't want to answer. She looked out the window and saw Aidan and Caleb heading back into the house. She let the curtain fall. "They're coming."

"So?" Mia asked with a laugh as she watched Jamie rush over to the sofa.

She leaped over Mia and plopped down on the cushion next to her. "Act natural," she ordered as she scrambled to an upright position.

Mia raised an eyebrow. "*I* am."

Caleb opened the front door, letting the scorching heat of the summer day billow in. Aidan walked into the living room, and he waited until Caleb had closed and locked the door. They both approached Mia and Jamie. Jamie saw their determined, almost grim expressions.

Where the hell had she gone wrong? Her plan to introduce the idea of a ménage à trois should have worked. She really hadn't expected any resistance to the idea. Now the whole weekend was ruined.

"What's up, guys?" Mia asked, breaking the tense silence.

"We want a threesome," Aidan said, "with Jamie."

Jamie couldn't hide her surprise. Aidan had agreed to the ménage à trois? How had Caleb managed that?

She recalled how they had their heads together while talking on the porch. Jamie's eyes narrowed with suspicion. What else did they want? Did Aidan have some stipulations? She didn't care as long as she could get Mia into the fun.

"Why not Mia instead of me?" she asked.

"Don't start, Jamie," Mia said quietly.

Jamie had to. She'd started this for Mia. The idea of a ménage à trois was for Mia to compare Aidan and Caleb. Of course, Jamie couldn't tell that to the guys.

But Mia was worried about the fact that she couldn't tell which guy she'd had sex with in the bathroom. Personally, Jamie didn't see that as a problem, but Mia was really concerned.

So was this how Mia could study Aidan's and Caleb's techniques? By watching them in a threesome? That might help, but Jamie didn't think so. She was all for hands-on learning.

"I suggest you do it right here," Mia said, as she rose from the sofa.

Here? In the living room? Jamie glanced at the carpet on the floor and shivered, knowing she was going to suffer rug burns.

"We'll need something sturdier than that sofa," Caleb said. "Like a straight-back chair."

"Of course," Mia said. "There's no way all three of you will fit on this. Stay here."

"Where are you going?" Jamie asked. Mia was going to watch, wasn't she?

"I'm getting one of the kitchen chairs."

"One second," Jamie said to the men as she followed Mia into the kitchen. She was trying to think of a way to include her friend, but how was she going to succeed when Mia was quite happy to stay in the shadows?

"Mia, this is great that Aidan agreed. Now we have to find a way for you and me to switch roles."

Mia gave Jamie a curious look. "Are you having second thoughts about a threesome?"

"Of course not."

"I'm not doing it."

Jamie huffed with annoyance. "Why are you giving up?"

"I'm not," Mia said. "You need to be patient."

"Fine." She'd wait until Aidan was far gone, on the verge of an orgasm, and she'd have Mia join them.

"Don't try to include me in," Mia warned, "especially when everything gets hot and heavy."

Jamie's eyes widened. "How did you know what I was thinking?"

Mia chuckled. "You're very easy to read."

God, she hoped not. Jamie tried to keep her expression blank and act as if Mia's words hadn't struck fear in her. She said nothing as she watched Mia hoist the chair and walk back to the living room.

Jamie knew she should be excited about taking part in a threesome. They didn't happen as often in her life as she would like.

But having Mia watch on the sidelines was going to be a problem.

Jamie slowly returned to the living room, not sure what to do. She wanted to do this—who could refuse two hot guys at the same time—but for once, she didn't have a strategy.

Mia placed the chair in the center of the carpet just as Caleb walked in the room from the other doorway. She didn't know exactly what Aidan and Caleb had in mind. Wouldn't it be easier for everyone if they lay down on the floor? In her opinion, it would offer lots of space to maneuver and little chance of falling. She guessed it went to show how little she knew about group sex.

Her lack of knowledge had never bothered her before. She was curious, but she would have to be patient. Watching Jamie in a threesome was enough for now. It had to be.

She walked back to the sofa and sat down just when Aidan blocked Jamie's entrance into the living room. Mia tucked her legs underneath her, enjoying.

Aidan reached for Jamie, holding her upper arms and turning her slightly so that Mia could see everything he would do to her. Caleb stood behind Jamie, his hands on her hips.

Aidan lowered his head and claimed Jamie's lips. By her muffled squeal, Mia knew he was grinding his mouth against hers. Mia pressed her lips together, imagining what it was like. She grinned when Jamie grasped Aidan's face with both hands and deepened the kiss.

Caleb glided his hands over Jamie's shoulders. He curled his fingers along her throat and jaw, gently pulling her away from Aidan. Jamie turned her head and kissed Caleb.

Aidan's hands slid up and down Jamie's waist. His touch was rough, drawing a gasp from Jamie. He covered her breasts with his hands and squeezed. His fingers looked large against Jamie's voluptuous curves.

Jamie arched back, thrusting her breasts deeper into Aidan's hands as she continued to kiss Caleb. She gasped against Caleb's mouth when Aidan thrust one hand down her shirt, stretching the camisole top to feel her naked breasts.

Jamie moaned and pulled her lips away from Caleb. But Caleb

captured her mouth and continued the long, wet kiss. Aidan grasped Jamie's chin, and his hands bumped against Caleb's. He turned her face toward him and kissed Jamie again, erasing the taste and feel of Caleb.

Mia's breath hitched in her throat as she watched the men fighting over Jamie. Would they compete over her own attention like this? Or would they try to prove which one was the better lover?

But it was more than sharing a woman. Caleb and Aidan were fighting for domination, for control.

From the looks of it, Jamie liked it. And why shouldn't she? Mia wondered. Because, really, Jamie was the one who was in control of these two men.

Aidan was the first to pull away, much to Mia's surprise. "Take off her shirt," he ordered Caleb. "I'll take off her shorts."

Mia wiggled with anticipation as Caleb grabbed Jamie's shirt and wrestled it off her. He stopped in the middle of his duty to cup her naked breasts and mold them in his hands.

Jamie moaned and closed her eyes when Caleb pulled at her nipples. Aidan wrenched Jamie's shorts off her hips. He hooked his fingers around her thong and dragged it down her long legs.

Mia hummed with longing as she watched her best friend stripped naked. She wished she was Jamie right this minute. She wanted two men fighting over her, tearing off her clothes.

Mia's skin prickled with awareness as she watched Caleb licking his way down Jamie's neck and back while his hands were all over her breasts. Aidan was pressing kisses up Jamie's stomach as he roamed his hands over her ass.

"It's . . . it's your turn . . . to get undressed," Jamie reminded them, having trouble forming words.

Aidan rose to his full height. He towered over Jamie, causing her to look up to him. "Undress me."

Mia shivered at those words. Had Jamie felt the same twinge? Was she eager to follow his orders, or was she going to resist him?

Jamie pulled off Aidan's shirt with such force that Mia was surprised it didn't rip. She was just as ruthless taking off his jeans and underwear. Aidan didn't move or help. He preferred watching Jamie with a grin as she pulled and yanked.

"Now me," Caleb said.

If Jamie was surprised by Caleb's command, she didn't show it. She turned to Caleb and undressed him. Her movements were slower as she helped him off with his shirt, sliding her hands along his abdomen as he pulled his shirt over his head. Her fingers danced along his flat stomach as she unbuttoned his fly. She stroked his legs as she pushed down his jeans and underwear.

Jamie was going to bend down to help Caleb discard his clothing when Aidan stopped her. He pulled her to her full height and pressed her hips against his, grinding his cock between her buttocks.

Aidan reached for Jamie's breasts and kneaded them so hard that Mia whimpered. She was tempted to touch her own tingling breasts and mimic Aidan's moves. But Mia knew it wouldn't be the same. She kept watching as her nipples puckered and stung.

Mia bit her lip, hiding a smile, when she saw Jamie granting her kisses to Caleb. She wondered how Aidan was going to handle that. Not well, she suspected.

Aidan did not wait for his turn. He placed his open mouth on Jamie's neck and began to suck. Jamie's knees sagged as she moaned. She curved her throat, accepting the love bite.

As Caleb continued to kiss Jamie, he slid his hands along her hips. He reached down to cup her mound and Jamie groaned, bucking her hips toward him. Mia saw Caleb rubbing her clit with one hand while dipping his other hand farther. He slid his finger into her pussy, and Jamie groaned against his mouth, parting her legs for him.

Mia rocked her hips as she watched Aidan and Caleb give Jamie double the pleasure. Mia really wanted to have two men pressing against her naked body. She wanted their hands all over her, their only concern to make her scream with pleasure.

Mia couldn't prevent envy from piercing her chest. Would she ever have two naked men determined to give her the wildest night of her life? She had told Aidan that she would wait, but she didn't feel so patient anymore.

Jamie pulled her mouth away from Caleb. "I want to suck your cock," she said breathlessly.

She knelt down and grabbed Caleb's cock with both hands. Jamie held him tightly as she placed her lips around the tip of his erection. Caleb sank his hands into Jamie's hair and murmured something Mia couldn't catch.

Aidan placed his hands on Jamie's shoulders. "Suck mine," he ordered.

She twisted around, reaching for Aidan with one hand, and her fingers barely wrapped around his cock. Jamie swirled her tongue along the tip, teasing him, until Caleb pulled her away.

As Mia watched her friend go back and forth, her mouth grew dry. She licked her lips, imagining what it felt like to be in Jamie's position. She would have Aidan demanding more of her attention, while Caleb would silently distract her. As Jamie mindlessly went from one man to the other, Mia noticed that Aidan's and Caleb's cocks were almost touching. Her pussy began to pulse at the erotic sight.

Aidan was the first to step away. "I want to be inside you now," he told Jamie.

He curled his arm around Jamie's waist and lifted her off her feet. Carrying her over to the chair, he sat down and turned her around to face him. Draping her legs over his hips, Jamie straddled Aidan.

Aidan grasped Jamie's waist and guided his cock against her entrance. Jamie held on to Aidan's shoulders as she slowly sank onto him, moaning and shaking until she took every inch of him.

Caleb stepped behind Jamie and tilted her head back to kiss her, his top lip pressing against her full bottom one. Jamie's fingers gripped Aidan's shoulders as she kissed Caleb back.

Mia was beginning to see how different Caleb and Aidan were as lovers. While Aidan demanded and took, Caleb didn't fight for attention. He was stealthy in getting what he wanted.

"Are you ready for Caleb?" Aidan asked as he pumped inside her.

Jamie could only nod, grinding against Aidan, meeting his thrust with the roll of her hips.

Aidan encircled her waist with his hand and thrust deeply into her. "Hold on tight," he said through clenched teeth.

Mia jolted upright when she saw Caleb approaching. For one brief moment she thought he would include her in the threesome. Her heart banged against her ribs and stopped when she saw Caleb halt at the coffee table.

Mia's spirits fell as she watched Caleb grab a bottle of lubricant that she hadn't seen before. She looked away and saw Aidan lean back on the chair, guiding Jamie forward. Aidan squeezed his eyes shut as the movement burrowed him deeper into Jamie. Mia's friend groaned and clamped her hands on the back of the chair.

Caleb walked back to Jamie and Aidan. Mia noticed that Jamie's ass was now jutting out invitingly for her lover. Caleb poured the lube in his hand and spread it up and down his erection. Mia squirmed as she heard the oil gliding between his hand and cock. He tipped the bottle again and poured some more lubricant into the palm of his hand.

He rubbed it on his fingertips and reached for Jamie. Sliding his finger along the cleft, he massaged her rosebud. Jamie tensed and rocked her hips as he worked the lubricant into her. Jamie gasped as Caleb sank his finger inside her hole.

Caleb massaged the oil deep inside Jamie, getting her ready for his rock-hard cock. Mia didn't know what he did—either curled his finger or brushed against a knot of nerves—because Jamie tensed and groaned.

He withdrew his finger and grasped the root of his cock. Caleb pressed the shiny wet tip against Jamie's anus. "Hold her still," Caleb said roughly. Aidan gripped Jamie's hips, his fingers digging into her flesh. He kept her motionless as Caleb slowly worked his way into Jamie.

Jamie's moan was deep and primitive as she rested her head on Aidan's chest, relying on his strength to hold her upright. Her shudders were visible from where Mia sat.

What was Jamie feeling? Mia couldn't imagine, although her friend's cries tugged at something deep inside her. From the expression on Jamie's face, it must be exquisite. Mia wondered if it bordered on pain and pleasure. It seemed to intensify with every move Caleb made.

Mia had never had anal sex. It didn't interest her, and she didn't think she was missing anything. She never heard anyone talk about it, as it was still considered taboo in Clover Bud. But watching

Jamie reach a level of ecstasy Mia had never experienced made her rethink that decision.

Jamie was panting hard as Caleb sank all the way into her. His knees visibly wobbled, and he squeezed his eyes shut. The look on his face was pure pleasure. "Okay," Caleb said, and held on to Jamie's hips, his hands overlapping Aidan's.

Sweat trailed down Aidan's face as he held still. Mia knew he was close to coming, and it was only his iron control that kept him from moving. Aidan's pump was shallow, but Jamie went rigid and gave a keening cry.

Wow, Mia thought as Jamie's body undulated when Caleb withdrew and thrust. One small move overwhelmed Jamie's senses. She was filled and stretched, and she couldn't stop shaking.

Mia watched, her mouth open with amazement, as Jamie took both men at the same time. Aidan and Caleb soon established a fast rhythm that drove Jamie wild. She matched their pace, her hips rocking back and forth until the scream caught in her throat. She was lying against Aidan's chest, shivers rippling through her limp muscles. Groans tugged from her throat as Aidan and Caleb continued to pump into her.

Caleb's thrusts grew erratic. He bucked hard against Jamie before he reared his head back and cried out. Jamie rocked her hips, grunting with pleasure. Aidan tilted his head back, hissing between his clenched teeth. He thrust deep into Jamie until he couldn't hold back any longer.

Mia watched the ruddy color flushing in Aidan's skin. His nostrils flared, and he gulped for air. His mouth sagged open, but no words came out as an orgasm was wrenched from his body.

Mia rubbed her thighs together as she watched Aidan slump against the chair, her pussy throbbing for the same intense pleasure they felt.

But she wasn't going to, Mia thought as she blinked back tears. She wasn't *allowed*, and it wasn't fair. She didn't care what Aidan said. It wasn't too soon. Hell, it wasn't soon enough! She wanted a ménage à trois more than anything else.

What would she have to do—what would she have to risk—to get a threesome before the day was over?

FIFTEEN

"What's wrong?"

Mia looked up, startled to see Caleb in her bedroom doorway. She had gone to her room once everyone had dispersed after the threesome. She needed some time alone to sort out her chaotic thoughts.

She could have sworn that she had closed the door to her bedroom, but it was wide-open, with Caleb standing at the threshold. His hair was dripping wet from the shower, and he wore only a pair of faded jeans. Caleb's body was sleek, but he didn't look anything like the hunter he had been the night before.

"Nothing is wrong," she lied as she curled up tight in her over-stuffed chair. "I'm just thinking."

Caleb looked around the bedroom and then down the hall. "Where's Aidan?" he asked.

She nodded toward the bathroom. "In the shower." She could hear the hiss and clink of the ancient water pipes.

Caleb leaned against the doorway and watched her closely. Mia began to fidget under his intense gaze.

"Did you have fight?" Caleb asked.

Mia shook her head. "No." She was doing everything to prevent it because she didn't want to ruin this weekend, but she and Aidan would probably have one very soon.

"What did you think of the threesome?" he finally asked.

"I thought it was wild," Mia admitted. She knew her eyes glowed with interest, and she felt her blood pumping hard in her veins. Watching Jamie with Caleb and Aidan had been like seeing an intricate, sensual dance. She had been swaying to their primitive beat and had wanted to join in.

She looked away before she said any more. She didn't want anyone to know that she'd felt left out, or that she realized she'd missed an amazing opportunity. It had been her choice, and she'd told Aidan she could be patient. She'd said she would wait until Aidan gave her permission, and she wouldn't go back on her word.

"You want one, too," Caleb said. It wasn't a question; it was a statement of fact.

"Yeah, but I have to . . ." Mia bit her lip when she recognized the wording she was using. She tried again. "I mean, I want to wait until Aidan agrees. I made that promise."

Caleb wrinkled his nose. "Stupid promise, if you ask me."

Mia hadn't thought so at the time. She wanted Aidan to know that her needs weren't spinning out of control, and that she could master them. Now she wasn't so sure.

"Why are you hanging back when Aidan is going full speed ahead?" Caleb asked. "It doesn't seem fair."

"You are as bad as Jamie." Mia frowned when she realized she hadn't seen her friend since the threesome. "By the way, where is she?"

"Sleeping."

Mia could understand that. Her friend had been aggressively

taken by two men. Jamie had surrendered to them—and to the powerful orgasm that had rocked her body. A delicious shudder swept through Mia, but she froze when she felt Caleb's attention still focused on her.

"What do we need to do to convince Aidan?" Caleb asked.

Mia went on alert. "For what?"

"For you to get a threesome."

She was afraid he was talking about that. Mia held up her hands as if to ward him off. Any interference would make the situation worse. "You don't need to get involved."

"I want to."

It was something she hadn't expected from Caleb. He usually kept to himself.

"I need time," she answered. And that was one precious commodity she was running out of. "Aidan needs to get used to the idea, and I need to show that I have discipline over my desires."

"Well, I can't help you there," Caleb said. "But I could set something up. The next time we have a ménage à trois, I'll include you when it's too late for him to refuse."

"Kind of like a tag team?" she asked with a laugh. "That's tempting, but no, thank you. I want to show him that I'm not going to break my promise the first chance I get."

Caleb gave her a look of admiration. "You do know that he may never let you have a threesome."

She gave a deep sigh, because the probability of that happening was great. "Then that's something I'll have to live with."

"You shouldn't have to."

Mia closed her eyes. Did Caleb realize that he was enticing her like the serpent had tempted Eve in the Garden of Eden?

"I knew the consequences," Mia said, unable to hide the hint of regret in her voice. "Now I just need to get used to them."

———

Aidan braced his hands on the bathroom sink and looked at himself in the clouded mirror. He swiped the condensation from his reflection as he listened to Mia and Caleb. Aidan didn't know how much of the conversation he had failed to hear while he was showering, but it was hard to miss what Mia was feeling.

He had known this was coming, just not so soon. Definitely not on the same day—the same afternoon—that Mia had made her offer. Aidan realized he shouldn't have let Mia see the threesome, but he thought that after doing so, she would hesitate about having one of her own.

Why he had thought that, he wasn't sure. Aidan shook his head and rubbed his hands over his face. Instead of backing down, she wanted one more than ever. Mia's sensual awakening was growing by leaps and bounds.

And that was what scared him. He had tutored Mia in the sexual arts, and she was surpassing him. There would be a day when he couldn't hold her back. Just as Mia was concerned that he wouldn't find her fascinating once her innocence vanished, he feared that she would find someone else who could truly bring out and intensify her sensual nature.

Aidan knew he had to let go. He had to trust that what he shared with Mia was strong enough to hold them together. If he held on too tight, she'd leave for sure.

He had to believe she wasn't like Lacey. His ex-girlfriend had thought she'd carte blanche with any man and any sexual situation. She hadn't understood why he liked to watch, and she hadn't cared.

Aidan remembered the last time Lacey had cuckolded him. She had dropped by the local gym where he worked. He hadn't thought anything of the visit since Lacey was a paying, yet infrequent, member.

But it was unusual that she didn't seek him out or let her presence be known to him. That should have been his first clue. During his break he had searched the gym and located her in the steam room next to the swimming pool. He had no premonition of what he would see when he opened the door.

Lacey was in the steam room with three men. While the others still had their towels on, Lacey had removed her bikini and lay on one of the wooden benches. Her arms were outstretched and her legs spread.

The three men were of various ages and sizes, but they were giving her all that she craved. The moans and long, guttural sighs had echoed in his ears.

The oldest man, who had white hair and a paunch, was sliding his cock in and out of Lacey's mouth. The youngest man crouched next to her, playing with and sucking on her breasts. The two men weren't familiar to Aidan, but he recognized the third lover as a coworker. The man tossed his towel to the side and pumped vigorously into Lacey.

Aidan stood at the door, unable to take his eyes off Lacey. He was reluctantly aroused, but most of all, he was disgusted. It didn't matter how overtly sensual Lacey had been, or how she had known no limits when it came to her sexuality. Aidan had no longer found pleasure in her pleasure. Instead, he had felt cheated.

As the three men serviced her, Lacey turned her head and saw Aidan at the steam room's door. Her eyes widened with surprise, and then she gave that sly smile he'd learned to hate.

She had smiled at him like that when she'd enjoyed a zipless fuck with a stranger on the dance floor at a nightclub. That smile reappeared weeks later when she stumbled out of the backseat of a car that had been filled with male classmates. When she made out with one of her sorority sisters in front of him, he was treated to that smile.

He had seen that smile far too often, and now he understood what it meant. Lacey had thought she was getting away with cheating on him. She hadn't cared if he had watched or not. Each time he had found her in a compromising situation, Lacey swore that she had done it to please him. She had known that he liked to watch, and she had only been performing for him.

It was all a lie. The only person Lacey had wanted to please was herself.

From that moment on, Aidan kept his voyeuristic tendencies a secret. He wouldn't let anyone use his fantasies against him. But now Mia had that power to hurt him. Would she use it?

He didn't think so. His gut instinct told him that she loved him. Mia wasn't a destructive person. She liked to create and share. Relationships were more important to her than the pursuit of pleasure.

And unlike Lacey and most of the women he had dated, Mia was looking for more than a challenge or a chance to experiment. She genuinely wanted the boundaries he placed on her. She felt safe. Mia could then follow her desires. She was eager to learn how, knowing that he was there to catch her.

Mia wasn't like Lacey. Yes, both women knew he liked to be a voyeur, but Mia wouldn't use it against him. He had to believe that, and it was time to prove that with action.

Aidan wrapped a towel around his hips and opened the bathroom door. He hesitated when he suffered a rare attack of nerves. He had to make this offer now or never. Aidan gritted his teeth and stepped over the threshold.

He looked in the direction of the bedroom and saw Mia curled in her chair. She flinched guiltily and darted her gaze away. Caleb, standing by the door, looked over his shoulder. As always, he had an unreadable expression.

"Are you ready for another threesome?" Aidan asked Caleb as he approached them.

"Jamie's sleeping," Caleb responded coolly.

"I meant with Mia."

Mia perked up, her face lighting up with tenuous excitement. "Seriously?" she asked, her voice cracking.

"As in now?" Caleb asked.

Aidan shrugged. "Yeah, now is good for me."

"I'm in," Caleb said.

Mia gave a whoop of joy and launched out of her chair, flinging herself at Aidan. When he caught her, she gave him an enthusiastic kiss, which Aidan matched.

"What changed your mind?" she asked against his lips.

"I know now that you can handle this," Aidan said. "You won't spin out of control. In fact, I believe it so much that I don't want to tie you down."

He saw the flicker of dismay on her face. "That might not be a good idea."

"Trust me," Aidan said as he pulled away. "Follow what I say and you'll be fine. Agreed?"

"Okay," she promised as the excitement shimmered in her blue eyes. "I'm ready."

He had no doubt. He braced his legs and folded his arms over his chest. "Kneel before Caleb."

She was surprised that he wanted her to do Caleb first, but she didn't say anything. She knelt in front of Caleb, who was gazing down at her. Trying to be the perfect submissive, Mia folded her hands on her lap and kept her gaze downward.

"Unzip his jeans," Aidan said, "and take them off him."

She followed his command, eagerly reaching for Caleb. Mia slowly unzipped his jeans, the only item of clothing he wore, and tugged the denim off his legs. Caleb stepped out of them and Mia tossed them aside. She immediately placed her hands on her lap and waited for Caleb's next command.

"Lick his balls."

Mia cupped Caleb's testicles and fondled them. Caleb clenched his hands as he tried to remain still. Mia leaned forward, inhaling his scent and smiling, before she licked one heavy sack with short laps of her tongue.

She continued massaging and licking Caleb's testicles, and Aidan knew she would keep doing so until he put a halt to it. Caleb might beg her to stop, Aidan thought as he gave a wry side-long look at the other man. Caleb was at that point of pleasure and pain where each touch was sweet torture.

Mia reached for Caleb's cock.

"No," Aidan said.

Mia jerked her hand back. Her eyes were wide, surprised that she had almost transgressed from the original command. She immediately placed her hand on her lap and dipped her head.

"Shit, Aidan . . ." Caleb said through his gritted teeth. "Let her do what she wants."

Aidan ignored him. "Just his balls," he told Mia.

She followed Aidan's orders, determined to make him proud. But it was more than that. As Aidan watched her, a coil of lust tightening around his chest, he could tell that Mia really wanted to taste Caleb's cock.

He also sensed that she wanted Caleb to come in her mouth. She would work hard to put him under spell and watch him cave in. Her mood surprised Aidan. Didn't she know that she weaved a sensual spell on him every night?

Mia was more powerful than she realized. Or maybe she did realize it. Aidan considered that as she swirled her tongue against Caleb's balls. That was why she was afraid to lose control and why she wanted to be tied down. She wrestled with the power all the time.

Caleb groaned and fell back against the wall, sinking his hands into Mia's hair as she sucked his balls. He gripped the long blond tresses and was about to guide her to kiss his cock.

"Now stop," Aidan said.

Both Mia and Caleb groaned. Mia moved a fraction away from Caleb, but Aidan knew that distance was not far enough to resist the temptation.

"Mia," he said in a stern voice, "come to me."

She reluctantly left Caleb and crawled over to Aidan. Once again, she knelt before him, her hands clasped on her lap, and her head was dipped with respect. He saw the flush in her cheeks and her swollen pink lips. Mia's tight nipples poked against her T-shirt. Her breathing was erratic, and the pulse point at the base of her neck beat visibly.

"Take off my towel," Aidan told her.

She peeled the damp cloth off his waist and revealed his nakedness. His cock was already rock-hard from watching Mia and Caleb. Mia stared at his cock and licked her lips, but she tossed the towel onto the floor and placed her hands on her lap like he had trained her all those months ago.

"Now suck my cock."

"No fair," Caleb complained as he rested heavily against the wall. It was as if Mia had drained the energy out of him.

Aidan smiled. He had never promised that a threesome would be fair play.

Mia grasped the length of Aidan's cock and swirled her tongue around him from the root to the crown. She was surprised when Aidan raised his arms and linked his hands behind his head. He loved how he stood before her like a barbarian king while she knelt at his feet like a woman in his harem.

Caleb stepped behind her and sank his hands into her hair. He massaged her scalp, and Mia wanted to melt into Caleb. She hummed with pleasure, and Aidan flinched from the vibrations.

Her world centered on the two men. She wanted to give Aidan pleasure as much as she wanted to receive it from Caleb. Her sex ached with anticipation as she wrapped her lips around Aidan.

She sucked him hard and with no finesse. It was all about power. It wasn't long before Aidan had to pull away, his breathing rough and choppy.

"Mia, stand up and take off your clothes."

She rose gracefully to her feet as Caleb let his hands fall away from her hair. Keeping her eyes on Aidan, she removed her shirt, revealing her naked breasts. She dropped the shirt to the floor, and with a spark of audacity, she faced Caleb.

Mia half expected Aidan to grab her shoulders and turn her around, but he didn't move. Once she realized that he wouldn't stop her, Mia stripped for Caleb, slowly wiggling out of her shorts and panties. She kicked her clothes to the side and placed her hands on her hips.

"Turn around," Aidan said.

She obeyed, expecting to see Aidan towering over her. Instead, he knelt down. Holding on to her bare legs, Aidan kissed a path from her ankle to her knees.

"Lean against Caleb," Aidan told her.

She felt Caleb spanning his fingers on her shoulders and guiding her back until she rested her spine against him. Mia tilted her face up and met his mouth with hers. She murmured her appreciation when Caleb wrapped his arms around her and played with her breasts.

She felt Aidan spread her legs and his mouth on her inner thigh. She inhaled sharply as her pussy creamed with anticipation. Aidan licked her labia over and over, purposely ignoring her clit. He drove his tongue into her pussy with enthusiasm, and Mia sagged against Caleb. She reached for Aidan, grabbing his hair in her fists and riding his face at a breathless pace until the sparks lit under her skin and shimmered over her eyes before she came hard.

Aidan continued licking her after she climaxed. Her knees were shaky, and she couldn't stand up on her own by the time Aidan stood up. "Caleb, take her to the bed," Aidan said.

Caleb swept her up and lowered her onto the bed, but Aidan stopped him. "I want her kneeling on the bed, facing the door. I want you right behind her."

Caleb did as he requested, and Mia wondered why he listened to Aidan. He could take her anytime, anywhere, but he didn't. He waited until Aidan said it was okay. It was as if he recognized and respected Aidan's prior claim on Mia.

She sighed with delight as Caleb ran his hands all over her. He knew how to touch her lightly, and she was panting for his next move. When Mia couldn't take it anymore, she hooked one arm over Caleb's shoulders and kissed him.

With Mia stretched against him, Caleb met her kiss and banded his arm across her chest. He speared his other hand down her stomach and spread her wet curls to caress her clit.

Aidan got on the bed and knelt before Mia. Reaching out, he grasped her chin and pulled her mouth away from Caleb's. Aidan tilted her face up and waited until she met his gaze; then he kissed her with a ferocity that took her breath away.

She couldn't stand much more. She loved having four hands roaming her body, teasing a climax out of her, but it was almost too much. She gasped as Caleb slid his fingers into her and pumped hard. Mia was already close to the edge, and it didn't take much for a small, intense orgasm to flow through her.

"Get on your hands and knees," Aidan told her as he gave her one more kiss.

Mia lowered her body, placing her palms on the unmade bed. Aidan's thick cock was in her face. She felt Caleb behind her, and she had a sense of déjà vu.

Aidan smiled and nodded, as if he knew exactly what she was thinking. "I've wanted to do this since Caleb first took you." He grabbed the root of his cock, his grip tight, and brushed the wet tip along her mouth. She parted her lips to take him.

"Not until I tell you to," he reminded her.

She groaned, the frustration bubbling inside her. At least Caleb continued to stroke her sex. She would find gratification from him.

His fingers flirted against her rosebud. She clenched her buttocks instinctively. She'd never been touched like that before. She wasn't sure if she liked it. It was so taboo.

As Aidan drew designs on her mouth and cheek with his cock, Caleb massaged and squeezed her ass. He dipped his finger in her core, and then slid his fingertip toward her anus. Mia wiggled from the intimate touch and started to shake with anticipation.

"You like that?" Aidan asked, motioning his head toward Caleb. From the look in his eye, he knew she did. He wanted her to say it out loud.

"Yes." But she wasn't sure if she was ready for anal sex. She squeezed her eyes closed as she considered the size and girth of Caleb's cock. She shied away from Caleb's touch.

"Just my finger," Caleb promised. "For now."

He circled his fingertip along her rosebud. Suddenly nothing existed but where his finger touched her. Aidan circled his cock around her mouth. She moaned, her world expanding.

"Open up," Aidan told her gently.

She parted her lips and darted her tongue along his cock. Her eyes widened when Caleb pressed his finger into her anus. It wasn't like anything she'd felt before. There was some discomfort, but it was more of an unfamiliar touch than anything else.

"Relax," Caleb whispered.

She did, and his finger slid past the puckered ring. She groaned as her nerve endings flared to life. Aidan took the opportunity to slide his cock deep in her mouth.

She sucked him as hard as she could and listened to his groan. He withdrew, shuddering, trying to make this moment last. Aidan watched as Caleb pumped his finger in her anus. She saw the dark pleasure flash across Aidan's face. She had never seen him look that intense before.

She jutted her ass, wiggling it from side to side. Caleb slowly withdrew his finger from her rosebud. "No," she wailed. She wanted more.

"Next time," Caleb promised. "And it will feel even better."

She couldn't imagine that, and she wanted a little taste of next time, but Caleb and Aidan denied her. Aidan cupped her face with his hands and fed her his cock. She licked and slurped his erection, wanting to give him as much pleasure as he had given her.

Caleb grabbed her hips, and his hard cock pressed against the folds of her sex. She moaned, long and loud, as he slowly entered her. His thrusts were short and shallow, designed to tease.

She pushed back, her flesh hungry for all of Caleb's cock. But that meant getting shallow thrusts from Aidan. She groaned, wishing she could have both buried deep inside her.

"Trust us," Aidan said.

She wondered if every emotion, every thought was broadcast on her face. They must have known that they were tormenting her. Did they also see that she wanted more? She wanted it harder, deeper, faster. She wanted it all.

Just when she thought she would have to take matters into her own hands, Aidan and Caleb started to thrust in tandem. Aidan plunged into her mouth as Caleb withdrew. Then Caleb gave a deep thrust, and Aidan retreated.

It was exquisite torture. Her mind was buzzing, her body humming with pleasure. They continued, on and on. The pleasure built inside her, tighter and tighter, until it sprang free.

Her climax was almost painful. She flinched, her body shaking as the intensity whipped through her. As she shook from the aftermath, her flesh clamped onto Caleb's cock, slowly wringing an orgasm from him.

Caleb reared back, his fingers digging into her hips. He pumped his cock into her so hard that she almost fell. He held on tighter, his thrusts fast and furious. Mia felt like she was being tossed around like a rag doll, dizzy and disoriented, until Caleb came hard.

Aidan watched it all, his movements growing coarse and uneven. He held Mia's head very still as he pumped into her mouth. Mia opened wide as he thrust into her mouth, almost hitting the back of her throat before he pulsed hotly in her mouth.

Caleb carefully withdrew from her and leaned back against the headboard with a groan. Aidan reluctantly let go of Mia, and she tumbled onto the bed, exhausted and sated. *So that was a threesome . . .* Mia thought with a tired smile. She was glad she'd had the courage to try it.

"Well, well, well."

Mia froze and lifted her head. She saw Jamie, proudly naked, standing at the door to the bedroom. Her hands were on her hips, and her head was tilted back in defiance.

A slow smile formed on Jamie's wide mouth. "I wondered what all the noise was about."

She wasn't angry, Mia realized with a spurt of relief. She was tired and curious.

"Is there room for one more?" Jamie asked as she strolled to the bed. It was going to be a snug fit, but her friend didn't seem to care.

Aidan groaned and tossed his arm over his eyes. "You women are insatiable."

"Room to sleep," Jamie corrected Aidan as she crawled over Caleb and wormed her way into a tight spot on the bed. "I need some rest before I go at it all night."

All night. Mia's core clenched with anticipation. The sun hadn't, set and she still had all night to explore wherever her desires and imagination led her. Mia smiled as she drifted into sleep. It was going to be a very long night.

SIXTEEN

Mia stirred awake, and she wasn't sure what had pulled her from a dreamless sleep. She had been comfortable and warm, as if she had been cradled. She didn't want to open her eyes but reluctantly peered through her lashes.

Her head was pillowed on Jamie's shoulder. Mia looked up and saw the mess of brown hair hiding most of Jamie's face. The only way she could tell if Jamie was asleep was the dreamy, goofy smile. Jamie would never smile like that once awake.

Mia lifted her head and snuggled against Aidan, her spine flush against his chest. He didn't stir. The bed was crowded with all four of them. They were a tangle of arms and legs. The warmth, sharing, and joy were something she hadn't expected to feel during the swap. She wondered if switching sex partners had been successful because they were friends.

She closed her eyes and was about to drift off into sleep when she felt a hand drift to her thigh. Her leg muscle tightened. She didn't know whose hand it was.

No, you do. She wasn't going to look down to see the hand. If she followed Jamie's advice on the other senses, she would know. She needed to concentrate on what she really felt and not on the consequences of whose hand it might be.

The long fingers spanned against the back of her thigh. Mia tried to ignore the tingling in her leg and focused. The way that the hand was positioned took Aidan out of the running. That left Caleb and Jamie.

She concentrated on how the hand caressed her thigh. The gentle exploration made her think of Caleb. He had touched her like that during their first night together. She smiled as she remembered that night when a fingernail grazed her leg.

Fingernail? Caleb kept his nails short because of his job as a handyman. This fingernail was long and tapered.

It was Jamie's hand.

Mia kept her eyes closed. She tried not to flinch or pull away. She knew Jamie wanted to have a sexual encounter with her. Was she ready for that?

She still couldn't believe that she didn't know her friend was bisexual. How could she have missed the signs? There were a lot of rumors about Jamie, and her sexuality had been one of them. Mia always assumed the rumors started because men and women were very aware of her sensuality.

And the sexiest woman she knew wanted her. The knowledge gave her a little buzz. It made her feel like she was just as sexy and beautiful as her friend.

But in all honesty, Mia didn't know how she would have reacted if Jamie had made a move before this weekend. Surprised. Worried. Concerned that any experimentation on her part would kill their friendship.

Because Mia wasn't interested in a sexual relationship with a woman, and Jamie wasn't in love with her. She knew that for certain. Mia wasn't sure, however, how far she was willing to go, but that was what this weekend was all about: exploring her boundaries.

Mia faked a yawn and stretched; the pull of muscles felt good. She noticed how Jamie snatched her hand away from Mia's thigh. She blinked her eyes open and smiled at Jamie. Her friend pushed her brown hair out of her eyes and gazed down at her.

"This is cozy," Mia said as she wiggled, her hip bumping against Jamie's.

Jamie bucked against Mia and then froze. She tried to move away but couldn't. "What time is it?" she asked in an obvious attempt to distract Mia from her instinctive move.

"I'm not sure. Looks like some time in the afternoon." She laid her hand on Jamie's waist and watched her friend's eyes widen. "Do you think we should let the guys sleep some more?"

"No way," Jamie said with great feeling. "We don't have that much time left."

Mia agreed. She wanted to pack as much pleasure in the remaining hours as she possibly could. "What should we do next?"

"Orgy."

Mia smiled at her friend's quick response. "Amazing how that was on the tip of your tongue," she teased. "But I'm not sure if we can do that. It was difficult getting Aidan to agree to a threesome."

Jamie made a face. "What's one more?"

"Yeah, we tried that argument," Mia reminded her. "It didn't get us anywhere."

"Okay, fine," Jamie said with a trace of impatience. "You come with the idea this time. Let's see how you do."

"Fine, I will. Think, think, think . . ." She waited a couple beats and then gave her best impression of when Jamie came up with a doozy of an idea. "I got it! Let's fool around, you and me."

Jamie's mouth sagged open. "Excuse me?"

"Oh, come on. Don't act all surprised. You told me years ago that guys love watching two women make out. That should encourage an orgy, right?"

Jamie opened and shut her mouth. Mia wondered if she had done the wrong thing. She was curious what it would be like to have sex with Jamie, but her friend wouldn't make the first move. Mia thought this was the best way to approach her. Either one could back down and there would be no hurt feelings.

Jamie opened her mouth again and hesitated before she asked, "Do you really think that's going to work?"

Triumph pulsed through Mia's veins, and she tried to keep an innocent expression. "Let's find out." Mia jabbed her elbow into Aidan's ribs. "Aidan?"

Jamie grabbed Mia's arm. "What are you doing?" she hissed.

"I need to ask Aidan first," Mia insisted. Aidan had taken a leap of faith letting her take part in a threesome. She knew that showing patience and obedience in bed made him more comfortable when she tested her boundaries. "Aidan honey?" she said as she gave a little nudge.

"Are you crazy?" Jamie asked. "Just make out now and apologize later."

Mia smiled and tilted her head so Aidan could hear her clearly. "Jamie wants to make out with me."

Aidan's eyes popped open. "Huh? What was that?"

Hmm . . . Maybe she should say that every morning when she needed him to wake up. "Do you want to watch me kiss Jamie?" she offered. It wasn't quite asking permission, and she hoped Aidan didn't call her on the infraction.

His dazed expression vanished and was replaced by a wicked gleam in his eye. "Go for it."

"Did you hear that, Jamie?" she asked as she turned around to face her friend. "But I'm new to this, so you need to take the lead."

"Like that was ever in question." Jamie tilted Mia's head. She brushed her lips against Mia's, tasting and exploring. Mia sensed Jamie was holding back, not wanting to scare Mia with her usual aggression and domination.

Mia parted her mouth open and darted her tongue into Jamie's mouth. Jamie gasped with delight before she tried to draw Mia deeper into her mouth. Mia took this opportunity to explore Jamie's mouth, but got distracted by Jamie's superior kissing technique. She was being easily seduced by her friend's clever tongue.

Jamie rubbed her hands over Mia's body, and Mia copied her friend's actions. Soon Mia's instinct and curiosity guided the way, and she glided her hands along Jamie's ass and pulled her closer. Jamie moaned and reached for Mia's breasts. She squeezed them hard, and Mia deepened the kiss.

Jamie pulled her mouth from Mia's and trailed kisses down her neck. Mia didn't stop Jamie when she began licking her way down to the small slope of her breasts. Jamie tested the weight and size of Mia's breasts, humming with approval, before licking around one of Mia's nipples.

Mia arched, cupping Jamie's head and driving her friend closer to her breasts. She wanted more than her friend's tongue. She wanted Jamie to suck and bite. Mia was so deep into Jamie's touch that she jumped when she felt Aidan shifting behind her.

"Keep going," he murmured in her ear as he spanned his hand along her waist.

"That was my plan all along," Mia whispered, gasping with

pleasure as Aidan nuzzled her throat before licking her ear. She really loved having her ear licked. Who knew?

He lifted his head to watch Jamie suck Mia's breasts, and growled with pleasure in Mia's ear. Curling his hand along Mia's knee, he hooked her leg over his. He then speared his hand into her wet curls and stroked her clit.

Mia loved having four hands and two mouths on her. They were attending to her needs and desires, and all she had to do was enjoy. The extreme pleasure was an embarrassment of riches.

Jamie stiffened, and Mia gave a little shriek. She saw Caleb rouse from his sleep, his hands creeping up Jamie's chest before settling possessively on her voluptuous breasts.

"Now this is a nice way to wake up," Caleb said, his voice rough with sleep.

Mia had to agree. Her core was pulsing, she felt Aidan's cock pressing against her ass, and her friend was teasing her breasts with her mouth. She didn't think it would be long until Caleb leaned over Jamie's head and claimed Mia's mouth.

"Do you want to have all three of us?" Aidan whispered in her ear.

Three lovers? Mia's moan seemed to vibrate from deep within her. If she had all three determined to please her, she would experience a sexual nirvana she couldn't imagine. The intense sensations alone would shatter her into a million pieces.

"No," she said, pulling away from Caleb. "I shouldn't."

"Shouldn't." The word echoed in her head. Her answer wasn't as strong as "won't" or "no." Yet she couldn't bring herself to say either of those.

If she indulged in three lovers, she would turn greedy for everything they had to offer. Aidan, Caleb, and Jamie would make her lose all control. No ties or binds would be able to contain her.

"Yes, you should," Aidan said, his hand on her hip, his fingers tantalizingly close to her mound.

She wanted to jump at Aidan's offer. Oh, how she wanted her three friends to guide her through this passage. It was scary and thrilling—and for one brief moment, she considered returning to her safe little world—going back to one lover, one set of rules.

"I'm here to catch you," Aidan assured her.

How did he know what she was worried about? And did he think she was silly for being afraid? Most people wanted to go wild in bed. She wanted to know that as long as she went as far as her sensual world could take her, she could always hurry back to the safe comfort she needed.

"Okay," she said, her voice trembling. "I want to take the three of you all at once."

Jamie's lips stilled on Mia's breasts, and she jerked her head up. "You want to do *what*?"

Mia looked directly in her friend's startled eyes. She didn't think she'd ever shocked Jamie quite like this before. For once, Mia enjoyed being the scandalous one.

Jamie continued to stare at Mia. "Exactly what is it that you're planning to do?"

Mia offered a tremulous smile. "I want to have sex with you"— she emphasized—"Caleb, and Aidan. At the same time."

"Jamie, hold Mia down so I can go get the handcuffs," Aidan said as he sat up.

"Get a blindfold while you're at it," Jamie said as she smiled at Mia.

Mia glared at her friend. "That won't be necessary."

"You won't be able to tell us apart," Jamie pointed out. "That's half the fun."

"Mia would be able to identify me," Aidan said with confidence. He rolled out of bed and walked to the dresser.

"Don't be too sure," Jamie retorted. "In fact, let's put money on it—*ouch!*"

Mia kicked her in the leg again. "What do you think you're doing?" she whispered fiercely. "You know . . ." Mia let her voice trail off. She couldn't risk saying any more. She hoped Aidan never found out that they had suggested a threesome because Mia couldn't tell the difference between Caleb and him.

"Stop worrying." Jamie climbed over Mia and pinned her arms to the mattress. "You're going to do fine."

"No, I'm not." She had been unable to tell which person had stroked her leg a few minutes ago.

"I wouldn't have suggested it otherwise," Jamie said in all seriousness.

"Yes, you would have," Mia whispered, her voice sharp and fast, "because you weren't thinking!"

"I am, too," Jamie said. "I'm thinking of you."

Mia huffed with disbelief. "Lovely way of showing it."

"You can tell the difference between the two," Jamie whispered in her ear.

"Shh!" Mia looked in the direction of Aidan, but she couldn't see him. She glanced at Caleb, who was deep in thought as he caressed her legs. Mia couldn't tell if he had heard, but she also couldn't tell if he would care if Mia's mind made him interchangeable with Aidan.

Aidan returned to the bed with four handcuffs and a blindfold. Mia stared at the gleaming metal and black velvet, unsure if she was going to pass this test.

She had passed every test Aidan had given her over the year, Mia realized as Caleb and Aidan cuffed her to the bed. The fact that she always rose to the occasion made Aidan think he was too soft on her, but Mia knew the truth. Aidan only tested her when he knew she was ready. He also knew that Mia's pride wouldn't allow her to fail.

But Aidan was misguided by the belief that she would know his touch in the dark. What would he do when he found out? She couldn't let that happen. She hadn't failed him yet, and she wasn't going to start now.

As Jamie placed the blindfold over Mia's eyes, Mia muttered darkly, "I'm going to get you for this."

"You're chained to a bed. I'd like to see you try," Jamie taunted back.

Suddenly Mia's surroundings were pitch-black. She craned her neck, trying to hear and predict what was coming at her next.

A mouth covered hers. It was warm and dry, but Mia still reeled back from the unexpected touch.

"Okay," Jamie said gleefully against her ear. "Who was that?"

Mia's heart hammered against her chest. She had no idea! "The kiss was too short," she complained. "I need another one."

She felt the mouth against her lips, and Mia tried to pick out the clues. The lips weren't full and lush, so she knew it wasn't Jamie.

Then who was it?

The man kissed her with teasing nibbles. The touch was assertive, but not aggressive. There was no hint of possession. "Caleb," she whispered without thinking.

The moment she said his name, she wanted to call it back. She hadn't meant to give an answer unless she had been absolutely certain.

"You're right!" Jamie said, her voice sounding farther away this time. "And you weren't sure of this game."

Mia still wasn't! She knew she had made a lucky guess. She had to be very careful.

Mia gasped as she felt the heel of a hand pressing against her mound.

"Who's touching you?" Jamie asked.

"You," Mia immediately replied. She bit her tongue, wishing she would be more careful. Then again, she had been one hundred percent positive with her answer. But there was that chance she was wrong, because she couldn't see anything thanks to the blindfold.

Jamie lifted her hand. "How did you know?" she asked.

"I just did." Mia didn't think there was any reason to mention that Jamie's manicure tipped her off.

"And now?" Jamie asked, clearly enjoying the test.

Mia felt two big hands massaging her left foot. She wanted to kick the person away as a thumb dug at the bottom of her foot and dragged along its length. The touch was almost ticklish.

It was a masculine hand, Mia noted as she felt the strength and callused skin. "Caleb again," she answered. Caleb had work-roughened hands. He had also rubbed her foot like that on their first night together.

"Okay, maybe this is too easy for her," Jamie complained. "We need to give her something really difficult."

"Where's Aidan?" Mia asked. He had been too quiet and hadn't participated in the game.

"Right here," Aidan replied, and placed a gentle kiss on her breast. Mia arched her back, wanting more than a kiss. The metal cuffs around her wrists rubbed her skin as they clanged against the bedposts.

"When do I get all three of you touching me at once?" she asked breathlessly.

Her stomach twisted, and this time it was from the excitement, although she was still fighting some nerves. She didn't know what she was getting herself into, and there was only so much Aidan could do to take care of her.

"Do you think you're ready for it?" Aidan asked.

"Yes!" she bit out impatiently. "Give me everything you've got!"

Aidan kissed her hard and stabbed his tongue past her lips. She felt his hands cradling her face as Caleb and Jamie stroked her body.

At first she could tell exactly what each person was doing. Jamie squeezed and pinched one of her breasts while Caleb sucked Mia's nipple on the other.

As the trio pleasured her, Mia slowly lost track with who was touching her breasts and who was kissing along her hip bone. The hands and mouths seemed to multiply, and she couldn't tell what they were going to do next.

She was dizzy with excitement, and the only thing Mia could do was surrender to the wild sensations spinning through her. Aidan would stop everything and catch her if she lost complete control.

Mia froze when she felt a hand on her clitoris. The touch was as light as a feather but gave quite an impact. Mia moaned as this lover captured the swollen nub between two fingers and pressed down.

Mia panted for air as the sting whipped through her. She couldn't concentrate on who was teasing her clit. Was it one of the men, or was it Jamie?

The last thought gave her a jolt, and the metal cuffs jangled harshly as she rocked her hips.

Her attention was torn away as someone squeezed her breasts, which felt heavy and full. She whimpered as this lover bit down on her nipple, sending a white-hot rush through her veins.

"More," she whispered shyly. She didn't want to be this greedy, but the hands and mouths were stirring up feelings she had tried so hard to hide.

She frowned when she felt something solid and warm against her ribs. Mia couldn't tell who it was or what he was doing. If only her arms were unchained, then she could investigate.

The solid warmth squeezed her like a vise. *Legs.* Mia clearly imagined knees and suddenly knew what was pressing against her armpits. But why was he touching her like this?

She felt the legs flex. Wet heat covered one of her breasts. The pressure rocked back and forth. Mia couldn't figure out what the lover was doing to her, but if felt good. Hard and slippery against her soft breast.

Jamie. Jamie was riding her breasts. Once Mia realized this, she was very aware of Jamie's juices wetting her nipples and trickling down the curve of her breast.

Oh, that feels so good. "More," Mia said as she rocked back and forth, matching Jamie's rhythm.

Jamie grunted loudly and swiveled her hips, crushing Mia's breasts with her weight. The lines between pleasure and pain blurred. Mia rocked from side to side, chasing the delicious sensations as Jamie bucked wildly against her.

Jamie's legs tightened. Mia gasped for breath as Jamie rode her fiercely. Jamie cried out as she climaxed, and then suddenly she wasn't there. Mia's breasts were free, and chilly air wafted over the sticky, swollen crests. Where had Jamie gone? Mia wondered as her body pulsed for completion.

She felt knees bumping against her armpits again. Only this time they were much bigger. It had to be either Caleb or Aidan. Mia wrestled with her bindings, trying to touch more of her male lover.

He cupped her face with his hands, and the other hands and mouth on her dimmed in her consciousness. Mia couldn't tell if the hands on her face were callused or not. All she could determine was that they were big and strong.

The man rubbed the tip of his cock firmly against her mouth. Outlining the shape of her lips, her lover was seeking entrance.

Seeking entrance . . . requesting permission. Mia parted her lips as she recognized her lover. *Caleb.*

He glided his cock past her lips, and she knew without a doubt that it was Caleb. His taste, his length, even the texture of his cock identified him.

"More," she ordered him and opened her mouth wider. Mia sucked the tip, drawing him deeper into her mouth. She heard Caleb's groan as he started to pump in her, each stroke careful and measured.

Mia murmured with pleasure as she sucked his cock, rubbing the roof of her mouth over a sensitive spot that tested Caleb's control. His hands tightened on her face as his pace quickened.

She felt someone's hands on her hips and pelvis. There was an intent in the way the person touched her. Jamie. She clasped Mia's mound with such possession that Mia wanted to melt against her friend's touch.

Jamie caressed Mia's clitoris in small circular movements, and Mia swayed her hips. Jamie's pattern and Caleb's rhythm fought against each other, yet brought Mia's arousal to a fevered pitch.

She felt Aidan's strong hands on the top of her legs. Mia imagined he was either kneeling between her spread thighs or standing at the foot of her bed. Her core pulsed with urgent need. She had to have Aidan deep inside her. She couldn't take the exquisite stimulation anymore.

Mia turned her head, allowing Caleb's cock to slip from her mouth. "More," she yelled impatiently as she rattled the chains that bound her.

She felt Aidan's hands slide underneath her legs and he grabbed her ass. Tilting her hips, he lifted her off the mattress. The angle of her pussy promised deep penetration.

When two fingers dipped into her core, Mia at first thought it was Aidan, but she realized that was impossible. *Jamie* was testing her wetness before withdrawing her fingers and smearing the moisture against Mia's aching clit.

The tip of Aidan's cock pressed against the folds of her sex as Caleb continued to slide his cock in and out of her mouth. Already she could tell one difference between the two men, and she couldn't understand why she had been previously confused about Aidan and Caleb.

Mia sighed around Caleb's cock as Aidan thrust into her pussy. She writhed under her lovers when Aidan stretched and filled her. Her flesh gripped him tightly.

She tried to meet Aidan's thrusts as she rocked against Jamie's fingers. Caleb pumped in her mouth, no longer able to control his rhythm.

Each lover would have driven her wild by himself. Together they overwhelmed her senses. Her body began to quake as the desire coiled tightly in her belly. Urgent need pressed against her from the inside out. She thought her skin would erupt and splinter.

Aidan thrust into her just as Jamie pressed down on her clit. Mia inhaled sharply, taking Caleb deep in her throat. That was all it took.

Intense pleasure clawed at her, the sensation so burning hot that it felt like ice. It ripped through her to the bone, and Mia screamed as she climaxed. She shook, the cuffs biting into her skin.

Her release was violent, pulling her in all directions. It should have made her feel weak and fragile. Instead, raw energy filled Mia. Three lovers had dominated her all at once, but she had never felt so powerful.

SEVENTEEN
SEVENTEEN

Hours later, Jamie was snuggled against her friends on Mia's big bed. She stared up at the canopy bed when she heard her friend give a sigh of regret.

She turned to look at Mia. "What are you thinking about?" Jamie whispered, her question startling her friend.

"I didn't know you were up."

Jamie lifted herself up on one arm. "You look so sad. Aren't you having fun?" She hoped Mia wasn't regretting this weekend.

"I am having a great time," Mia assured her. "Almost every one of my fantasies has come true. It's all thanks to you guys."

"Then what's the problem?"

Mia gave a little shrug. "You got to explore and have sex with another guy. Aidan got to watch. I got to tie up Aidan. But what about Caleb?"

Jamie looked over her shoulder and saw Caleb sleeping soundly. "You're right. He's been granting everyone else their wishes, but no on has done the same for him."

Mia thought for a moment. "What's his sexual fantasy?"

Jamie tried to recall. The only thing he had asked for was seeing her and Mia have sex. Jamie knew that wasn't *his* fantasy. He might want to watch, but it was really something he wanted to give to her. "I don't know."

"You don't know?" Mia's voice rose with indignation. "You've been with him all this time and you have no clue what he likes?"

Jamie's shoulders tensed defensively. "Hey, you didn't know Aidan likes to watch you having sex with another man. How were you going to figure that one out on your own?"

"That's different," Mia insisted. "Aidan was hiding that from me. He didn't think I would understand. But Caleb doesn't have any reason to hide from you."

"Don't be too sure about that," Jamie muttered, but she knew what Mia was saying. Caleb didn't have to hide his sexual fantasies from her. Jamie was all for people having exotic fetishes and extreme sex, the wilder the better.

But it turned out that she had been as judgmental about sex as her neighbors. The comparison made Jamie sick to her stomach, but she couldn't deny it. Jamie hadn't understood and had interfered with Mia's submissive nature. She had thought her friend should act like a modern-day woman both in and out of bed.

Yet surrendering to a dominant male was Mia's fantasy. Jamie didn't understand it and had tried to show Mia the error of her ways. It had been wrong of her. If Jamie wanted to be a good friend, then she needed to leave Mia's wishes alone.

Maybe that was the same problem with Caleb. Jamie gave him another glance. He might have a very traditional sex fantasy. Jamie found it difficult to believe since Caleb was the most adventurous and fascinating lover she had had, but it was possible.

234 ■ Jenesi Ash

"We need to correct this oversight," Mia decided, her eyes gleaming with anticipation. "The next time we have sex, we're focusing on Caleb."

"Good idea." Jamie wanted to match Mia's enthusiasm since she truly felt it was a good idea. Jamie just wished she had come up with the idea first. She should have thought of it days ago. It was yet another example of how selfish she was.

Jamie rarely indulged in self-analyzing, but she couldn't ignore it anymore. This weekend had really had its ups and downs. She had lived out a fantasy few could claim, but she had discovered she wasn't a thoughtful, attentive lover. For someone who prided herself on her sexual prowess and a multitude of lovers, this was painful to swallow.

But she could change her ways, starting now. Jamie always felt better when she took action. Time was not on her side to make up for the past, so she probably had one chance to make it right with Caleb. Now if she only knew what he wanted . . .

"Give me some clues," Mia told Jamie. "What does he like?"

"Everything." His enthusiasm for her body, and his passion for her, never wavered. Caleb was always eager to have sex, no matter what she had planned.

Mia rolled her eyes. "That can't be possible."

"He hasn't said that he liked one position over another. There hasn't been one thing that he doesn't like. He won't refuse me anything . . ." Jamie's voice trailed off. Everything she'd said was true. Why hadn't she noticed any of this before?

Mia pursed her lips and glared at Jamie with envy. "You don't realize how lucky you are."

"I'm beginning to." And right before she was walking away from it all without a backward glance.

"Well, did he say anything when you guys argued?" Mia continued to prompt Jamie for ideas. "What about the makeup sex? Did he want to do anything in particular?"

Jamie felt her cheeks grow sizzling hot. She remembered how Caleb had pinned her against the shower wall. He had been role-playing, acting like Mia. It hadn't been his fantasy, but hers. She couldn't tell Mia that!

"Well?" Mia waited expectedly. "Don't tell me 'nothing.' You haven't blushed that way for years. What did he want to do?"

"There was some mention of a dildo," Jamie said slowly, watching Mia blush in return. She knew her friend was remembering how she had walked into the room while Jamie mounted Caleb. After she had seen that, Mia immediately agreed to the swap.

"Anything else?" Mia asked in a strangled voice.

"When we argued, he said he didn't want to be left out again."

"That shouldn't be a problem this time around since the focus is all on him." Mia fell silent and gnawed her bottom lip. "Jamie, go find your strap-on."

"Ooh, Mia!" she teased, waggling her eyebrows. "You're taking charge. I like that."

"Stop it." Mia narrowed her eyes. "I've taken charge a lot of times this weekend. Now go get your toy."

"Don't you need to talk to Aidan about this first?" Jamie motioned at Aidan tucked behind Mia.

"Ooh, Jamie!" Mia mimicked. "You're telling me to go ask for permission? I like that."

Jamie was going to playfully punch on Mia's arm when a voice stopped her in her tracks.

"Are you going to ask for permission or not?" Aidan asked, his voice rough with sleep.

Jamie and Mia looked at each other with wide eyes. Damn. How did Aidan always hear their conversations at the worst possible times? Couldn't he be like every other man and tune them out?

"How long have you been up, honey?" Mia asked, her voice high.

"Long enough to know what you guys are planning." Aidan slowly opened his eyes. "You want a threesome with Caleb."

Jamie was suddenly very aware of Caleb lying behind her. He hadn't stirred, but that didn't mean anything. Was he awake as well? Dread twisted in her stomach. Had he heard how little she knew about him?

She was afraid to turn around and see the hurt in Caleb's eyes. *Please be asleep. . . . Oh, please be asleep. . . .* She felt the rise and fall of his chest, and listened intently to the rhythm of his breathing. She determined that he was asleep, and then she sagged with relief.

"You really need to stop eavesdropping," Mia chided Aidan.

"And you really need to stop making these plans. First you wanted to swap and then you asked for a ménage à trois. Now you've decided to take it upon yourself to create a sexual fantasy for Caleb."

"What's your point?" Jamie asked.

Aidan leveled her with a warning look. "Maybe he doesn't want to take part in your plans."

Jamie's gaze clashed with Mia's. Could that be possible? Could Caleb be perfectly content with how this weekend was shaping up? "Nah . . ." they said in unison.

"You're probably right," Aidan admitted. "But if this backfires, remember that I had nothing to do with it."

Mia perked up. "Are you saying I can do this?" she asked him.

Aidan paused. "Yes, go ahead."

Mia squealed with delight. "Thank you!" She turned and cra-dled Aidan's hands. Jamie hushed her in case she woke up Caleb, but Mia wasn't listening as she claimed Aidan's mouth with her own.

When Mia pulled back from her kiss, she asked Aidan, "What are your conditions?"

Jamie shook her head in disgust. Why hadn't her friend thought of this before pouring on the gratitude? The girl needed to learn how to negotiate.

Aidan's eyes darkened as he softly announced, "I'm next to get a threesome with you and Jamie."

Mia looked over her shoulder at Jamie and smiled. "I think we can arrange that."

Watching Mia's eyes widen with delight, Jamie refrained from making any snide comments about Mia's readiness. She didn't know why Aidan was now gung ho about Mia's participation, but she wouldn't question it. She only had time to enjoy it for today.

"I'll go get the strap-on," Jamie offered. She carefully got out of bed so as not to disturb Caleb. As she headed for the attic, Jamie wondered if it was necessary to get the toy. The harness was her bit of fun because she enjoyed the power. But would Caleb pick that kind of sex over any other?

Retrieving the strap-on, Jamie stared at the black vinyl harness in her hands. She knew Caleb enjoyed taking it in the ass, so she might as well bring it in case he wanted it. Caleb was always full of surprises, and it was best to be prepared.

What she really needed to make sure she was doing was focusing on Caleb's pleasure. He would turn everything around to be her fantasy lover. And she had the habit of taking without giving back.

Jamie sighed heavily. *Remember, you're changing all that. Start-ing now.* She was going to give Caleb what he wanted in bed, even if it was something she wouldn't normally do. There weren't many things on that imagined list, but Caleb knew every one of them. If he wanted to, he would request one of those, and Jamie would take the task gladly.

She wouldn't think about how she would be the last time they were together. This might be her only chance to say goodbye to him. And if he chose to have Mia over her, Jamie would graciously step to the sidelines.

Maybe she had learned something during her night with Aidan. Jamie shook her head wryly as she gathered the lubricant, mini-vibrator, and purple dildo. She was ready to deprive herself of satisfaction. She was willing to stand back and be patient. Jamie didn't think she was going to act like that every time she had sex, and she wasn't sure it was an aberration. She would do it for Caleb, and only for him.

Jamie returned to Mia's bedroom and found Aidan out of bed and sitting in the overstuffed chair. Mia was kneeling in the bed, waiting for her arrival. Jamie stumbled to a stop, taking in the erotic sight of Mia's nakedness.

Mia's blond hair fell past her shoulders in waves. She was smiling at Aidan, her blue eyes lighting up with joy. Mia's innocence and fresh face were part of her beauty. Jamie knew why all the men drooled over Mia, but they never noticed the sly tilt of Mia's lips or her sensual nature.

The men of Clover Bud were always too busy ogling Mia's body. Mia had never appreciated what she had; she had been too busy envying Jamie's lush curves. Jamie didn't know why Mia complained.

Mia's silky-smooth skin whetted Jamie's appetite. Would it taste sweet or earthy? Jamie's gaze slid down Mia's body, resting on her small breasts. She knew they fit perfectly in her hands. Jamie's pulse began to race as she imagined Mia straddling her, wiggling her hips, and rubbing her pussy on Jamie's. Jamie abruptly looked away before Mia could interpret her staggered expression.

"Why are you sitting there?" Jamie asked Aidan. She didn't care if she sounded brusque. She was too busy ignoring Mia. "Caleb's fantasy probably doesn't include you watching him."

"You don't know that."

"Call it a hunch."

"Let's find out for ourselves." Aidan leaned back and rested his hands on his stomach, lacing his fingers together. "Go wake him up."

Jamie looked at Caleb. He was sleeping so soundly that she was almost reluctant to wake him up. No, that wasn't true, Jamie admitted to herself. In the past, she'd had no qualms about shaking him awake when she was aroused. Just looking at him was making her blood heat up.

No, she was hesitating because Caleb's secret fantasy would be something she wouldn't expect. She would have proof that she didn't really know the one man she felt closest to.

He won't tell us his secret fantasy.

Jamie frowned, wondering where that thought had come from. Caleb was quiet and mysterious, but he would tell her if she asked. He trusted her when she wanted to do all sorts of things to him. Wouldn't he trust her to make his wildest dreams come true?

"Mia and I will wake him up," Jamie decided. "Mia help me get Caleb to the middle of the bed."

Jamie walked over to Caleb's side and, with Mia's assistance, rolled him to the center of the mattress. Caleb yawned and stretched, slowing waking up.

"Quickly," Jamie whispered. "Lie down next to him."

As Mia cuddled up against Caleb, pressing her breasts to his spine, Jamie got into bed and spread her hands on his chest.

Jamie caressed Caleb, wanting to tease him fully awake. She didn't know what Mia was doing to him, but it didn't matter as long as Caleb enjoyed it.

As she pressed her mouth against his, Jamie hooked her leg over Caleb's and bumped her foot against Mia's. Mia jerked her foot away, the sudden movement gaining Caleb's attention.

He blinked his eyes open and saw Jamie. Her heart gave a flip as she watched his sleepy smile. Then she saw confusion sweep across his face. Jamie knew he felt Mia's hand and mouth on him.

"Mia and I came up with a great idea," she told Caleb as she kissed along his jaw. "We want to grant you one fantasy."

She felt his muscles bunch. It was so quick she would have missed it if she hadn't been pressed against him. Was he playing it cool even though he liked the idea, or did the offer send a chill down his spine? She wished she could read his feelings better, or had the easy, nonverbal communication Mia shared with Aidan.

"I don't have any fantasies," Caleb said.

Aha! Jamie almost smiled at Caleb's answer. She had been correct, knowing he wouldn't share his deepest wish.

"None at all?" Mia asked, and Jamie saw her friend kissing along Caleb's shoulders. "That's not good. Maybe we should make one up for him. What do you say, Jamie?"

"I like that idea," Jamie answered as she stole another kiss from Caleb. "What about you, Caleb?"

"Uh . . . where's Aidan?" he asked quickly, changing the subject.

"Sitting on the chair watching us," Mia informed Caleb before she reached around him and rubbed his chest. "Why do you ask? You don't think you can handle us at the same time?"

Caleb moved on his back and smiled at Mia. "I think I can handle it. What do you have planned?"

"What would you like us to do?" Mia asked.

"Hmm . . ." Caleb laced his fingers behind his head and pondered the question. "I want Mia to start by sucking each of my toes before licking her way up my body."

"Suck your toes?" Jamie pressed her lips together before she commented on that fantasy. She glanced at Mia to see how she was coping with the request. Her friend was blushing but holding back a smile. From the looks of it, Caleb and Mia were enjoying a private joke.

"What would you like me to do?" Jamie asked Caleb.

"Start at my mouth and lick your way down. You and Mia will meet at my cock."

What was Caleb planning? Was he still trying to hook her up with Mia? She hoped not. This was supposed to be for *him*, and it was going to be hard to resist acting on one of her fantasies when he was handing it to her.

Jamie brushed her mouth against Caleb's. She swiped her tongue along his bottom lip before slowly moving down to his chin. Using short, quick flicks, she lapped along Caleb's neck and chest. He tasted warm and masculine.

Glancing down, Jamie saw Mia industriously sucking Caleb's toes and humming with pleasure over her task.

Jamie darted her tongue against one of Caleb's flat nipples. She swirled the tip of her tongue, over and over, until she felt the nub harden. Jamie gave a little nip with the edge of her teeth and felt Caleb flinch. Then she moved on to the next nipple.

As Jamie licked her way down Caleb's stomach, finding the taste of his skin addictive, she reached his cock before Mia. Her friend was still licking her way up Caleb's inner thigh.

Jamie covered the tip of his cock with her mouth when Caleb stopped her. "Lick, but don't suck," he said between harsh breaths. "Not yet."

Jamie thought it was an unusual request, but she did what he had asked. It was Caleb's fantasy after all.

She licked his erection with long, wet strokes before rimming the head with a flirty twirl of her tongue. Cupping his balls in her hands, she laved the heavy, tight sacks, enjoying how Caleb twitched under her touch.

Mia reached Caleb's groin and began to lavish attention on his cock. As Jamie gave Caleb long, leisurely strokes with her tongue, Mia made short laps. She jerked back when her tongue met with Jamie's.

"Keep going . . . please," Caleb said roughly.

Mia returned to her task, licking and kissing his balls before working her up his warm cock. She outlined the ridges and knobby veins of his thick penis. And her tongue once again met Jamie's. After the briefest pauses, Mia continued licking Caleb's cock.

Jamie invaded Mia's territory so she could parry with Mia's tongue and Caleb's cock. Soon it was hard to tell who she was licking more—Caleb or Mia?

She heard a far-off moan and glanced at Caleb. But it didn't sound like him—it sounded more like Aidan. Jamie raised her head and saw Aidan clenching his cock with one hand and pumping. His eyes were glazed with lust as he watched Mia fight over Caleb's erection.

Caleb slowly rose into a sitting position and grabbed for Jamie. He clasped one hand at her jaw and held her in place to bestow a hard kiss on her mouth.

He then reached for Mia and wrapped an arm around her waist. Mia fell clumsily against his chest as he claimed a kiss from her.

"Tell me what you want," Jamie murmured, rubbing her hand all over his chest. "I can give it to you."

She felt an amazing energy saying those words: *I can give it to you.* There was nothing submissive about granting wishes. The power was raw and addictive. She understood why Caleb wanted to make every one of her fantasies come true.

He looked at Jamie. "I want you to take me in the ass while I sink into Mia's pussy."

Piercing hot excitement forked through Jamie like lightning. "Are you sure?" she asked, her voice wobbly.

His eyes gleamed as he watched Jamie suppress her reaction. "Go get your strap-on."

Jamie and Mia exchanged a smile. "It's already here on the bed." Jamie reached for the vinyl harness.

"Have Mia help you put it on," Caleb told her.

"But I can—" Jamie stopped when she saw the hurt lurking in his gaze.

"I insist," he said.

Jamie crawled out of bed, and Mia knelt on the mattress in front of her. As Jamie instructed her friend, she gingerly stepped into the harness Mia held. Mia adjusted the straps and buckles, her fingers brushing against Jamie's mound. Jamie was tempted to take Mia's hand and slide it underneath her harness.

"Mia," Caleb said, "please rub the lubricant on Jamie's dildo."

Mia cast a quick, curious look at Caleb, but didn't say a word as she reached for the bottle. She poured the silky lube in the palm of her hand and grasped the dildo protruding from Jamie's crotch.

Jamie watched, fascinated, as Mia glided her slender hands along the purple cock. Jamie wiggled, her pussy becoming hot and wet as if Mia were actually touching her.

"Very good," Caleb said to Mia. "Now lie down on the bed and put your head on the pillow."

As Mia followed Caleb's orders, Jamie grabbed the bottle of lube. Caleb settled on top of Mia, bracing his arms and legs on either side of her. Mia stared up at Caleb, her eyes filled with joy-ful anticipation.

Caleb dipped his head and kissed Mia with long, exploratory kisses that had her arching and writhing against him. As Jamie poured lube in her hand, she watched Caleb cup Mia's sex. Mia gasped, her voice high as he rubbed his fingers along her wet, swollen folds.

Kneeling behind Caleb, Jamie saw the pleasure in Mia's eyes. When Jamie rubbed the lube against Caleb's puckered hole, he must have touched Mia the same way. They moved their bodies in unison as their low grunts mingled.

Jamie slid her fingertip past Caleb's rosebud, and he bucked against her hand. Mia rocked her hips against Caleb's touch. Again and again, it was as if Mia responded to Jamie's touch while Caleb acted as the conduit.

When Caleb couldn't take any more of her teasing touch, he clutched Mia's hips and slowly sank into her. Mia's long sigh conveyed ecstasy in its purest form. Mia turned to see Aidan, who continued to watch. He slowly pumped his cock as if he wanted the sensations to last as long as possible.

Jamie grabbed one of Caleb's hips, her fingers digging into his flesh as she guided the tip of her dildo against his hole. She slowly pushed into him as he growled with pleasure.

Once he took all of her dildo, Jamie placed both hands on his hips and started to thrust. She couldn't see Caleb's face, but from every tremble and groan, she knew how to maximize each move she made.

Jamie could, however, watch Mia's face. Mia whimpered and bit her lip as she watched Aidan. Each thrust Jamie made started a chain reaction. It was as if she was having sex with both of them at the same time.

Jamie reached down and turned on the mini vibe nestled against her clit. She trembled, heat washing over her, as the powerful toy pulsated.

Jamie thrust harder and faster, causing Caleb to move at the same rough pace. Mia's eyes rolled back as she tossed her head from side to side. Mia froze, her mouth sagging open as she gave a silent scream. She continued to shake as Caleb's thrusts became wild. He reared back, nearly unseating Jamie as he found his release.

Caleb collapsed on top of Mia, who lay limply on the bed. Jamie was tempted to keep thrusting until she found satisfaction. She wanted to achieve the same blissful state as her friends. Jamie hesitated and then reached down to turn off the mini vibe.

Her body rebelled over the decision. She wasn't used to self-denial. But this wasn't her fantasy. It was Caleb's.

Or was it? She studied Caleb, who was slumped over Mia. Mia looked dazed as she gulped for air, continuing to watch Aidan. Aidan gripped his aroused cock, but didn't come. Living out his voyeuristic fantasy had been his ultimate goal, and he had achieved it.

Once again, Caleb had made everyone's fantasies come true. But Jamie felt as if she'd failed Caleb for not granting a fantasy that was solely for him. She needed another chance to get it right, but time was not on her side.

EIGHTEEN

EIGHTEEN

"I'm so excited!" Jamie exclaimed as she unzipped her duffel bag and stuffed some shorts and tank tops inside. "Just a couple more hours and I am out of here."

"It's hard to believe," Mia said, trying to hide her sadness. She gathered Jamie's supplies from the bathroom and walked back to where her friend stood by the foot of her bed. "Do you really have to go?"

"Yeah, I do," Jamie said, her excitement fizzling as she struggled with the bag's zipper. "I need to get out now before I—" She stopped. "Before I get crazy."

That was not what she was going to say. Mia watched how Jamie made a point not to look at her, and she knew what her friend had almost said. Jamie had to get out before she made a move on Mia. She had to leave before she hurt the one lasting relationship she had ever known.

Mia wished she knew the right thing to say, or the perfect solution so that Jamie would stay and be happy. She knew her friend wasn't in love with her or even hoped for a romantic relationship.

Jamie wanted the status of their relationship to turn into "friends with benefits."

Surprisingly, Mia wasn't opposed to the idea. She didn't know what had brought that on. She wasn't interested in women, but she was intrigued by the idea of having sex with Jamie.

From the corner of her eye, she silently took in Jamie's appearance. Jamie's long dark hair was a wavy mess, but that didn't distract from her beauty. If anything, Mia found the soft brown tangles enticing. She wanted to play with Jamie's hair and sink her hands in, twisting the strands around her fingers and making it impossible for Jamie to get away.

But her friend's hair was not as tempting as her lips. Mia rubbed her lips together as she stared at Jamie's wide mouth. The memory of Jamie's kisses made Mia blush. She liked the aggression Jamie had displayed. It contrasted with the fruity gloss she had smeared on Mia's lips. And when Jamie had darted her tongue into her mouth, Mia had thought it was the most forbidden kiss she'd ever received.

And that was what intrigued her the most: the forbidden. She associated that word a lot with Jamie. Mia wasn't sure if she wanted to pick up the torch of being the naughtiest woman in town once Jamie left. She liked flirting with the forbidden, but she didn't want to publicize it the way Jamie did.

But Jamie seemed to recognize the limits. If she'd had any personal relationships with the women in town, it was a closely guarded secret. Mia couldn't imagine who Jamie would want to hook up with. Mia wasn't interested in locking lips with a woman around town.

However, she wanted to kiss Jamie again. She was curious how it would feel to have Jamie's mouth on her pussy. An erotic shudder rippled through Mia as she imagined Jamie's face pressed against her mound, kissing her clit.

"Mia?" Jamie waved her fingers in front of Mia's face. "Hey, Earth to Mia."

Mia jerked and the daydream disappeared with a poof. "I'm sorry. What did you say?" Mia asked, desperately trying to ignore the throb between her legs.

Jamie gave her a strange look. "Is everything okay?"

"Yeah, sure," Mia said as she dumped the containers on the bed. "Everything is fine. I'm just going to miss you."

"Aww . . ." Jamie threw her arms around Mia and gave her a fierce hug. "I know what you mean, but we'll still be best friends."

"Absolutely." Mia stood in Jamie's tight embrace and closed her eyes.

"And you have Aidan now," Jamie said brightly.

"It won't be the same," Mia said as she inhaled her friend's scent.

"Of course not," Jamie agreed, "but he'll be there when you need him."

"You're right." Did she sound as distracted as she felt? The only thing she seemed to be aware of was Jamie's lush, full breasts pressing against her small, firm curves. Mia drew back when she felt her nipples tightening, not wanting Jamie to know she was getting aroused from the friendly gestured.

Was this what Jamie had to endure? Mia thought as she stepped out of her friend's hug. It was no wonder Jamie found it urgent to leave Clover Bud. Wanting to be close and touching Mia but running the risk of getting too close must have been hard.

Mia didn't know how long Jamie had felt this way, but she admired her friend's restraint. Mia was struggling with these very new feelings, and she was already tempted to run her hands over Jamie and nuzzle her face into Jamie's neck.

She had to step away. *Make up a reason and just do it.* "I'm going to . . . uh . . ." Mia tried to think of an excuse to create some physical distance and regain her composure. "I'll check the bathroom one more time to make sure you're not leaving anything behind."

"It's no rush," Jamie said as Mia hurried away. "I'm leaving first thing tomorrow morning."

"*You* are?" Mia teased as her heart thumped. She turned around and headed straight to the bathroom. "You can't get out of bed bright and early."

Mia didn't look back and threw herself into her task. She systematically went through the drawers and shelves, but her mind was elsewhere. She felt bad about pushing Jamie away. It wasn't like her. It was like . . . the way Jamie had acted for the past two months. That must have been when Jamie became attracted to her!

Mia didn't know what had caused it. What had she done to gain Jamie's attention? Perhaps it was not one thing, but a natural progression until one day Jamie found herself desiring her best friend.

"Jamie? Mia? Are you up there?"

Mia heard Caleb calling them. She stepped out of the bathroom and saw him at the foot of the stairs. "What do you need?" she asked Caleb.

"Now there's a leading question," he said with a smile as he climbed the stairs.

His smile disappeared when he saw Jamie packing up the last of her things. "Why are you doing that now?"

"Ask Mia," Jamie grumbled. "Something about birds eating worms."

" 'The early bird catches the worm,' " Mia repeated. "Like you haven't heard me say that a million times."

Caleb stared at the suitcases and took a step down the stairs.

"If you're doing this, then I'm going back to my apartment. I need to get a change of clothes and collect my mail." He took another step down. "Stuff like that."

Mia watched Caleb's retreat with concern. "We don't have that much left other than packing Jamie's car."

Caleb blanched at Mia's words. "Aidan can help with that."

"But you'll come back later, right?" Mia asked. "Jamie and I are planning a threesome with Aidan."

"Start without me," Caleb offered.

That surprised Mia. Caleb had really come full circle since the beginning of the weekend when he hadn't wanted to be left out of anything. "Are you sure you don't want to be here for that? Because I thought you told Jamie—"

"I can make an exception this time," he said as he turned and walked down the remaining steps. "I'm not into watching like Aidan is."

"But . . ." Mia watched Caleb leave. He disappeared from her view, and she heard the back door open and close. Mia turned to Jamie to share a look, but her friend had already returned to her packing.

"He's really not taking it well about your moving," Mia said softly. "You need to talk to him."

"I have, and there is nothing more to say." Jamie's tone was cold, but Mia knew she was hiding from her. "Now please, Mia, let's not ruin this weekend with this discussion."

"Fine." Mia held her hands up in surrender. "I won't say another word about it."

"We'll see about that," Jamie grumbled. "There! I'm done packing." She tossed her hands in the air. "Tada!"

Mia walked over to where Jamie stood proudly. She placed her hands on her hips and surveyed the pile of mismatched luggage and stuffed boxes. "I thought you were giving away most of your stuff."

"I did. These are my essentials."

Mia shook her head. "Your idea of traveling light is way different from mine," she said. "I don't think it will all fit into your car."

"It's all how you organize the trunk," Jamie said breezily. "I'll be fine."

"You'll have to show me," Mia said, because she didn't see it happening. "Are you ready to move all this to your car?"

Jamie swallowed a sigh. "I'm ready when you are."

Mia and Jamie stared at the luggage and then looked at each other. "Aidan!" they called out.

Minutes later they heard Aidan reach the foot of the steps. "What?" he asked. "I was just going to start a game on the Xbox."

Mia knew what that meant. Their emergency had better include massive blood loss and/or impending natural disaster. "We need your help."

Aidan groaned and stamped up the stairs. "If this is a spider you want me to kill . . ."

"No, I promise," Mia said. She waited until Aidan reached the attic before she said, "We need to move Jamie's stuff to her car."

Aidan stared at the towering pile. "Forget it." He turned to go back downstairs.

"Please, Aidan?" Mia curled her arms around his and batted her eyelashes. "We need a strong guy—"

"Oh, Gawd." Jamie rolled her eyes.

Mia knew Jamie couldn't stand the helpless-woman routine, but it really worked on Aidan.

"Ask Caleb," he told her.

"He went to his apartment to pick up some things. We want to get this done so we can keep swapping until Jamie has to leave."

Aidan's eyes sparkled when she said the word "swapping." "How about you give me my threesome now, and then I'll carry all that crap."

"First of all, this is not crap," Jamie said, offended. "Second, you don't get the reward before you do the work."

"Jamie!" Did her friend not realize what she just said? "We aren't bartering with sex!" Although, the idea sounded kind of fun. . . .

"If I did the work first, I would be too tired to enjoy my reward," Aidan insisted.

"He makes a good point," Mia said. The truth was, she didn't want to wait for another threesome. "What do you say, Jamie?"

Her friend gave a long, exaggerated sigh. "Well, I guess we'll let Aidan have his way this time."

Aidan's mouth twitched, but he didn't point out the obvious: he always got his way.

"Okay, Aidan," Mia said. "This is your threesome. How do you want it to go?"

Aidan rubbed his hands together. "First I want to see you and Jamie kiss."

"Why does that not surprise me?" Mia asked Jamie as she stood in front of her friend. The sparky feeling inside her, however, astonished her. She really was looking forward to kissing Jamie. "Are you ready?"

Jamie responded by grabbing Mia at the waist and pulling her close. She kissed Mia roughly, their lips grinding, before her tongue delved into Mia's mouth.

Mia moaned and linked her arms around Jamie's shoulders. She liked how her breasts strained against her friend's. Kissing Jamie made her feel so naughty. Her hands roamed over her friend's back before she flattened her palms on the woman's ass. Jamie broke off the kiss abruptly and stepped back.

"You taste good," Mia said as she licked her lips. It was such an innocent comment, yet Jamie looked like she was going to grab Mia again for another long, luscious kiss.

Aidan was suddenly standing behind Jamie. "Mia, help me take off Jamie's clothes."

Mia obeyed the order automatically, her hands bumping Aidan's. She stripped off her friend's shirt and shorts, brushing her fingers along the curve of her breast or the small of her back. Sometimes the touches were accidental, but most of the time she did it on purpose.

Then Aidan took over, removing Jamie's bra and panties. Mia watched as Aidan kissed and fondled Jamie. She wanted to join in but knew she had to wait for Aidan's command. She was shocked when he never gave it.

As Jamie stepped out of her panties, Aidan told her to help him strip Mia of her clothes. This time he stood behind Mia, kissing her face and throat as Jamie took off Mia's shorts and shirt. Once Jamie was finished with her task, she watched Aidan leisurely remove Mia's underwear.

"Now me," Aidan said, his voice getting a little rougher. "I want you two to take off my clothes. Mia, get behind me, and, Jamie, you get in front."

Mia was unsettled by Aidan's demand. She was used to being the center of attention. She was always in the spotlight, and now she was relegated to the shadows.

Was she getting too greedy? Mia wondered as she and Jamie took off Aidan's clothes. She didn't want to begrudge Jamie any pleasure. They had shared so much, and now wasn't the time for her to become stingy.

But Aidan was *hers*, and what they had together was special. When she was with him, Mia felt cherished and loved. Why had she complained that it might not be enough?

Her greed hadn't started this weekend, Mia realized as she smoothed her palms over the defined muscles of Aidan's back. She had developed it over the course of the year.

All this time she thought she had worked for each pleasure she had received, but the truth was that Aidan gave her everything she wanted. He looked after and guided her through one sensual awakening after the next. Aidan did it because he cared for her. And she had taken him for granted.

Stunned by these revelations, Mia clung to Aidan's bare shoulders and curled against his spine. She closed her eyes, inhaling his scent and enjoying his strength and warmth. She pressed her mouth against his shoulder blade, thankful that he spoiled her yet again by giving her this weekend.

Who knew how long it would have taken her to appreciate what she had with him?

"Mia, did I tell you to kiss me?" Aidan drawled.

Mia smiled against his back. "No, you didn't," she replied and reluctantly stepped back.

"Jamie, go sit down on the bed, legs out in front of you."

Mia saw her friend bristle at his tone. She noticed the familiar flash of attitude in Jamie's eyes and knew she was about five seconds away from telling Aidan what he could do with that suggestion.

"You will lie back against Mia," he continued.

Mia wasn't sure where he was going with this, but she would trust him. She silently followed Jamie to the bed. Her friend sat in the middle, and Mia crawled onto the mattress and sat behind her, her legs on either side of Jamie.

"Jamie, lean back on Mia."

Jamie offered no complaints as she reclined. Mia caught her, and her hands rested on Jamie's ribs, just under her big breasts.

Mia was tempted to clamp her hands on Jamie's breasts and knead the mounds until her friend cried out with pleasure. The need was so great that her hands tingled.

Aidan crawled between Jamie's legs and gently caressed her feet. Jamie squirmed under his touch.

"Mia, you have one task to fulfill," Aidan said as he rubbed Jamie's feet. "You must stay in that position and please Jamie until she begs for more."

"Please her?" The command was unlike any Aidan had given her. It was vague, and the results were out of her control. "Please her how?"

"That will be based on your imagination and experience," he answered.

Mia stared at Aidan. What the hell was he talking about? "And then what?" she asked.

"You'll find out," he said patiently, but she saw the glint of warning in his eye. She was not to question his commands.

"Come on, Mia," Jamie said as she settled comfortably against her. "I want to see how you're going to tease me."

Did Jamie think Mia would back down from the challenge? She was about to be proven wrong, Mia decided as she slid her hands over Jamie's breasts.

Fondling another woman's breasts was an unfamiliar feeling. Mia was genuinely curious, pressing Jamie's breasts together and discovering what pleased her friend.

She was surprised at how heavy Jamie's breasts were. It was no wonder that soft, fleeting touches against her nipples went unnoticed. Mia found that she had to pinch and squeeze to elicit a response.

Mia glanced down at Aidan and found him stroking Jamie's pussy. He rubbed her clit with one hand while gliding his fingers along the wet folds of her sex. Jamie purred and stretched against his hands, murmuring her encouragement for more.

But she hadn't begged.

Mia was determined to make her friend plead for more. She remembered how Jamie insisted that Mia liked having her ear licked. That sounded like something Jamie would prefer.

As she massaged Jamie's breasts, Mia dipped her head and darted her tongue along her friend's ear. Jamie hissed and tucked her head. Mia licked the rim of the outer ear before stabbing the tip of her tongue in Jamie's ear canal. She felt the shivers rippling through her friend.

Mia was curious to see what Jamie's response would be like if her touches were rougher. She slid her mouth down, bared her teeth, and bit Jamie's earlobe.

Jamie cried out Mia's name and tried to tug away, but Mia wouldn't let go. She liked the way the fierce yank made Jamie shudder with pleasure.

Jamie looped an arm around Mia's neck and shoulder. Mia let go of Jamie's ear just as her friend turned to kiss her.

Their lips met, and Mia inhaled sharply when she felt a jolt. She liked kissing Jamie a lot, and she didn't know what that meant. It was different from kissing Aidan or Caleb. With Jamie, she felt like she was embarking on a mysterious adventure. But that made no sense to Mia, because she had known Jamie almost all her life.

Mia lifted her head and glanced down at Aidan. He watched

them both, his eyes glittering with lust as he pumped his fingers inside Jamie.

Jamie rooted for Mia's mouth. "Kiss me again."

Mia shook her head. "I want to lick your ear," she confessed as she darted her tongue out and flicked it on the curve of her ear.

Jamie trembled. "Kiss me, Mia. Please."

Mia glanced at Aidan. "Does that count as begging?"

"I believe it does."

"Don't stop," Jamie told Mia, her low voice smoky and seductive.

Mia whispered in her ear. "Later," she promised and slicked her tongue against Jamie's lobe.

Aidan withdrew his fingers from Jamie. "Move to the side, ladies."

They scooted over to the edge of the bed and Aidan lay down in the center of the mattress. Mia saw how his erect cock slapped against his stomach. He had gotten incredibly aroused watching her with Jamie.

"Mia"—Aidan reached for her—"I want you to ride my cock."

Mia gladly straddled his hips. Her core was already wet with anticipation as she slowly sank onto his cock. Mia tossed her head back and moaned as the fire streaked through her.

"Don't move," Aidan said.

Don't move? Oh, Aidan was cruel. Her muscles strained to rock, to dance. She barely controlled herself as she felt the pulse twitching in Aidan's cock. She really needed to ride him hard.

"And you"—Aidan motioned for Jamie—"will face Mia and ride my mouth."

Mia's muscles were quivering as her control started to slip. It was too difficult to stay still as she watched Jamie straddle Aidan's mouth and ride his tongue.

She saw Jamie's eyes widen and her mouth slacken as the pleasure bloomed inside her. Jamie slid her hands over her face and in her long brown hair as she rocked against Aidan's mouth.

Mia couldn't stand it anymore. She refused to wait. To hell with her perfect obedience. She had to ride. She rolled her hips slowly and heard Aidan groan. Jamie closed her eyes, and she swayed, the vibrations of his voice offering another dimension to his touch.

Mia realized that she could add to their pleasure. She placed her hands on Aidan's chest and rode his cock a little faster, moving her hips from side to side. She felt the power bubbling inside her. Every surprise move she made, Aidan's pleasure increased. Jamie felt each deep roll of her hips.

Jamie's face flushed, and her eyes half closed. It was only a matter of moments before her friend would climax. Jamie leaned forward and clasped her hand at the back of Mia's head. She tugged Mia forward and kissed her clumsily as she rode Aidan's tongue.

Mia pulled back slightly and mouthed, *Jamie.*

Jamie frowned. "What?" she asked. She tilted her head to the side to hear Mia more clearly.

Mia smiled when Jamie fell for her ruse. She stopped riding Aidan's cock as Jamie leaned closer. Mia caught Jamie's earlobe with her teeth.

Jamie shrieked as the intense orgasm crashed through her. Mia didn't let go as Jamie bore down on Aidan's mouth.

When Aidan grabbed Mia's hips and started thrusting deep inside her, she let go of Jamie. Her friend's ear was bright pink, and she noticed teeth marks on the earlobe.

The sight triggered Mia's release. She arched her back and gave a low, guttural moan as the heat washed over her. It was like nothing she had experienced before.

And she felt it all because she had branded Jamie in the most primal way. Mia's core twitched at the sight of her teeth marks. Now if only she were brave enough to back up the symbol of possession with action.

NINETEEN

"Our weekend is almost over," Jamie said.

"Don't remind me," Mia whined as she leaned against Aidan's chest and snuggled into his warmth.

The dinner they were having was probably the nicest meal she'd had in a long time. The menu was simple: takeout pizza and a six-pack of beer that Caleb had thoughtfully brought to the house when he had returned.

The dress code was casual. They wore a mix of T-shirts and shorts. The location was sparse: on Jamie's bed, their legs criss-crossed as they gobbled up the food. Mia realized this was the last meal she was going to have with her best friend.

"How do you want to end it?" Jamie persisted with her questions.

Mia flinched until she realized Jamie was talking about the swapping. She knew it was easier for her friend to discuss their sexual arrangement than her leaving town.

"I don't know," Mia said with a halfhearted shrug. "I haven't given it much thought."

"I made sure this weekend would happen for you." Jamie pointed a finger at Mia. "You should get to decide how to end it. If I have to do it, you're not going to be happy with my choice."

Mia looked at her friends clustered on the bed. The possibilities of how to end the swap were suddenly endless. She could have Aidan, Caleb, or Jamie. She could have just one or all three at the same time.

She could do whatever she wanted. And if she had the time, she probably would have.

But she didn't want to make the decision how to finish the swap. Half the fun for her was surrendering to whatever happened. The one thing she had learned about herself this weekend was that she didn't like making decisions in bed. She wanted it to feel like she was surrendering herself to the fates when, in actuality, Aidan was pulling the strings and keeping an eye out for her.

If she didn't like making the choices, she wasn't going to start now. She would let them make it. But if she tossed the chance in their laps, Aidan and Jamie would squabble over it. Caleb would sit back and watch the fireworks.

She needed to be smart about this. She would make them work for the privilege of choosing, but while she was at it, she wanted to reenact one of her favorite moments during the weekend.

"Okay"—Mia made a loud clap with her hands—"here are the rules."

"Oh, God," Jamie made a face. "Mia, the point of the weekend is no rules."

"Listen up, because I'm only going to say this once," Mia said as she glared at her friend. "I'm going to turn off the lights in the house."

Caleb smiled as he realized what she had planned.

"Mia, where are you going with this?" Aidan asked.

"Once I turn off the lights," Mia continued, "I'll tell you guys I'm ready."

"For what?" Jamie asked, squinting her eyes with confusion.

"Think of it as hide-and-seek," Mia explained. "You can't turn on the lights and whoever finds me first gets me."

"Gets you get you?" Jamie wanted to clarify.

"Yeah, this is a one-time-only deal. They get me, any way he"— she looked at Aidan and Caleb—"or she"—she looked at Jamie's stunned face—"wants me."

"Seriously?" Jamie's voice cracked.

"Yes." Mia looked at Aidan, knowing she hadn't talked it over with him. He didn't seem perturbed by the oversight. His dark eyes gleamed with interest, and he looked forward to the game.

"I'm going to turn off all the lights now. Otherwise it won't work." Mia got up from the bed and walked over to the wall next to the stairs. Gripping the banister, she turned off the attic light.

The light from the mudroom gleamed up the stairs. "Now stay here until I call out that I'm ready." Mia knew they probably wouldn't follow the rules, but at least she was getting a head start.

Mia took the stairs, wondering if she was ready for this. Anyone could catch her. There was no way she could cheat or play it safe. Was she ready?

She turned off the light in the mudroom and went straight for the kitchen. What if Jamie caught her? Mia had never had sex with a woman. It had never been a fantasy of hers.

But it was Jamie's fantasy to claim her, Mia thought as she turned off the kitchen lights. She liked being someone's fantasy— especially when that someone was so sexy.

She walked into the dining room, checking that the curtains were firmly closed. The last thing she needed was moonlight advertising her whereabouts. She crossed over to the living room and turned off the lone light before she headed to the media room and bedroom.

When those lights were off, she went down the hall and turned off the bathroom light. Then she had to put her hand on the wall to find her way back to the door leading to the attic.

The atmosphere pulsed with energy. She smiled, liking the idea that these three people, all of them important to her, were ready to compete for her body. She'd like to think it was because she knew how to give and receive pleasure.

Mia took a deep breath. This was it. There was no turning back. One thing she knew for certain was that she wanted the swap to end this way. "I'm ready," she called out.

Her eyes widened when she heard the pounding of footsteps on the steps. She hadn't expected them to be at the top of the stairs. She hurried back into the hall and dashed into the bathroom just as she heard their feet hit the mudroom.

"I'll go through the kitchen," Jamie said, "You guys go the other way. We'll find her quicker than if we were in the same room."

"But—" Caleb said and was interrupted.

"Okay," Aidan said. "We'll meet in the media room. Yell if you find her."

Jamie agreed. "Same goes for you."

Mia held her breath as she heard the others start searching for her. She pressed her hand against her stomach as excitement twisted inside her. Her pursuers weren't in the same room, and she was getting jumpy.

"Hey, man!" Aidan said in the hallway, his voice very close to where she hid. "Watch where you put your hands."

"Sorry," Caleb apologized. "I can't see a damn thing."

"Listen." Aidan's voice dropped into a whisper. "Jamie really wants to win. Let's make sure it happens."

Oh, yeah, Mia thought with a smile. Aidan wanted to see her hook up with Jamie.

"I don't know about that," Caleb said. "Are you sure Mia wants it that way?"

Mia could have given Caleb a big, fat kiss. It was good to hear a man other than Aidan looking out for her.

"Yes," Aidan agreed impatiently. "Otherwise she wouldn't have made it a possibility."

"If you say so," Caleb responded. "We'll let Jamie win. But don't let Jamie think for a minute that we didn't try hard."

"Deal."

"Ow!" Caleb said in a hiss. "Aidan, watch where you put your hands."

"Sorry."

Mia could barely stand the anticipation building inside her. She was going to get Jamie. Or, rather, Jamie was going to get her.

Jamie, her best friend, who liked to conquer her sex partners. The woman who was aggressive in life and in bed. The one person who had turned Clover Bud topsy-turvy by means of her sex drive alone.

Mia carefully exhaled as Aidan and Caleb moved past the bathroom door. She listened to them walk down the hallway, bumping against the wall and door.

"How does Mia expect us to find her way out here?" Aidan muttered.

"You get used to it after a while," Caleb said.

"Say what?" Aidan asked in a lethally soft voice.

There was a significant pause. "Nothing," Caleb said casually.

Mia heard them at the farthest end of the hallway. She took a step out of the bathroom, her heart knocking against her chest, as she heard them moving toward the media room.

If she wanted to cheat or play it safe, she could easily walk into them and declare Caleb and Aidan the winner. But she wasn't going to. She didn't want to.

With her arms outstretched, she headed in the direction of her bedroom. It was as dark as Aidan had complained about. She banged her fingers against something hard. Mia pressed her lips, swallowing back a whimper, and looked in the direction of the media room.

No one showed any kind of reaction that they heard her. No sudden movements, no quick footsteps in her direction. In fact, there was no sound at all. It was eerie, and if anything popped out at her, she was going to freak.

Mia slowly made her way into the bedroom, recognizing the the texture of the carpeting on her bare feet. Now where should she wait to be caught? She recalled the layout of her room.

The bed? No, too obvious. Jamie was in it for the chase, so Mia couldn't show that she had already surrendered. The chair? No, it was still too easy for Jamie.

Mia felt around for the door, and once she found it, she quietly felt around the edges. She flattened her hands against the wall and slowly made her way into the room. Pressing her back against the wall next to the door, she found the wallpaper scratchy on her skin.

Mia listened intently for any noise in the house. It wasn't long before Jamie bumped into Aidan and Caleb.

"Gotcha!" Jamie crowed. Mia heard a huge clatter and what sounded like a thud.

"Jamie, it's me, Caleb," he said, his voice sounding strange.

"Damn," Jamie said. "I thought you were Mia."

"Is that how you're going to greet her? By slamming her against the wall and shoving your tongue down her throat?"

"You got a better plan?"

Mia's eyes widened. Had Jamie gotten the best of Caleb and pinned him to the wall? Just how strong was Jamie?

And the way she tackled Caleb—Jamie planned to do the same to her. Mia shivered, and she pressed her legs together, but it didn't relieve the ache in her belly.

"Where could she be?" Jamie asked, her voice drifting closer.

"We'll cover the rooms you looked into," Aidan said. "You cover where we've been. Meet us at the door leading to the attic."

This is it. Mia pressed herself as close as she could to the wall. It would be a matter of minutes before Jamie found her. She heard another bump in the media room. Jamie was closing in.

Jamie banged against the wall and muffled a curse. It sounded so close to Mia. At this rate, Jamie was going to be in a very impatient mood when she found Mia.

Mia sensed rather than heard Jamie enter the bedroom. The tension was palpable. Her breath caught in her throat when fingertips brushed along her shoulder.

Jamie hesitated and then wrapped her hand around Mia's shoulder. "Gotcha," she whispered.

Mia heard the triumph and excitement shimmering in her friend's voice. Mia's breathing snagged in her throat. She couldn't move or say anything as Jamie slammed her mouth against hers. She pressed her body against Mia's, their breasts smashed against one another.

Jamie's hands were all over Mia's body, taking, grabbing, and claiming. Mia's pussy started to throb. She wanted this. She wanted Jamie.

"Oh, baby," Jamie crooned. "You are in for it now."

Mia bucked her hips against Jamie's. "What do you have planned?"

"Wait and see." Jamie slapped her hand on the bedroom wall until she found the light switch. Mia blinked as the lights flared on. She stared at her friend, who held her in a tight grasp.

Jamie looked like a wild woman, a conqueror. Mia's friend licked her lips in anticipation and shook her head to call out, "I found her!"

Mia looked down at Jamie's hand cupping her breast. Her nails dug lightly into Mia's curves. Mia realized Jamie was going to make the most of this moment. The thought drenched Mia's sex.

She heard the men turn on the other lights as they headed for the bedroom. Aidan was the first to appear. He took one look at Jamie pressing Mia into the wall with a possessive claim on Mia's breast. His eyes flared with lust.

"Caleb," Jamie said, barely glancing at him, "would you find my strap-on? It was in my bathroom next to the sink the last time I saw it today."

The strap-on? Mia's eyes widened as her core squeezed tightly. Jamie was going to take her with a dildo?

"Sure," Caleb said, and Mia heard his quick footsteps heading toward the attic.

"Aidan," Jamie said without taking her eyes off Mia, "carry Mia to her bed and then hold her arms down."

Mia was shaking, knowing she was really in for a wild time with Jamie. Her friend knew what she needed, like being restrained and having Aidan there. She had also picked up on Mia's curiosity about strap-on. Mia wasn't sure how Jamie had figured that one out, but it didn't matter. She was going to give Mia a fantasy night.

Aidan silently scooped Mia up and carried her to the bed. He lowered her gently. "Are you sure about this?" he asked.

She nodded, her heart pounding hard. "Are you?" She really hoped he was, because she did not want to give this fantasy up. It would be very difficult for her to make a decision without following Caleb's orders.

"Oh, yeah." Aidan's voice was a sexy growl.

She looked up when she heard Caleb enter the room. He held the cleaned dildo in his hands. The long purple cock looked bigger than she remembered.

"Put that on the chair. I'm not ready for it," Jamie told Caleb. "Then hold down Mia's other arm."

Jamie crawled onto the bed and over Mia's body. Her movements made Mia think of a jungle cat on the prowl. Jamie lowered her head and kissed Mia, her tongue delving into Mia's mouth. She rubbed her hands all over Mia's throat and breasts, tweaking and pinching Mia's nipples. Mia moaned and arched her spine.

Jamie bent down and captured one of the nipples with her mouth. She sucked hard, and Mia could barely stand it. When Jamie released her nipple, Mia couldn't stop shaking.

Jamie placed her mouth on Mia's stomach and kissed a trail in a straight line. Mia glanced up at Aidan and saw his ruddy complexion and tight jaw. His eyes gleamed, and she knew that this man loved watching her have sex with another woman.

Mia gasped when Jamie's mouth brushed against her pubic hair. Her eyes widened as Jamie licked her wet slit. Jamie's tongue dragged along the folds of Mia's sex. Mia widened her legs and humped against Jamie's mouth.

Jamie dove in deeper, groaning with pleasure as she licked and tasted Mia. Jamie devoured her, and Mia writhed helplessly, urging her friend to go deeper.

Mia was so aroused it wouldn't take much for her to climax. She had to squeeze her inner muscles to stop the first gentle orgasmic ripple from happening when Jamie raised her head and said, "Caleb, help me with the strap-on."

Mia watched as Jamie stepped into the vinyl strap-on, and then placed a small vibrator into a pouch that would stimulate her clit. The dildo looked monstrous and foreign against Jamie's body.

Mia felt a moment's apprehension as Jamie settled between her legs. Mia was aroused and wanted a rock-hard cock inside her, but she might not be ready for this dildo. Mia took a deep breath as Jamie stretched her wet pussy with the dildo. The silicone was cold against her flesh as Jamie thrust into her.

Mia would never forget the look on Jamie's face when she sank into Mia's pussy. Jamie looked victorious, triumphant. She reached and clutched Mia's breasts as she withdrew, only to thrust deeper.

Mia loved watching Jamie master her. Her long brown hair fell in waves around her face. Her large breasts jiggled and swayed with every move. Jamie was the sexiest woman Mia had ever seen.

Her thrust became hard and fast, and Mia matched each thrust with a bucking of her own. She would swivel her hips as Jamie pumped into her, make Jamie work for every thrust.

But she didn't count on the fact that Jamie would outlast a mortal man. With each grunt and thrust, Mia realized that Jamie wanted—needed—for her to reach an orgasm. Only then would Jamie surrender to the swirling sensations inside her.

But she couldn't reach that point, and she didn't know why. She wanted to come, longed for it as desire twisted inside her until she couldn't breathe.

Jamie stiffened, and Mia knew that the vibe had done something to her. Her friend tossed her head back and cried out, slumping against Mia's sweat-soaked skin. Her arms and legs were shaking, and goose bumps dotted her flesh.

Caleb reached for Jamie and lifted her away from Mia. He laid her beside her friend. Jamie sighed when her head hit the pillow as Caleb stripped the harness from her hips.

Aidan let go of Mia's arms and crawled between her legs. He claimed her mouth with his, and his possessive kiss stole her breath. Aidan hooked her knees around his hips and entered her with one thrust. Mia reached up and stretched her arms, subconsciously seeking for something to hold on to. There was nothing to hold her down as Aidan drove his cock into her.

Mia tossed her head from side to side. She needed something to hold on to, something to hold her down. *Jamie.* Jamie was strong enough for both of them.

Mia looked to the side and saw Jamie watching her with glazed eyes. Caleb was on top of her, pumping his long cock into her wetness.

Their gaze held for a split second. Mia saw the gratitude and affection in Jamie's eyes. Mia tried to smile, but she was suddenly gasping for air as the climax she had fought so hard to gain slammed into her.

TWENTY

Jamie lay on her bed, watching the sunrise. She studied Caleb as he slept. She was somewhat envious that he could sleep while she had been awake for hours.

Today was the day. She planned to leave and not look back. She should be excited, and she was. But she felt like she had some unfinished business. Some regrets.

She didn't regret her encounter with Mia. All this time she had been afraid that she would make the wrong move and destroy years of friendship. Instead, their moments together were the pinnacle. They had changed Jamie and Mia's relationship, but they hadn't ruined it.

But she still had to go. She was too interfering, too protective of Mia. She could see now how happy Mia was with Aidan. Aidan might not be Jamie's choice of mate, but he was perfect for Mia.

And as strange as it sounded, she hoped Mia would share her home with Aidan. The guy looked out for her. He saw that Mia was the best thing that had ever happened in his life, and he was going to take care of her.

It was too bad it had taken Jamie so long to realize what the best thing that had ever happened to her was. She had almost walked away from it. From him.

She reached out and stroked Caleb's face. Her heart started to pump fiercely. She wasn't sure what she should do. If she was smart, she would walk away without looking back. No need to ruin a perfectly good thing. Every relationship had a beginning and an end. She wanted her relationship with Caleb to end on a good note.

But, secretly, she didn't want it to end.

Jamie placed a gentle kiss on his brow, then brushed her lips against his eyes and cheeks. By the time she kissed his mouth, he was kissing her back.

She moved and Caleb's hand shot out. He held on to her tight, instinctively. "Don't go."

She didn't know if he meant getting out of bed or out of Clover Bud. He might have meant both. She cupped his cheeks and deepened the kiss.

Caleb rolled over, and she was underneath him. She blinked, not familiar with this position. She was usually on top; she'd never liked being pinned down or at a disadvantage. Only this time, she felt cherished, loved.

She arched up and kissed him, sliding her hands all over him. He was lean and wiry, his flesh warm and supple. She grabbed his ass with both hands and dug her fingers in, bucking her hips to meet his groin.

Caleb's hands were all over her, urgent and desperate. It was as if he were afraid he didn't have enough time to do all he wanted.

He kissed a path from her neck to her breasts. He paid special attention to them, massaging and squeezing, kissing and licking, until her nipples poked against his tongue.

He continued to kiss down to her pussy. Her tummy did a

little flip as he settled between her thighs, hooking her knees over his shoulders.

She closed her eyes and gasped at the first flick of his tongue against her clit. He worshipped the bud with his tongue until she couldn't take it anymore. She clutched at his head, begging for him to move on, but he wouldn't listen.

He licked her pussy, with quick, short flicks that drove her crazy. She was wet from his touch.

He dipped his finger into her pussy, and she bucked as her wet flesh gripped him, drawing him in. He pumped into her and continued to lick.

An orgasm rippled through her. She wanted to flip him over and ride him hard, but she held back, barely. She wouldn't tell him what to do. This was all about him.

He slowly kissed his way back up to her mouth. She tasted her arousal on his lips. After sliding his hands underneath her ass and tilting her hips up, he pressed his cock against her entrance.

His gaze connected with hers. There was something about the way he looked at her. It was too intense. She wanted to look away, but she couldn't. He was saying goodbye to her, letting her know how much he was going to miss her.

He slowly slid his cock into her. When he'd sheathed himself completely, he placed his palms on the mattress next to her head and began to thrust.

His thrusts were measured, as if he was memorizing everything about them: the feel and scent of their arousal; the way she looked underneath him.

She wrapped her legs around his hips. She wouldn't make him move faster. She'd let him set the pace and follow it. She'd surrender to him, to this moment, and not be afraid that it would weaken her.

But then, Caleb never made her feel weak. She felt confident and powerful when she was with him. She wanted to conquer him, but she never really did. His quiet strength and acceptance made doing so impossible.

Caleb's hips began to pump faster. She saw the tightening of his face, the flexing of his muscles. He was about to come, but he was holding back. He wanted to make this last for as long as possible. Forever, if he had a say in it.

He couldn't continue. Caleb squeezed his eyes, in pleasure and in regret, as he pulsed inside her. When he surrendered to the last, Jamie reached for him and held him close. They were hot, sweaty, and breathing hard, but she didn't want to let go.

She took a couple minutes to gain her courage. It was surprisingly difficult to make this offer, and she realized why. There was no guarantee that this was going to work out, or that Caleb would agree to it since he had stopped talking about it a week ago, but she had to give it try or regret not doing so.

"This might be bad timing since I'm going to be leaving in a couple of hours," Jamie said softly, "but . . ."

She felt Caleb go rigid, his muscles locking. Tension washed off him in waves. "Don't say it," he warned her.

Don't say it? Why did he think it would be so bad to have it out in the open?

He lifted his head and glared at her. "I don't want to hear what you have to say," he told her through clenched teeth. He actually looked angry that she would make this attempt. "Don't ruin this moment."

"But this is—"

"I mean it, Jamie." Caleb's cold tone was something she had never heard him used. She would have remembered it, especially if it had been directed to her. "Do not say another word."

"Okay, fine." She looked away and pressed her lips together.

"Good." He laid his head back down on her chest.

"I won't ask you to leave with me."

His head jerked up. "Leave?" His eyes were filled with disbelief. "As in leave Clover Bud? With you?"

She nodded, unable to remember the last time she had ever felt this nervous. "But I won't say it."

"Jamie . . ." His voice wavered, and she knew she had pushed him too far.

Jamie sighed. "I should have given you more notice, I know. . . ."

"Why are you asking me now?" he asked, watching her cautiously.

She took a deep breath. "I've been up for a couple of hours, thinking about all I've done and all I've regretted."

He looked surprised. "You regret this weekend?"

"Hell, no," she said with great feeling. "My only regret for this weekend is that we should have done it sooner."

Caleb laughed, and Jamie felt a little bit better. She always did when Caleb smiled at her.

"It turns out that I don't regret a lot of things," Jamie said. "In fact, you will be my only regret."

"You regret me?" Confusion and hurt shimmered in his eyes. "The time we spent together?"

"I'm going to regret not knowing the real you," she confessed, feeling very vulnerable. "I feel close to you, and I tell you things I don't even tell my best friend, but I don't know enough about you."

His expression darkened. "You might regret finding out."

She knew she could tell him that that would never happen, but she saw the old pain in Caleb's eyes and knew it had happened to him before. She could only tell him what she knew. "I'm ready to take that chance."

Caleb studied her expression, and Jamie could tell that he was afraid to trust his sudden good fortune. "Exactly what do you want from me?" he asked.

"I want you to leave town with me, and we can learn more about each other. I'm ready to leave Clover Bud, but I'm not ready to walk away from you."

Caleb began to smile. "That's all I needed to hear."

"Is that all you're taking?" Mia asked in horror as she stared at Caleb's backpack and suitcase.

"What do you mean?" Jamie interrupted. "I had to get rid of some stuff so Caleb could get his things in the car."

"Yeah, it's a little thing called compromise," Mia told Jamie. "Couples do it all the time."

"Well, it sucks," Jamie decided. "But I'll get the hang of it."

"I think that's everything," Caleb said as he tossed his bags in the car and closed the door.

"I can't believe you're going." Tears pricked Mia's eyes.

Jamie looked at her as if she was going crazy. "I told you for years that I had to get out of this place."

Yeah, but I didn't think that you would ever do it. "Are you ever coming back?"

Jamie nodded, "I'll drop by every chance I get."

"And continue what we started this weekend?" Mia asked and waggled her eyebrows just like Jamie always did.

Jamie thought about that for a second. "Do you think it'll be the same?"

"Good point." Mia would rather leave their weekend as a great memory than try to recapture the magic. "Everything changes."

"We don't," Jamie protested.

"Yeah, we do, but the important stuff stays the same." Mia gave her friend a hug. She felt no spark or discomfort being so close. She felt like she was trying to hold on to her best friend. "I'm really going to miss you."

Jamie held her tight. "I'm going to miss you, too."

"And I admit it," Mia said as she stepped out of the embrace, "I'm glad you are taking Caleb with you. He's good for you."

"But am I good for him?"

Mia recognized that Jamie was serious. "I think you are."

"You have to say that," Jamie said with the roll of her eyes. "You're my best friend. Bye, Mia."

"Bye." Mia felt the tears clawing in her throat and could barely choke out her next words. "Thank you."

"It was my pleasure," Jamie said with a wicked smile.

Jamie paused and looked at Mia. She smiled and gave her another hug. Mia held on tight.

"Okay, you guys," Caleb said beside them, "stop hugging each other like that."

Mia smiled. "Is he getting jealous?" she asked Jamie.

"Hardly," Caleb answered. "Hug someone like that around here, and people are going to get ideas."

"The right ideas," Jamie said with a sly smile.

Mia let go of Jamie and heard the front screen door slam shut. She turned to see Aidan dressed in his gym clothes. "Aidan, where are you going?"

"It's Monday morning," he reminded her as he walked down the path to the sidewalk where they stood. "Most people go to work."

"Hello? Do you know what day this is?" Jamie asked him. "I'm leaving Clover Bud." Her news didn't warrant a flicker in Aidan's expression. "Forever."

Aidan was not impressed. "You'll be back."

Jamie pursed her lips. "Don't bet on it."

Aidan hugged Jamie goodbye, and Mia smiled when Jamie pinched him audaciously on his butt. Aidan didn't say anything but gave her a look to be careful. He clapped his hand on Caleb's shoulder. "You're a brave man," Aidan told him.

"We need to hit the road," Jamie announced.

"I thought you weren't on a schedule," Mia said. "Where are you going?"

"Wherever the road takes us," Jamie said, her smile wide with excitement.

Mia privately thought it sounded like hell, but kept her encouraging smile firmly in place. "Be careful."

"Only if you'll be adventurous."

"I'm serious," Mia said.

"So am I," Jamie mimicked Mia's tone.

Mia sighed. She knew Jamie worried about her just like she worried about her friend. "Okay, I'll try."

"I expect to hear reports of your wild life." Jamie turned and saw Caleb opening the driver's-side door. "Hey, hey, hey! I'm driving."

Was there any doubt? Mia watched with amusement as Jamie got into the driver's seat and powered up the engine.

"Seat belt," Caleb reminded Jamie as he sat in the passenger seat. Jamie rolled her eyes and silently put it on.

And that was when Mia started to relax. Jamie would be in good hands.

Jamie rolled down the window and waved. "Bye!"

"Be good!" Mia called out.

Jamie stuck her head out the window. "Be bad!" She floored the gas pedal and went careening down the old cobblestone street.

Mia waved, watching Jamie leave until she couldn't see the car anymore. Mia kept looking at the empty street as if Jamie would suddenly do a U-turn and come back. But that wasn't going to happen. Mia gave a heartfelt sigh and rested her head against Aidan's shoulder.

"She'll call," Aidan predicted.

Mia wasn't so sure. Jamie wasn't one to write or call.

"And she'll definitely be back," he added.

"I don't know about that," Mia said as she stepped away from Aidan, "especially when she finds out she doesn't have a place to stay anymore."

"What are you talking about?"

"I have plans for that attic."

"You're renting it out?" He frowned and folded his arms across his chest. "I don't know if I like that idea."

"I don't think I could rent it out to anyone," Mia said. "Jamie was already a part of my life, so that made it easier."

"Oh. Then what do you plan to do with it?" he asked, following her up the path to her house. "Are you going to make it a craft room? I know you've talked about it, but come on! Do you really need all that room for scrapbooking?"

"That's one option," she said. "I am going to need to put my stuff somewhere when you move in."

She felt rather than saw Aidan stop walking. She looked over her shoulder. He was standing still and staring at her. "That is, if you're still interested," she said.

He hesitated. "Are you sure about this?"

Her smile was confident. "Absolutely."

Aidan swung his arm around her waist and gathered her close to him. He leaned down for a kiss, and she tilted her head away.

"Hey, hey. This is Clover Bud," she reminded him with a teasing smile. "There are no public displays of affection. People will get all sorts of ideas."

"I'm having all sorts of ideas right now," he growled in her ear.

"Really?" she asked, knowing that her eyes were probably as bright and sunny as she felt. "Like what?"

He looked up at the house. "I want dibs on the attic."

She blinked and frowned. That wasn't the answer she had been expecting. "That's what you're thinking about?"

"Oh, yeah." His voice was low and gravelly. "After this weekend, I think it would make the perfect playground for us."

"Really?" She took a step toward the house. "Well, why don't you show me what you have in mind?"

"Tonight," he promised.

She didn't think she wanted to wait that long. "Right now," she insisted.

"I have to go to work," he said with a reluctant smile. "I used almost all my sick days for this weekend."

"Guess what." She grabbed the front of his T-shirt. Walking backward, she lured him to the front door. "You've had a relapse. You're going to have to stay inside for at least another day."